War of the Gypsy: The Sword of Rhiannon: Book Two

By
Melissa E. Beckwith

War of the Gypsy
Book Two: The Sword of Rhiannon
© by Melissa E. Beckwith 2016

Cover design and book editing done by www.Fiction-Atlas.com

Cover Art by Jackie Felix: https://jackiefelixart.deviantart.com/

Formatting by Affordable Formatting:
https://www.facebook.com/affordableformatting

Map by Cornelia Yoder, www.corneliayoder.com

Special thanks to my Proof Reader, Amy Marshall-Waddell

Woodland Cottage Publications
ISBN: 978-0-692-05257-0

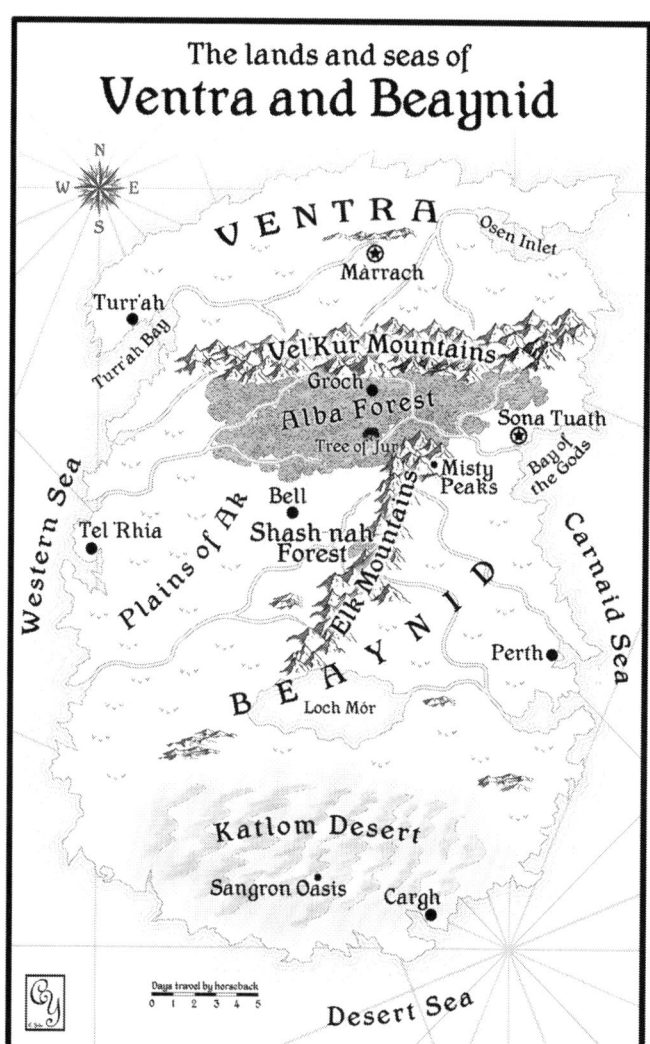

The lands and seas of
Ventra and Beaynid

To my three perfect, little gifts: my children. Nathaniel, Kyia-Lynn & Antoinette

PROLOGUE

Crimson waves curled and spit as they rolled out onto a brown sandy beach. The salty wind bit at her as she stood on the lonely bluff looking over the beach. White seabirds floated effortlessly on the breeze as they curiously watched the woman.

Baobh Dark-Water—or Baobh Basilias as she was known now—bent down and gently brushed a dark-skinned hand across a small weather-worn stone, affectionately tracing the name Raven Dark-Water with her slender fingers. "Mother," she whispered. "If only you could see what I have become." Her words were quickly whipped away on the wind as a single tear slipped down her cheek. She remembered chiseling her mother's name in the stone so many years ago; it was almost like a dream. Tenderly, she brushed away the dirt that had gathered over the years as if to erase her mother's memory.

She stood, walking a short distance to where the edge of the Alba Forest gave up the land, and a ramshackle old hut stubbornly stood under the impotent rays of an overcast sun. The wood of the structure had long since faded to gray and parts of the roof were blown completely off. Baobh slowly stepped over the threshold; the door had fallen away. Oiled deerskin shutters still hung over the windows, dancing in the moist wind, stirring up motes of thick dust.

What was left of a rug, lay in pieces near a darkened fireplace, and a blackened pot hung silently over half-burned logs still lying on cold clay bricks.

A lump formed in Baobh's stomach as she looked around her childhood home. A discarded doll, a shredded blanket and some pots and pans were all that was left of the life that she and her mother had lived here, on the edge of the forest, so close to Castle Sona Tuath. This is where a young mother tried to keep her child safe after the Basilias' had turned their backs on them. She walked over and picked up the old doll, turning it over in her hands. Her mother had made it.

Her dear, sweet mother. Too timid and ashamed to go after what she and her daughter were owed. Baobh sighed, remembering her childhood living in the shack on this rocky, grassy bluff. It was not an easy existence here, the two of them all alone. Being Goyor, finding food in the forest was never a problem, but theirs was a lonely life scratched from the sand, surf and the relentless, howling wind. She dropped the doll, it silently hit the dirty floor, sending wisps of dust into the cool air, and she fought the urge to cough.

As High Prince Eric's only child, she was heir to the Sona Tuathan throne. She had heard the rumors that the prince and his wife had had a baby, but none was found, and Baobh made sure all the Basilias were dead when she had taken Sona Tuath. There was none that could challenge her claim to the throne, bastard or not.

She walked over to an ancient silver mirror that hung crookedly on the wall. It was covered with dust, and a long crack ran across its face. She carefully ran her fingers over the surface, leaving thin lines where she could dully see her image in the glass. She looked a lot like her mother.

Her mother had been one of Queen Danielle's handmaidens. Fresh from Ghroc and wanting adventure, her mother was naïve and had given in to the teenage Eric's advances. Eric had been enthralled with the exotic beauty of the Goyor, and when she had told him she was with child, he wanted desperately to marry her. In fact, her mother had told her that they had tried to run away together. King Lund and Queen Danielle had different plans though and quickly expelled her pregnant mother from Sona Tuath.

It seemed that High Prince Eric had been heartbroken because it had taken the king and queen a full twelve years to find him a suitable wife and many years after that before rumors of a royal pregnancy started to circulate. Baobh sighed again and almost felt bad at ordering her father's execution all those long years ago. It had to be done, though, she reasoned. There had to be none left that could challenge her right to the throne. And it seemed to her that if he had wanted to badly enough, throughout all those years, he could have found a way to sneak from the castle to be with them.

Baobh sighed and walked up to one of the small windows in the shack and held up the leather flap. It crumbled and fell from her hand landing in broken bits onto the floor. She looked out the window and saw gray clouds scuttle across a gray sky pushed by an incessant wind. As if carried by the wind, her childhood memories flowed from her troubled mind.

She thought back to all those solitary years they spent on this windblown bluff. Her mother would spend hours staring down at the gleaming, white castle seemingly willing her lover to appear. But he never did. Mother kept them safe, made repairs to the shack as best she could, kept them fed and clothed. Theirs was a desolate, desperate existence because she and her mother were not good enough for Beaynidan royalty. Her stomach tightened, and her hands gripped tightly at the window sill, splintered wood biting into her fingers. Anger boiled up inside of her. She remembered when word finally drifted up to them that the High Prince of Sona Tuath had taken a bride. Her mother's wistful, melancholy mood suddenly darkened into utter despair. Within a week she was bedridden, refusing to eat. Her beautiful mother withered before her eyes, turning to a wretched, old woman. Her dark eyes, once so bright, clouded with worthlessness, her smooth skin shriveled and scaled away. Her lustrous, shiny hair that she had meticulously kept braided eventually turned dull and fell from her head.

Finally, her mother had died. Her breath and memory blowing away on the agitated, ever-howling wind scouring away at her young daughter's life. Tears formed and then fell from Baobh's cheeks as she remembered cleaning the shell of what had been her mother's body, hauling her out to the grave she had dug herself then rolling her mother into the earth and covering her over.

Her hand went up to the Necklace of Ventra that proudly hung around her slender neck. No one would dare challenge her with such a powerful weapon at her disposal.

She angrily swatted her tears away, and her full lips curled into a bitter smile. She had learned of the necklace in Ghroc after her mother had been returned to the earth. Baobh went as a girl on the cusp of womanhood. She had not been sure that the Goyor would let in a half-blood spawn from one of their own who had defected so many years earlier.

But Journey-Of-The-Moon and her uncle, Fire-Caller, had welcomed her with open arms. Baobh took a deep breath and turned back to look upon the shack. She did feel bad for the way she left Ghroc. She truly regretted that she had had to kill Sun-Song and prayed to Pom-Ni that he would forgive her. But she was not like other Goyor. Though she worshiped Pom-Ni, even erecting a temple for him in the middle of Sona Tuath, her life was not for tending the dirt. She was born to rule, the daughter of kings, and now the Queen of Beaynid! She had more important things to do than shepherd the forest.

At length, Baobh slowly walked from the shack back out into the chilled wind that always howled through Sona Tuath. The sun was about to set, and she had been away too long. She turned her dark eyes up to the gray heavens and said a silent prayer to Pom-Ni as she melted into the form of a raven, in memory of her lost mother, and then silently floated away upon the salty wind.

CHAPTER ONE

The halls of Màrrach so strong and grand,
The halls of Màrrach will always stand.
Thousands of warriors drink and tell their story,
Centuries of warrior's voices raised in glory.
Verna protects her children in her land so vast,
Yes, the halls of Màrrach will always last.
— The Halls of Màrrach; Kyia Kossi

The wavering light of thousands of scented candles danced in time to the lively music filling the Royal Palace of Màrrach in the land of Ventra. The band of minstrels had traveled with the visiting king and queen who now sat at the bustling, crowded table with Ventra's royal family: the Kossis.

Small, fair-haired men and women dashed around to keep wine glasses and jeweled goblets filled and the table cleared of forgotten dishes, only to bring out more food. The table was filled with silver platters holding large chunks of pork and venison. Steam rose and curled from mounds of bread in every shape and texture, and shiny silver bowls offered cooked potatoes, broccoli, turnips, and carrots.

Dancing girls, also supplied by the visiting royalty, spun

and whirled around with jingling bells and tiny finger cymbals. A mighty fire roared in a fireplace so big it took up almost half of one marbled wall. The sound of talk and laughter rose and fell like an angry sea and filled every crevice of the grand dining hall. Rhiannon Kossi and her beloved confidant and interpreter, Tim, sat quietly eating their meal. She wished they would have been allowed to take their meal in her chambers like they had done so many times over the long weeks they had been in Màrrach. Rhiannon felt completely out of place. Stuffing some roasted pork into her mouth she planned her escape, but then sighed, realizing this was a special dinner and she would be expected to stay.

She nervously adjusted the thin, golden circlet resting on her dark hair. It had been swept up into thousands of tiny braids studded with a spray of gemstones that winked in the uneven candlelight. It had taken three servants all afternoon to produce such a spectacular mass of braids and jewels. She wore a deep red, sleeveless top made of the softest satin she had ever felt. The neckline was cut low to show her diamond-shaped birthmark. It was tight fitting, and the hem came to just under her breasts where hundreds of golden beads danced as she moved. A delicate rope of gold and rubies clasped her waist. Her low-cut, loose-fitting pants were made of matching silk and golden hems and flowed freely down to the floor covering her slippered feet. Rhiannon felt vulnerable and exposed in her royal costume. She missed her jeans and flannel shirts from home.

After a while she got bored, and Rhiannon's eyes wandered over to the visiting royals. The man was short and round and had balding grayish-brown hair. A thick golden crown encrusted with emeralds and rubies circled his head. Rhiannon thought it was garish and the colors clashed. He wore a silk shirt of the crispest white she had ever seen. It had a profusion of ruffles at the neck and cuffs. Over his shirt, he wore a tunic of bright yellow and black. The crest of a tawny-colored spit of land surrounded by red-colored water was upon his chest. His chubby fingers pulled at the meat on his plate, then shoved a massive piece into his mouth. Jewels on his fingers sparkled in the light.

She then let her eyes slip to his queen who sat demurely at his left. Her hair was also graying from brown and was held in a severe bun at the back of her head. She wore a smaller crown of gold, also with red and green gems. Her dress mimicked her husband's in color: bright yellow and black. Her neckline was low, and her pale chest was covered with ropes of gold and chunks of emerald. She was thin, almost sickly and her pallor looked washed out in the golden light. Her lined expression was pinched. It seemed she was unhappy at the Archigos' hospitality.

The young woman that Rhiannon assumed was their daughter was dressed in a blush-colored dress. The neckline swooped down to expose the tiny rounds of two pale breasts. Around her long, thin neck snaked many necklaces of sparkling gold and rubies. Her mousy brown hair was done up in several small plaits, and a tiny circlet of gold with small chips of emerald and ruby sat atop her head. Her face was powdered, and her lips painted red. She looked, perhaps, fourteen or fifteen.

She was in an animated conversation with Shankee's

son who was about her age. A small piece of her hair had come out of its braid, and she was mindlessly twirling it around one delicate finger. She was smiling and laughing at everything the young man said. He looked very uncomfortable but clearly took his diplomatic duties seriously. She seemed far older than her fresh looks suggested. Rhiannon surmised that this young girl was already proficient in the art of seduction and briefly felt sorry for her parents.

Rhiannon was wondering who they were when Shankee finally stood up.

"Tonight, is a special night," she spoke out loudly, her voice ringing in the crystal. Tim quickly translated Shankee's words for Rhiannon. "Some of you already know, but a few of you do not," she nodded her head in acknowledgment of the squatty looking, overly dressed couple. She continued, "I would like to announce the arrival of Rhiannon Kossi, the daughter of our great empress, Sernia!" Shankee held out an elegant, silk draped arm towards Rhiannon, gem-studded bracelets glimmering in the light. There were gasps and then all fell silent. "Will you please rise, Rhiannon?"

"She wants you to stand up, milady," Tim whispered, and reluctantly Rhiannon stood. Her heart pounded in her ears, and her mouth went dry. She gave a nervous smile and mechanical nods. She turned to the visiting guests and bowed her head slightly in acknowledgment.

"Rhiannon, may I present to you the King and Queen of Yellow Island and their daughter, Princess Jocelyn."

Shankee smiled magnanimously and motioned towards their guests as Tim interpreted.

At the mention of Yellow Island, Rhiannon gasped. Her hands clenched into white-knuckled fists. "Murderers!" Rhiannon screamed and pointed across the table at the King and Queen of Yellow Island, the ridiculous golden bracelets they gave her to wear clashed together making a tinkling noise. Suddenly the room was quiet. The only sound was the hiss of the fire. Everyone looked at Rhiannon with wide eyes and open mouths. Rhiannon could see recognition in the old king's eyes. She knew he understood her. "You sent your army to kill thousands of men who only fought for their freedom from the very woman who murdered my mother! Even now she holds my father in her dungeons."

"Return to your place, Rhiannon!" Shankee ordered in clear Jurian.

Rhiannon ignored Shankee's orders and went on, "You are in bed with Baobh, and when I become empress, you'll be made to pay for your bad choice in allies!" She picked up a small knife from beside her plate, gripping it in a moist hand.

King Umar jumped from the table. "You will not speak to a king in that manner!" he howled in Jurian. The Priests of Jur must have traveled as far as Yellow Island since he knew the language.

"You are nothing but a coward!" Rhiannon screamed and threw the knife so hard it sailed past several startled people and embedded itself in the table just inches from the king's fat gut.

The queen shrieked, and their daughter quietly

snickered, trying to hide her amusement behind a napkin. Instantly two Yellow Island Guardsmen were standing on either side of their king with their swords drawn, looking menacingly at Rhiannon.

The crowd looked from Rhiannon back to Shankee expecting violence. "Be seated, Rhiannon. These are our guests!" Shankee ordered.

"I will not share a meal with an ally of Baobh! And while he's here, he'd better watch his back." Rhiannon narrowed her dark eyes at him, then ran from the room. Tim jumped up and quickly followed her.

Rhiannon angrily paced across the soft, carpeted floors of her apartments drinking whiskey from a small crystal glass. Her mind raced as furious energy radiated from her body and out into the room. Tim sat nervously on one of the upholstered chairs fiddling with one of Rhiannon's daggers that she had been practicing with lately. "Do you really mean to kill King Umar?" he asked.

"Yes." She did not hesitate.

"Tonight?" Tim's eyes grew wide.

"No." She finally sighed.

"Good, because I am certain that would start a war."

"Well, if they were fighting us, they would leave the rebellion alone, and I know we could beat them!" Rhiannon started to scheme but quickly abandoned the thought. She could not start a war within weeks of her return to Ventra.

"You are not serious?"

"No," she sighed again, then took a deep drink of her liquor. "I am frustrated, though. I can't believe Shankee had the gall to bring them here when I told her Yellow Island had a huge part in all but wiping out the rebellion!"

"Perhaps she invited them here to ascertain whether or not they were planning on helping Beaynid try and take Màrrach when they were done with the rebellion." Rhiannon looked over at Tim, unconvinced. "She does have the responsibility of diplomacy."

"I know exactly where she can shove her diplomacy!"

L ater that night, Rhiannon sat on a blanket spread out near one of the small ponds in the vast park-like solarium. The ducks had long since swam off into the cattails and nested for the night. The air was chilly, yet not nearly as cold as it was outside. It had snowed three days after Flath had left for Beaynid and a thick blanket still covered Màrrach.

Rhiannon spent time in the gardens every night. She found it relaxing. She spent time thinking about her father or trying to recall memories of her mother or the first six years of her life, here in Màrrach. Most of the time, her thoughts would drift to Flath. Once she thought she had seen him lurking near a tree in the flickering glow of a burning torch. But it had turned out to be the mysterious warrior who, whenever she spotted him, would slowly walk away, as if defeated.

The pax lay stretched out next to her on the blanket, her rough purring almost singing Rhiannon to sleep. The cat had grown considerably, losing the black spots of her youth and the warriors and their servants had finally grown accustomed to seeing the beast at her side.

As she had so many times before, she thought of Flath. She hoped he fared well and wondered if the rebellion yet lived. Sometimes her heart ached so badly she could not think of much else than the utter pain of missing him.

Her long legs were drawn up, and she rested her cheek on her red, silk covered knees. She had torn out all the braids and gemstones earlier and now wore her hair unbound. It spilled over her shoulders and down her back in a sleek, black sheet. She squeezed her eyes shut and tried to push out all her racing thoughts. The enormity of the situation was far beyond what she could comprehend. How could she ever lead the mighty nation of Ventra? Especially into a war they did not want, to protect people they hated.

Suddenly, she was brought out of her thoughts. Her skin prickled, and she knew that she was being watched. He had come again. She spotted him as he stood under a large white oak, quietly staring at her. Curiosity forced her to wave an arm in the air motioning him to come near. His body slightly jerked, as if he was surprised, but reluctantly started walking toward her. When he stood before her, she patted the ground inviting him to sit and he quietly obliged.

He looked much like the rest of the Archigos: high cheekbones, bronzed skin, straight dark hair and deep black eyes. He was as tall as Flath, but his body was sleeker, his bones a little finer. His hair was braided and fell to the middle of his back. His appearance was not lacking. He was quite handsome in a mysterious, dangerous kind of way.

He stretched out long muscled legs and leaned back on one arm. She could see red and blue tattoos circling up his biceps in an interpretation of a snake figure. He continued looking at her as though waiting for her to say something.

Rhiannon sighed and looked out over the pond again. She wondered if he would speak to her and if so, would he lower himself to speak to her in Jurian? Her hand was resting on the grass, and she jumped when she felt him take it into his. He held her hand tenderly examining every freckle and crease in the flicker of firelight. Finally, he stopped at a faint scar—nothing more than a tiny white line. He rubbed a calloused finger over it, and then let her hand go.

"It really is you, Rhiannon." He spoke quietly in Jurian. She did not reply but examined the scar on the back of her hand. "Do you remember when you got that?" he asked, indicating her hand with a nod.

"No."

"It was almost spring, right before you left with your parents." He looked out at the pond as if conjuring memories long dimmed by time. "We had been warned by the stable master, but we still snuck into the stables and crept way back to the last stall." She watched him intently not able to look away. "I was afraid and didn't want to go any further, but you insisted." His lips curved into a smile. "So, we slipped through the stable door to get a better look at the new foal. The mare was surprised but didn't seem too nervous, so we just kept getting closer and closer to the colt. I remember how you laughed when he tried to stand, but fell down in the straw." He looked into her eyes. "Finally, we got too close, and the mare grew angry and started stomping and snorting like a huge scary beast. She reared up and was going to come down on my head, but you pushed me out of the way, and her hoof landed on your hand, splitting it open!"

"I remember!" Rhiannon gasped. "You pulled me out of the stall then ran screaming out of the stables yelling for the stable master."

"Yes, and I was so worried when they carried you up to your mother."

"I do remember it now."

"Do you recall the whipping I received?"

"Yes," she said, laughing.

"I didn't think it was so humorous. It had been your idea," he said, smirking.

She studied him in the flickering light. "I can't believe it's you, Shih 'Ni!" she said, reaching over and hugging him tightly.

He clumsily wrapped his thick arms around her and squeezed. "I thought you were dead," he whispered.

She let go of him. "No, not dead—just lost."

CHAPTER TWO

Wisps of clouds across a broad blue sky
This is where the tiny Oread live and die.
Purple mountains at your back; fertile valley at your feet
Work of your hands, bounty of your harvest; all is complete.
Laughter of your children float on the breeze
Warm hearths glow even under a deep freeze.
To serve is the call of the goddess
So our knee will always bow to the Empress.
—Oread; Author Unknown

Rhiannon leaned against the rough bark of a naked oak. She was breathing heavily, and sweat streamed down her face despite the icy wind. The tip of her sword rested on the frozen earth as she sucked in the crisp air. She wiped the sweat from her face and watched as Tim sparred with a young Archigos boy around his own age, named Xev. The boys had gotten along well, and he provided Tim with some much-needed camaraderie. Tim's new Venturien sword glinted in the sunlight showing small figures of animals and twisted Venturien symbols from hilt to tip.

Shih 'Ni sheathed his sword. "You need a break?"

She gave him a withering look, sheathed her sword and walked over and sat down on a cold, stone bench. She dipped a bright copper cup into a bucket of water that was sitting on the bench and took a long drink, then handed it to Shih 'Ni who came and sat down next to her.

"We've been doing this for weeks, when does it get easier?"

"Well, with such poor conditioning, this is going to take some time."

"Thanks for your confidence!" She grabbed the cup from him and dumped the rest of the water over his head.

He yelped and jumped up quickly. "That's freezing!" he protested, wiping the cold water from his leather tunic. After taking the cup back, he sat down next to her again. "You'll be ready for battle soon enough, Rhiannon."

"Not soon enough." She shook her head. "I have so much that I still need to learn before I can help Flath and the rebellion rid Beaynid of Baobh," she looked over at Shih Ni. "So, I must learn quickly." She looked down at her hands. Her hands were wrapped in leather strips to give her a better grip and to lend her blistered palms some protection. She slowly turned her hands over noticing how worn they looked. The cloth strips were stained brown with streaks of blood.

"Already making plans to go to war? And you're not even officially the empress yet!" Shih Ni gave her a sideways glance.

"Of course, I'm making plans, most of the men who were fighting with the rebellion were slaughtered or seriously injured by Yellow Island. Their only hope lies with us."

"And why should it concern us? Do you think the Seuns would come to our aid if it were us who were in trouble? I think not! Those self-righteous pale-skins would just as soon spit in our faces!"

"Well, maybe it's time for things to change." Rhiannon looked down at her leather boots, black with dampness.

"You will have better luck moving a mountain. Do you think your warriors will just follow you into a battle to help a people who we despise? You can't change generations of hate and distrust with the snap of your fingers, Rhiannon." His tone softened. "You'll have to give your warriors a better reason to follow you than just to help out a man you fancy."

Rhiannon looked up, fury bubbled inside her. "Baobh murdered my mother and is holding my father captive! Is that a good enough reason?"

Before Shih Ni could answer, they spotted Shankee and another woman approaching, heads bent in discussion. Shankee's youngest child, Tam 'Lyn, followed close behind his mother and was trailed by a small, fluffy black and white dog. He was six-years-old and the very image of his mother. He stopped in momentary awe of a man and woman sparring. His little eyes grew wide as the warriors moved, grunting with effort, the sing of steel ringing out into the cold air. Discovering his mother walking away, he turned and ran after her as fast as his short, little legs could take him.

Shih 'Ni and Rhiannon stood and bowed when Shankee stopped before them. Tim had appeared at her shoulder, ready to offer his services as her translator. Shih 'Ni could have easily translated, of course, but Tim did not want to relinquish his job.

"Good morning, cousin." Shankee smiled at her as Tim interpreted.

Rhiannon beamed, and something stirred in her heart at the family sentiment. She was glad that Shankee was no longer angry with her about how Rhiannon spoke to the King of Yellow Island. "Good morning, Shankee."

"This is Kyia. I have asked her to tutor you in Venn. I think the lessons will be good for you and will help you remember your language." Tim motioned to the young woman standing next to Shankee. He went on translating Shankee's words, turning them into something recognizable.

"She can also instruct you in the ways of royalty and remind you of our culture as well as introduce you to other women," Shankee glanced over to Shih 'Ni, and then to Tim and Xev. "I think it will be good for you to have some female friends to confide in."

"Thank you, Shankee," Rhiannon replied.

"I look forward to our first lesson. How is tonight after we eat?" Kyia asked in Jurian and smiled.

"After dinner will be fine."

"Good, I'll meet you in the solarium at the western pond near the panther bench."

With that, Kyia bowed to Rhiannon, and the two women left—Shankee's son running to keep up with the women who quietly spoke, paying no heed to his effort.

Rhiannon turned around to head back to their sparring box but stopped when she noticed a strange look on Shih 'Ni's face. "Do you know Kyia?"

"We were betrothed," he stated, then walked into the

sparring box and unsheathed his sword. "Are you going to continue your training so that we may take over the world, or are you still too tired to carry on?" he asked sarcastically.

That evening Rhiannon sat at her writing table. A petite, white-haired woman and a slightly taller man of equal complexion and features had brought up her dinner and a bottle of dark red wine. Many nights she and Tim ate in the grand dining room with Shankee, her family, and their various guests—however, she was tired and sore and did not feel like socializing on this night. She picked at her food and finished her third glass of wine, then turned her attention to the half-written letter that laid out before her. Xev had promised that his brother could travel to Beaynid and deliver the letter to Flath. Rhiannon was skeptical because the road across the Vel' Kur Mountains was impassible this time of year. However, she decided to give him a chance when he said his brother would be traveling out of Turr'ah by ship.

Looking down at the scrolling ink drying on the paper like a trail of black blood on a sheet of ice, she turned to the small pile of crumpled up attempts she had made earlier and shook her head. She asked if he was well and how his men were faring. She inquired about the status of the rebellion and then told him of what she had been doing over the long months since he had left.

What she wanted to say, however, was that she missed him terribly and wanted to see him. She wanted to ask him to come and rule with her in Màrrach after Baobh's defeat. She wanted to tell him that she loved him. However, those things were best left unsaid until they could be spoken face to face.

Finally, she finished the letter with a reassurance that as soon as she took control of Màrrach, she and her warriors would travel to Beaynid to aid in the rebellion. She begged him to be careful then signed her name with love. Carefully, she folded the letter and placed it into the envelope, then sealed it with hot wax. The royal seal of Màrrach stared back at her from the envelope. An unexplainable feeling of pride washed over her as she marveled at the intricacies of the little silver stamp. Suddenly she realized, somewhere, in the middle of what had started out to be the bleakest part of her life, she had made the decision to stay. Like the soft petals of a fading flower, she had dropped the memories of a Montana ranch, broken promises, and an uncomplicated life.

The crackling of the fireplace brought Rhiannon back to the moment. It was time for her first lesson with Kyia. Rhiannon made her way down to the solarium as Luna ran on ahead and the pax silently padded along next to her. She had affectionately named her Etâhpe'o-poeso, which means big cat in the old speech of the native people of Montana. She called the cat Poeso for short. The winter sun had sunk into darkness, and brilliant ice chipped stars twinkled in the northern sky. The world outside was painted in the sparkle of frozen fields and barren trees, but inside, the everlasting spring of the colossal solarium park continued the rituals of birth, growth, and bloom.

Just as she'd said, Kyia was waiting on the bench next to the western pond. Dappled rosewood was magnificently carved into the life-sized forms of crouching panthers—their emerald eyes sparkled in the fluttering torchlight. She playfully rubbed Luna's head. The she-wolf had run up to her and rested her head in the woman's lap.

"It's good to see you, Lady Rhiannon." Kyia jumped up and dipped into a clumsy bow.

"Thank you," she replied, feeling awkward, and then sat.

Like all other warriors, Kyia wore tiny beaded braids within her loose hair. Kyia's typical Archigos features were softened with plump cheeks and a slightly shorter, more petite frame. Most of the other Archigos women she had seen were tall and muscular with sharp angular faces—the men even more so. Kyia, however, had a certain softness to her. Her curves were plump, and her hands were delicate and her fingers, slender.

Even her cinnamon brown eyes were not as the inky dark pools of most she had seen in Màrrach.

"Are you ready to begin your lesson, Empress?"

"I don't feel much like an empress," Rhiannon replied.

"Empress Shankee asked me to help you remember our tongue and our customs. You were born an empress, milady, you don't need anyone to show you how."

"I don't know if I will ever be good enough to rule Màrrach." She looked down at her slippered feet. "I certainly don't know how to handle a sword too well." Rhiannon laughed awkwardly.

"Empress Shankee has told me you are making fine

progress. Archigos children start learning very early the techniques of warfare and weaponry, and even how to command a war-horse. It takes a long time to make an Archigos warrior, milady."

"I don't have that much time." Rhiannon started stroking the soft fur atop Poeso's head.

Kyia laughed softly. "Why are you in such a hurry? You have a lifetime ahead of you."

"Shankee hasn't told you?"

"That you wish to aid the rebellion? Yes, she has told me that you approached her and told her of your plans."

"Kyia, Baobh has my father. I don't even know if he's still alive, but if he is, I must free him. Surely you understand."

Kyia took a deep breath. "Yes, milady, I do understand your desire to free your father. But he is not an Archigos, nor is he the mate of an Archigos empress any longer. I don't know if you will be successful in convincing our warriors to leave their homes and children—possibly never to return—just to free an outlander."

"He was the husband of their empress, and he's my father, not quite someone of no importance." A tear slipped down Rhiannon's cheek. "I will go with or without the help of my people. Did Shankee tell you that also?"

"Yes, she did." Kyia rested her warm hand on top of Rhiannon's. "You have a strong conviction, milady. Let's just hope it will be stronger than the hatred that burns in the hearts of our people."

Rhiannon looked out over the still water, and neither spoke for a long time. She wondered what her mother would have done. She knew her father must have had some kind of protection or position of importance while her mother still lived, but if what Kyia said was true, he was no longer considered an Archigos—even if only by association —thus, the Archigos were under no obligation to rescue him. She had hoped that the Archigos would be the answer to freeing her father. Now she doubted they would aid her in her personal crusade.

And then there was the matter of her mother's necklace. A very valuable possession the Archigos had great pride in receiving, they say, from their goddess, Verna. Shankee seemed to believe that Baobh would not use it against the Archigos, but Rhiannon knew she would, eventually.

Kyia finally started to speak. "A very wise, very old woman once told me that a pure heart could stand alone or lead many, but the outcome would always be the same: truth and goodness would prevail." Kyia looked at Rhiannon and smiled. "I will follow you, Rhiannon." Rhiannon looked into the young woman's eyes and knew it to be true.

The dreams that had haunted her sleep for so long had stopped as soon as she stepped on the other side of that blasted tree. Tonight, though, Rhiannon dreamed again, but this time she was able to picture the man's face. Her dream took her to him, then around Beaynid and finally into the very gates of Sona Tuath. She found a small passageway draped with sticky cobwebs, then descended the twisting stone steps into the bowels of the castle. From the midst of the dream, she could see her father crumpled in the corner of a dark, damp prison. Thinking him dead, she ran calling out to him, but when she finally reached his withered form, he turned to meet her gaze. Watery blue eyes stared back, and a weak smile formed on his haggard face. She knew then he was still alive, and her tortured mind could ease itself and allow her to fall back into an empty sleep. Poeso's rough purr was momentarily halted while Rhiannon stirred under the blankets, but then the pax resumed her rhythmic night song.

"It's time you saw what lies about in Màrrach, Lady Kossi," Kyia announced as she met Rhiannon coming from the sparring fields the next day.

Rhiannon wiped the sweat from her brow. "Now?"

She smiled, "Yes, milady. It's a clear afternoon and not too cold for the horses."

Rhiannon looked around for Tim and finally spotted him chatting away in a group of young would-be warriors.

"Well, okay. Can you give me a few minutes to wash up?"

"Of course, milady. I'll meet you at your stable in thirty minutes." She bowed and was off before Rhiannon could object.

A half an hour later, dressed in a thick woolen tunic and breeches, she trudged out of the palace and down the marbled steps out into the cold—Poeso, contentedly following.

When Rhiannon reached Zellan's paddock, Kyia was standing there with him, and her mount saddled and ready to go. Rhiannon noticed there were thousands of horses in fenced pastures as far as she could see. Most of them were trained war horses belonging to warriors, but many, it seemed, were wild and restless. Small, fair-skinned grooms and trainers and other servants buzzed about like bees in a ripe hive. The activity in the paddock and huge stables were, by far, the most active area she had seen yet.

Seeing Rhiannon's interest in the horses, Kyia explained. "One of our biggest trade is in the selling of our horses. Horses from Ventra are highly sought after by nobles and royalty and rich merchants. We ship them out to the entire known world. We do not train them in our way, of course, that is a secret that none but the Archigos know." She smiled. "We are known by all as horse lords as well as warriors."

Rhiannon turned her attention back to Kyia. "It's really fascinating to see so many horses in one place."

Kyia laughed and swung up onto her mount's back. "Are you ready for your tour, Lady Rhiannon?"

Carefully, they made their way into the snow and away from the massive palace compounds of Màrrach and headed towards the vast growing fields now covered with an endless blanket of white. Bare, damp orchards covered the small hills surrounding the servant's cottages. As far as the eye could see were fruit and nut trees of all different kinds, now hibernating under the cool sun.

"You can't see them from here, but over those hills are other fields and orchards. These are watered from the Spring of Eternal Life. The produce they provide is sweeter and can last much longer than regular fruit and vegetables. This is why we always have fresh fruit and vegetables even in the darkest of winters." Kyia said something softly to her horse, and they started out again. "The Velk Trees are also planted there. These are the trees whose leaves we burn as a sacrifice to Verna. You can identify the trees by their pristine, white bark, and in the spring and summer, their bright, golden leaves." Rhiannon nodded, trying to file all this information away.

Kyia looked back at Rhiannon and continued to explain the sources of Ventra's seemingly endless riches. "I'm sure you've heard of the Del' Nort mine." She paused.

"Isn't that where the stones from my mother's necklace came from?" Rhiannon urged Zellan up to Kyia's mount.

"Yes. We mine thousands of other precious gems that are crafted into stunning jewelry. The bigger gems we sell raw. These are also taken to Turr'ah and sent out with the trading parties. This is where Ventra gets most of her wealth." Kyia explained matter-of-factly as they continued through the frozen countryside.

The air was cold and dry causing Rhiannon's face and fingers to numb. Huge, white clouds floated by, carried south by a frigid northern wind. She pulled her thick fur coat tighter around her shoulders and kneed Zellan forward.

They came up to a barren meadow lightly dusted with snow. A few hearty blades of grass poked through making a delicious meal for dozens of rabbits. Rhiannon pulled her fur-lined cap down further over her cold ears as Kyia patiently pointed out all things of interest and various landmarks, saying the word first in Jur, then in Venn. Six large supply wagons came over a sloping hill and headed towards the royal palace. Large Clydesdales trudged through the snow pulling wagons fully stocked with casks of liquor. Two white-haired men sat atop the wagon, flanked by warrioress' on each side.

"They travel east to Turr'ah every month to pick up imported drink," Kyia pointed to the disappearing wagon.

"Who are all those little servants around Màrrach," Rhiannon asked.

"You don't remember the Mountain People?" Kyia arched an eyebrow.

"No." Rhiannon looked out to a field where groups of the people were harvesting potatoes and yams and other cold weather vegetables.

"We call them Oread for short. It means 'small in stature' in Venn." Kyia hitched a shoulder in a half-shrug. "Well, the Oreads have been here for a long time. In fact, it's said that the mountain itself gave birth to the very first Oread shortly after the creation of everything."

"They've been here longer than the Archigos?" Rhiannon wiped her sleeve under her red nose. The air had gotten colder as the sun rested on the mountain range.

"They were the first inhabitants of Ventra," Kyia explained, "Legend says that when the Archigos arrived in Ventra, the Oread were jealous and would not share this land. The Archigos were not as mighty in number as we are today, in fact, the Oread far outnumbered the Archigos.

"Despite the hostility they received, the Archigos Empress decided to settle here in the valley due to its fertile soil and rich hunting ground," Kyia swept her arm around the vast land.

"It's a beautiful place," Rhiannon whispered.

"Every day the Oread grew to hate the Archigos more but knew that although they had the advantage in numbers, they could not defeat the skilled Archigos warriors. Finally, they devised a plan to drive the Archigos away, as the story goes." Kyia pulled her mare a little further away from Zellan's curious advances. "Back then we didn't have the grand palaces as we do now," she went on, "We lived in tents and mud huts all along these hills. One night a group of Oread snuck into the Archigos camp late at night and kidnapped the empress. They thought if the empress suddenly came up missing the rest of the Archigos would just leave in search of a more hospitable place to settle."

"They didn't think the Archigos would suspect the Oread of taking their empress?" Rhiannon asked, as she slid out of her saddle and stretched sore muscles.

"Well, as the legend has it, the Oread are quite simple minded."

Rhiannon snorted in reply as she kicked the snow from her boots. Kyia slid from her mount as well. Wrapping the reins around the low branch of a leafless sycamore tree, she arched her back in a lingering stretch. "So," Kyia started again, "They brought the empress back to their village and tried to devise a way to kill her,"

"Nice bunch of people," Rhiannon interjected.

Kyia gave her a smile. "Just before they were to behead

the empress, Taber, the chieftain of the Oread, saw the empress's beauty and fell in love with her immediately!" Rhiannon gave Kyia a disbelieving look. "I didn't write the legend, milady," Kyia chuckled, and then started again. "They kept the empress well-hidden while the Archigos scoured Ventra looking for their leader. But they never found where the Oread had hidden her.

"All the while Taber tried to win the affections of the empress. At first, the empress wouldn't have anything to do with the man, but he persisted and finally won her over due to his gentle ways. Finally, the empress took him back to the Archigos as her mate. Neither the Oread nor the Archigos were happy about this arrangement, however, and it caused even more enmity between the two races.

"One night a few of the more hateful of the Oread snuck into the Archigos camp and into the empress's tent. The empress and her mate woke, but the group of Oread overpowered them both and murdered them right there in their own bed."

"So, what happened?" Rhiannon prodded after Kyia paused a little too long.

"Our legends say that because the Oread had murdered the Archigos empress, the goddess Verna was greatly angered and tried to kill the Oread. However, the mountain woke to hear the screams of her children and began to fight with Verna. The earth shook, great boulders were loosed from the mountain's slopes, and huge trees snapped in half because of the violent quaking. Finally, Verna overpowered the Great Mother Mountain, but because Verna could see her deep sorrow for her children she promised to let the Oread live.

"Consequently, instead of destroying the Oread she gave them to the Archigos as servants and to make sure they would never again challenge the Archigos, Verna caused them to shrink into the small people that they are today." Kyia took a deep breath, and then let it out slowly as it turned to mist and floated away. "Before the empress and her mate were murdered, however, she had given birth to a baby girl who later became Empress. So, it's said that Archigos have a little Oread in our blood."

"Interesting. And what do the Oreads have to say about all of that?"

"Nothing. It's been this way for centuries, milady. They accept their fate."

Suddenly a loud crack snapped through the cold air. Rhiannon and Kyia turned around to see a massive bear charging towards them. Kyia's mare reared, tearing its reins from the small branch they were wrapped around and quickly disappeared over a small hill. Zellan screamed and sidestepped just as the giant bear barreled past him. Rhiannon jumped out of the way barely missing the beast's giant claws. Quickly she jumped to her feet and drew her sword. The bear stood up on its hind legs and bellowed. She could feel its hot breath as she stared into its yellow eyes.

Kyia ran up next to her, sword drawn. "Milady back away, slowly." But Rhiannon was frozen and could not move. The bear's sick yellow eyes held her in a web she could not break free from no matter how hard she resisted. Her blood ran cold, and her heart leaped in her chest. She gripped her sword tighter to try and stop her hand from shaking. "Rhiannon, move back!" Kyia screamed and shoved her back. Rhiannon tried to open her mouth. Sweat formed and began to roll down her brow as she tried to find her voice, but she remained silent.

A scream came from behind Rhiannon, and the sound of beating wings descended upon them. Poeso slashed the bear's shoulder with long, sharp claws. The Bear roared and swatted at the pax as she tried to slash at the bear's face.

Kyia took the opportunity to grab Rhiannon's arm and pull her back towards Zellan who nervously stamped the frozen earth but refused to leave Rhiannon.

"Get on your horse, milady." Kyia continued to pull her back with one hand while holding on tightly to her sword with the other.

Rhiannon still could not find her voice, nor could she look away from the huge creature that was now engaged in a battle with Poeso. The great, black bear stepped out of the way just missing a flesh-tearing swipe from the pax, then quickly spun around and delivered a hard blow to the winged cat, knocking her from the air. She screamed and hit the ground with a loud thud. Without missing a step, the bear charged towards Rhiannon and Kyia.

"Get on your horse!" Kyia screamed and pushed Rhiannon towards Zellan, and then turned to face the snarling beast, her sword held tightly in front of her.

Rhiannon felt as though her body was being swallowed by mud and no matter how hard she tried, she could not break free. A massive weight descended upon her like a great stone, and she began to shake as she watched the enormous bear close in on them.

Kyia dodged the bear's large paw, its claws slightly raking across her coat sleeve. Quickly she spun around and sliced across its chest. Blood sprayed the white snow, and the beast opened its mouth only to have a woman's scream emerge from its massive jaws.

The weight was suddenly gone as Rhiannon reached out and grabbed Kyia's arm, pulling her out of the way just as the bear brought its huge head down in an effort to tear her in half. Rhiannon sheathed her sword and scrambled on to Zellan's back.

"Let's go, Kyia!" she screamed as she pulled the smaller woman up behind her and kneed Zellan into a gallop. Poeso stood and shook the snow from her fur, then quickly took to the air after Rhiannon. As they crested the small hill, they heard the long wail of an enraged woman. Rhiannon looked back, but nothing except blood-stained snow where the great bear once stood.

~

"Goyor," Kyia answered Shankee later in her royal parlor.

"Are you certain?"

"Yes empress, I'm sure it was a Goyor." Kyia stood before Shankee. The older woman folded her arms and slowly walked over to the massive fireplace, staring into the crackling yellow flames and rocked from one foot to the other. Rhiannon looked over to Kyia, brows arched in a questioning manner for which Kyia just shrugged her shoulders. Tim stood silently by Rhiannon's side, his face etched with worry.

"It's starting all over again, then," Shankee spoke softly into the blazing fire. Tim whispered a translation into Rhiannon's ear. Then Shankee turned and walked over to stand in front of Rhiannon. "I watched as your mother was hunted, just as you are being hunted now." There was a slight, humorless smile in her black eyes as she remembered long-buried memories. "I was a young woman of fifteen years, and I remember how that evil shape-changer hunted your mother until she was forced into hiding, waiting for the Tree of Jur to open in the spring so that they could take you to your father's world and keep you safe until you were old enough to return and take the throne." The fire threw sputtering shadows across Shankee's drawn face giving her an eerie glow. Tim carefully translated Shankee's every word. A tear slipped down Rhiannon's cheek as she stared defiantly into Shankee's cold eyes.

"Your mother and father bundled you up in the middle of the night and disappeared. I thought it was finally over. I was sure the Goyor would not come back to Màrrach." Shankee's lips curled into a strange, bitter smile. "Twenty-four years later she has returned, though it's your blood she now craves. Quite ironic, don't you think?"

Shankee walked over to a large cabinet, pulled out a crystal decanter and poured herself a cup full of dark liquid. She closed her eyes and smelled the bitter wine, then took a long, slow drink. After a while, she turned back towards

Kyia. "She will not leave the palace without an escort, and she will not go beyond the palace courtyard, or stables, under any circumstance." Kyia nodded in acknowledgment.

Shankee put the cup down and walked back up to Rhiannon. "You need to pick a mate, Rhiannon, and produce an heir before you end up like your mother. I do not intend to live the rest of my life as a proxy empress."

Fury burned inside her chest as Tim translated Shankee's words. "You do not have to be proxy empress any longer, cousin. Make me empress now, and I will relieve you of your burden!" Tim stuttered as he spoke the words to Shankee. Kyia moved closer to Rhiannon.

Shankee laughed a humorless sound. "You're so sure of yourself, Rhiannon. However, you still have much to learn before you take the throne. You want to march our warriors off on some personal battle that none will come back from!"

"Do you think hiding is a better idea?" Rhiannon screamed.

"I think it's better until you can produce an heir and then it will not be of my concern any longer." Shankee folded her arms across her chest and looked at Rhiannon insolently, as Tim interpreted.

"You're a coward, Shankee!" Rhiannon screamed. "You're not an empress! You will not lead your people into battle to stop the evil that took your empress's life."

Shankee's lips pursed and she drew her brows into a frown. "You know nothing of commanding a nation. You're ignorant." Tim swallowed and looked up at Rhiannon, then nervously translated Shankee's words. Kyia turned her eyes to the floor.

Suddenly, Rhiannon grabbed Shankee by the arm and squeezed tightly. "I am Sernia's daughter, the Empress of Ventra, and I will fight!" Rhiannon stated with emotion and in perfect Venn and then walked from the room.

CHAPTER THREE

It is said the Archigos came to Ventra from a far-off land across the Carniad Sea. There is rumor they are somehow related to a race of Forest Folk, though this has never been proven. Whatever their origins, they have been living and ruling in Ventra for many generations.
—Ventra, Land of Ice and Warriors; G. P. Love

The cold winter weeks crept by much the same as the weeks before had. Still angered by Shankee's words, Rhiannon refused to speak to her and ate her meals with Tim and Kyia or Shih 'Ni in one of the smaller dining rooms. Whenever Rhiannon was alone in the quiet of her bedchamber Shankee's cold words echoed in her head.

Impelled by absolute determination, Rhiannon's fighting skills steadily improved. She also found that the twisty, harsh words of Venn slipped more easily from her mouth. Some of the words she remembered from long ago, but most she had to learn anew. Kyia had proved to be a patient, skilled teacher.

While not quite as patient as Kyia, Shih 'Ni's passion for the blade was infectious and Rhiannon found she loved the sing of steel, the zing of piercing arrow and even the precision of the shiny, small axes. His movements were fluid and graceful. He could move with such speed and power the enemy did not have a chance. Rhiannon studied his moves carefully and practiced relentlessly to try and duplicate Shih 'Ni's controlled, deadly style.

It was an unusually warm day for the end of December, melting snow lay in dirty clumps dotting the winter landscape. The sparring fields were full of warriors taking advantage of the break in the bitter cold to warm up stiff muscles and remember old techniques. Shih 'Ni sat on a stone bench tenderly rubbing a cloth over the gleaming blade of his sword. In the heat of practice, he had shed his tunic. Muscles and sinew rolled and bulged under taut skin shimmering with sweat. His jet-black hair was tightly braided and hung between his broad shoulders. The swirling red and blue tattooed dots that pronounced him a high-level warrior, and the Archigos Master-at-Arms, scrolled importantly across chest and shoulders. He seemed oblivious to the yearning stares and bubbly giggles of a group of girls not far off.

Archigos children were taught the sword from a very young age and continued to train until their twentieth year when they were pronounced warriors and welcomed into the fold. It was not until then that they could join in battle. It had been peaceful since Shankee took the throne as proxy empress, so most young warriors had yet to fight in battle. Still, the sparring and training carried on as it had for centuries.

In the distance, Rhiannon could see the rise of two more massive buildings that made up the three palace compounds of Màrrach. The Royal Palace or Verna's Palace, where she and the rest of the royal family lived, along with the most valued warriors and their families, was the largest of the three. Except for size, all three were identical in design and color right down to the huge solariums that filled the middle of the structures with eternal spring and the many statues of gods and goddesses dispersed around and in the palaces. The two lesser palaces were called Tec 'Lo after the Sun Goddess and Nei 'Rum after the Moon Goddess. Kyia had told Rhiannon that each goddess was inferior to Verna, of course, but was worshiped and held in high veneration by the Archigos just the same.

As Kyia had recited the legends of the sun and moon goddesses, Rhiannon's memory stirred, and the faint sound of her mother's voice began to fill her mind. She remembered her mother's recounting of the story of the beautiful sisters, Tec 'Lo and Nei 'Rum. As the legend went, they were twins born to an Archigos empress many, many years ago. As the girls grew, they began to look less and less like Archigos and even less like sisters. One had curls the color of fire and shown so brightly in the daylight that it was almost blinding to look at. The other had hair, fine and luminescent white, that had the most unearthly glow about it under the moon's light.

Finally, the time arrived for the girls to pick their mates. Both girls bore the red diamond above their breast, so it was determined that the first sister to bear a female child would take the throne. One at a time the girls made their way through Màrrach looking for a mate. They were presented with the most powerful male warriors in the kingdom, and each girl silently made their pick, telling no one of their choices, for it was to be a secret until the marriage ceremony called Nikah.

Finally, the wedding day arrived and the men they had picked weeks earlier were summoned to the Grand Palace. The room fell silent as only one man walked in. As he approached the sisters, they realized that they had chosen the same man! Immediately a violent fight broke out between the sisters. As blood began to spill, Verna decided to take action and appeared in the room before the sisters. For their disgraceful acts, Verna told them she was going to send the sisters far off from one another. The sisters looked confused and frightened, for they had never been separated. They begged Verna not to send them away, but the goddess would not change her mind. Verna then told the girls that because they spilled each other's blood, they would never see each other again. Verna turned Tec 'Lo into the sun, and Nei 'Rum became the moon. They each ruled the earth, but at different times and never saw each other again.

Rhiannon was brought out of her memories by the ring of steel. Shih 'Ni was sparring with one of the young girls that had been bashfully watching him before. Archigos men were more powerful. Nothing could be done about that. It was just physiology. Archigos women were strong in their own right and had the added advantage of being quicker. This young, future warrioress was lacking in all the skill that Shih "Ni had, but all could tell it was not his skills as a warrior she was interested in at the moment.

Luna began barking and captured Rhiannon's attention. The pax, who had been contentedly napping on a stone bench sat up, yawned, and then bent down into a deep stretch. Rhiannon followed Luna's sight and saw a large raven circling above them. Luna's bark increased in urgency. Poeso growled, and in a flurry of feathers, the pax took flight after the raven. They narrowly missed colliding in air, and then the bird swooped and headed for the forest with the pax close behind. Luna ran off over the snow-covered hills after Poeso and then disappeared behind a stand of pine trees.

Assuming the pax was hungry and Luna, just bored, Rhiannon began to clean her own blade wondering why Shih 'Ni had not chosen a mate yet, or rather, why a woman had not chosen him, as was the custom. Neither he nor Kyia would speak of their ill-fated betrothal, which made Rhiannon wonder even more, but she decided to wait until one of them opened up.

The song of the blades ended, and the young woman slowly walked back to her friends. Shih 'Ni pulled his tunic on and sat down next to Rhiannon. "You have quite a fan club there, big guy."

"What's a fan club?" He gave her a questioning look.

"Those girls seem to be mighty interested in your fighting technique." Rhiannon chuckled and carefully sheathed her sword.

"Oh," he flashed Rhiannon a smile. "Are you jealous, Empress Kossi?"

She laughed and gave him a shove. "Jealous? No! I have better things to worry about."

"Is that so? Will you ever choose a mate, or are you planning on living forever and being Màrrach's last empress?"

"All in due time, Shih 'Ni." Rhiannon looked south toward the towering mountain range that separated Ventra from Beaynid.

"Or, have you already chosen a mate?" Shih 'Ni's voice was soft as he watched Rhiannon.

"What makes you say that?" She looked back over at him.

"Shankee told me you favor that Seun gypsy who's leading the rebellion against Sona Tuath."

Rhiannon bit back a retort. "Shankee and I haven't had more than five short conversations since I arrived, how would she know who I favor?"

"I saw how you and that Seun embraced before he left. Everyone could see how you feel about the man." Shih 'Ni held her eyes. She opened her mouth as if to say something, but quickly closed it again. "They will never accept him, Rhiannon," Shih 'Ni said, finally.

"It's not up to anyone but me and Flath. I don't care what everyone else thinks!"

"Rhiannon, you're an empress now, you must always consider your people in all that you do."

"Maybe it's time for my people to change how they feel, then. Besides, Shankee's husband isn't an Archigos, and neither was my father."

"They're not Seuns, either," Shih 'Ni countered.

"Why do you Archigos have to be so hard-headed?"

"We've had this conversation before."

"And we'll keep having it until this hatred is squelched."

Shih 'Ni sighed and looked away. "You are a very different woman, Rhiannon Kossi."

"It wasn't so long ago that I was in my own place far away from here, living my simple life and my biggest worry was trying to make my father happy." A cool wind blew up from the north and ruffled her onyx hair. "Now I don't even know if I'll ever see my father again." She turned to Shih 'Ni, "I will change the way my warriors feel about the Seun people."

"It's a hard battle you've chosen for yourself, Rhiannon. Is he worth it?"

She looked very deeply into his eyes, his soul laid bare, "Yes," she whispered, and she saw the pain blister across his eyes.

Shih 'Ni sheathed his sword and walked away. It was then that she realized his feelings had grown into more than a friendship. She watched him as he walked toward the palace straight, tall and strong. He was a very proud, impressive man whose presence was one of unmistakable power. He would make an ideal leader and a perfect tjaty for an empress. But her heart was already given to someone else.

"**D**o you like being here?" Rhiannon lay on her belly on top of the cool green grass later that afternoon. Her chin rested on folded arms as she watched a pair of brilliantly painted black swans drift across one of the huge solarium's ponds.

"I do, very much, milady," Tim answered as he lay next to Rhiannon.

"Do you miss the fighting?"

"To tell you the truth, I am quite glad to be here," Tim turned towards her, "not that I am a coward, milady, but 'tis quite comfortable here." He was silent for a moment, then, "and I did not want to leave you by yourself."

Rhiannon smiled and looked over at him. "Thank you, Tim. Your company has made this whole ordeal much more bearable." She studied the peaks and hollows of his face. The bruises had long since faded, but his light skinned, freckled face would never be the same. There was a scar that ran from this left eyebrow and disappeared into his curly red hair. Another scar cut across the pink softness of his bottom lip forever marring his appearance. However, the biggest change in Tim was the guarded look in his eyes. She did not think he was aware of it, but the blue of his eyes, which were once the color of a summer sky, were now a shade darker, like an angry winter sky, as if the light in his soul had diminished a bit. She felt the sting of guilt, I have done this to him.

Tim rolled over onto his back, rested his head in his hands and stared up at the clear glass dome above. The sounds of birds calling to one another floated on a sweet breeze and mingled with the splashing of a waterfall. A persistent peacock shimmered into an iridescent fan then slowly followed after an oblivious peahen. A few snow-white bunnies hopped across the manicured lawn under a blooming rhododendron.

The pax lay fast asleep next to Rhiannon, her coarse

purring sawed out a lazy tune for a winter afternoon. She was fully-grown now and the injuries she had suffered when Rhiannon had first found her had healed. She had received no more than a few scratches in the fight with Baobh and had recovered from that also. She was the size of a large cougar, but curiously her weight was like that of a housecat. Her wings were glossy and powerful and spanned some twenty-five feet when fully outstretched. She was quite a sight and was almost always close by Rhiannon. Luna had grown accustomed to Poeso as well, and sometimes the two would wrestle around in a playful ball of fur and feathers.

"You remind me a lot of her," Tim finally said.

"Of who?"

"My sister, Rachel."

"I do?"

"Yes. She was quite outspoken and a bit of a tomboy, too."

"I'm a tomboy, huh?"

"Well, I mean… you… uh," Tim fumbled.

Rhiannon's body convulsed with laughter. "It's okay, Tim. I know I'm a bit rough. But after meeting my family," she rolled over onto her back and waved an arm to encompass the palace. "You can see it's not my fault."

Tim smiled. "You have a point, milady," he said and then went on. "She was very beautiful too. Not dark like you, but she had the most brilliant red hair that hung to her hips, and her skin was like cream." Tim swiped at an inquisitive bee buzzing around his head. "You and Rachel do not look alike, but your personalities are much the same."

"Well, then, I'm very privileged. I wish I could have met your sister, Tim."

"She would have loved you. She might have even tried to get you to take her back to Màrrach with you!" A broad smile crossed Tim's face.

"Do you miss home?" Rhiannon asked.

"Sometimes more than others. I miss my father, mostly."

"I hope someday you will take me to Bell to meet your father."

"He'll like you right off, milady!" Tim answered, excitedly.

Rhiannon rolled over on her side and propped herself up on one elbow. "You know, Tim, you're like the little brother I never had." Tim stiffened and was silent. They passed the next several moments in quiet contemplation.

Finally, Rhiannon's stomach growled loudly. Poeso stopped purring and looked up at her. Convinced nothing was wrong she closed her enormous eyes and slipped back into her nap. "I think it's dinner time," she said as she stood up and brushed grass blades from her long, beaded tunic and leggings. Poeso followed.

Tim and Rhiannon made their way through the solarium, continuing in silence, the pax following along. As they reached the end of the park, he turned towards Rhiannon. "I would be honored to be your brother, Rhiannon."

Rhiannon stopped and turned to face the young man.

The sentiment had taken her by surprise and emotion tightened her throat making it hard for her to reply. His bright blue eyes twinkled in the dying light as a tear slipped down his pale cheek. Rhiannon grabbed Tim in her arms and hugged him tightly. "Oh Tim, you've already proven yourself a wonderful confidant and brother."

"I am sorry that I was not able to prevent them from taking your mother's little stone."

Poeso rubbed against Rhiannon's leg, and she reached down and smoothed the big cat's furry head. "That wasn't your fault, Tim, I'll get it back soon enough."

"Do you think you can convince the Archigos to go into battle against Baobh?"

"I don't know," she sighed. "But I will go and help Flath whether these stubborn people come with me or not."

"Come, now. We're not all that bad." A calm voice said in Venn. Shankee walked out of the dying light and stood before them. She was not as tall as Rhiannon, but just as lean and muscled. Her long black hair was braided and fell over one shoulder. Tiny pins studded with diamonds dotted her dark hair. The gems of her crown winked in the light.

"Hello Shankee," Rhiannon said tightly and gave a slight bow. Happily, Rhiannon had picked up enough Venn to converse.

"I see you're still determined to send your warriors into Beaynid."

Rhiannon listened intently making sure she understood each word. "My father is rotting away in a..." she tried to find the right word, "...dungeon ... in Sona Tuath. I will free him as soon as I'm able." Rhiannon raised her chin in defiance. Tim sighed, bracing for the fight that would surely ensue.

"So, you would sacrifice the lives of valuable warriors for the chance of rescuing an old man?"

"The people of Beaynid are suffering under the rule of Baobh! She asks for more coin than they can afford and even takes their harvest, leaving little for the people to eat. They are on the brink of a famine! They need to be freed from her..." she cursed herself for not being more fluent. Then Tim whispered an appropriate adjective. "... tyrannical rule. The rebellion can't do it alone. Does the suffering of thousands of innocents mean nothing to the Archigos?"

"We have no business in Beaynid fighting their wars or freeing their oppressed. They're not a concern of Ventra."

"Baobh murdered my mother, your empress! And now she's after me! Does that mean nothing to you?" Rhiannon began to shake with emotion.

Shankee's face darkened, and she took a deep breath. "Here's something that you don't know, cousin. Baobh murdered my mother also." Her voice was but a whisper. She moved closer to Rhiannon, her piercing dark eyes holding hers. "My mother raised the warriors and went after her sister's killer. But my parents never returned, nor a brother and sister. Many did not return." Rhiannon's eyes grew wide.

Shankee took a deep breath and then continued. "Baobh has power that you cannot imagine. It's even been rumored that she has been blessed by the Goyor god. You will not be able to defeat her, especially since she has the necklace."

Rhiannon folded her arms across her chest. "It has been foretold that I am the one who will destroy her."

Shankee's plump lips curved into a humorless smile. "So you gamble with the lives of your warriors and your kingdom on the word of a few crazy prophecy keepers?"

"You do not believe the prophecy?" Tim blurted out and then was immediately sorry.

Shankee's eyes went from Tim back to Rhiannon. "This world has always been filled with prophecies, some small and simple, others large and intricate, but most have been nothing but a liquor-induced dream." She looked back down at Tim. "So, no. I do not believe in the prophecy."

"Am I just to wait here until she finally kills me too?"

"If she does not perceive you as a threat, she will eventually find more important things to do."

"I will get my father out of Sona Tuath and retrieve my mother's necklace, with or without, the help of the Archigos, be sure of that, cousin."

"Now who's being stubborn?"

Rhiannon clenched her fists, hissed something under her breath, then turned and left the palace heading for the stables. She was not to leave the palace without an escort, but she did not care.

Zellan was in the royal stables contentedly munching on grain when he saw Rhiannon and ran over to the fence happily greeting her. She felt sorry for him since she had not spent much time with him lately. However, Shih 'Ni told her that soon her training would include fighting from the back of a horse. He also said that Zellan was in need of some intense training himself. "An Archigos' War-Horse is one of our best weapons." He had said. Rhiannon smiled at the thought of Shih 'Ni. He was so serious when it came to training—much like Flath—yet so different at the same time.

Rhiannon quickly climbed over the paddock bars and threw her arms around Zellan's thick neck. His winter coat was shaggy, yet he retained his deep black sheen. He was warm and smelled of hay and dirt. The grooms took good care of him, but it was her that Zellan needed the most.

Tim and Poeso walked up to the fence. Poeso sat, sniffing the air, while Tim scampered over the wooden beams and dropped into the paddock. "Are you alright, milady?" Rhiannon did not answer. She just kept holding on to Zellan. He tried again, "Milady?"

"Tim, if we are to be brother and sister I must insist that you stop calling me that."

"But—,"

"No buts, you can call me Rhiannon or sister, no more Lady Kossi or milady, or my-greatness, or god-like-one, or…whatever." Rhiannon let go of Zellan and ducked under his big head to stand in front of Tim. "Okay?"

"You are royalty, though," Tim said stubbornly.

"I thought we were siblings." Rhiannon smiled and reached out and ruffled his ruddy hair.

"You are due honor and respect. I cannot address you like a commoner."

Rhiannon laughed. "Tim, I am a commoner. I have to eat and sleep and use the privy just like everyone else."

"But you are an empress!" Tim was getting flustered.

"Maybe I don't want to be." Rhiannon turned and

looked up at the sky painted with streaks of red, pink and yellow as the huge orange ball disappeared behind large purple hills. Luna walked up looking a bit muddy. She shook her thick coat and then sat down near the pax.

"I do not see where you have a choice," Tim reasoned.

"Let's run away, Tim," she turned towards him and took his hands in hers, "let's pack up and leave tonight. If we really ride hard, we can meet Flath inside of a month."

"Milady that is a horrible idea! You cannot just run away from your responsibilities!"

"You heard Shankee. Maybe this prophecy is just something someone conjured up and started spreading around."

"The fact still remains, you are Sernia's daughter, and as such, you are the Empress of Ventra. You cannot deny that any longer; prophecy or not."

"Maybe I wasn't meant to be the Empress. Shankee has done a good job up until now. Why can't she just keep Ventra and let me go?" Rhiannon threw her hands in the air.

Tim put his arm around her. "Remember the siochair?"

"Of course, I don't think I'll ever forget them." A shiver ran down her back at the recollection of the cold, dead water and the tiny beings that lived within.

"Remember when they told us all that you were the rightful Empress of Ventra. Not only that," he hesitated. "But they also told Ian that you would be his queen someday as well." Rhiannon was silent, lost in recollection. "Since he is a Seun the siochair meant you would also become the Queen of Beaynid someday."

Rhiannon had tried to forget all that had happened that

bitter night when she and Flath had almost lost their lives. It seemed so long ago, yet she could still feel the wet, cold pond and the siochair's commanding voices still echoed in her ears. "That's impossible!"

"No? The siochair are wise beyond our comprehension. They know what is to come."

"How could that be possible? I have nothing to do with the throne of Beaynid? Not to mention I'm an Archigos—the sworn enemy of all Seuns."

"Perhaps you were meant to overthrow Baobh and take the throne of Beaynid as your own and then bring the Archigos and the Seuns together."

Zellan nudged Rhiannon, so she began stroking the stallion's dark head once again. "That's ludicrous!" Rhiannon laughed. "There has to be someone that was related to the Basilias' that will materialize after Baobh's ousted. I don't want to be the Queen of Beaynid. It's hard enough being the Empress of Ventra…and I'm not even officially the empress yet!"

"All of the Basilias' were killed when Baobh took Sona Tuath." Tim reached out and patted Zellan's soft nose.

"I can't believe that no one survived. Not a cousin or a nephew or someone's brother-in-law?"

"If I have my history right, King Lund and Queen Danielle had three children. High Prince Eric was the oldest and was married to Princess Lorena. He also had two other sons, twins: Prince Tam and Prince Lon; neither was married. Almost all of them were killed in the castle, but High Prince Eric and Princess Lorena escaped. Some say they had their infant with them, but only the bodies of Eric and Lorena were found, so it is believed that either they had no child, to begin with, or their baby was killed with them, and its body was dragged off by some wild beast."

"That's horrible!" Rhiannon gasped.

"Life is hard for royals too, I presume." Tim shrugged.

"The king and the queen had no brothers or sisters?" Rhiannon quit rubbing Zellan for a moment and was shoved by a powerful muzzle as a reminder of his presence.

"I am afraid King Lund was an only child, and the queen's three sisters died from some blood fever."

"Well, what happens in a case like that? Who will rule Beaynid?"

"I do not know Rhiannon. We will have to wait and see. Perhaps it will be you!" Tim smiled.

"Perhaps not," she retorted.

L ater that night a fire crackled and danced bathing her room in an orange glow. The air was hot and dry though she knew outside it was blistering cold. The weather had turned frigid and had covered the land in a harsh blizzard.

Rhiannon turned over and stared up at the high marble ceiling above her massive bed. She threw her blankets off and rubbed her eyes. Beads of sweat formed across her forehead in the overbearing heat of the room. One of the palace servants must have just come in and fed the fire because it was roaring.

Something had awakened her from a fitful sleep, and

now she felt like a roast pig baking away in an oven. Poeso was stretched out across a pile of blankets lost in a deep sleep. She could hear Luna snoring from the floor around the foot of her bed. "Great, everyone's having a nice sleep but me," she mumbled softly.

Not being able to stand it any longer she pulled herself out of bed and walked across the marbled floors that were covered with thick woven carpets to the giant shutters. Gleaming ivory inlaid the exotic tortoiseshell wood shutters polished to a shine. With a heave, Rhiannon opened one great shutter. It made a quiet squeak, but then glided open to reveal the bitter cold night air.

Under the illumination of a full moon, she could see the land below lay gripped in winter's iron hand; it had snowed again. All branches were bare, leaves long decomposed. Drifts of snow covered the frozen ground and lay glowing under the gray moonlight as far as the eye could see. In the distance, she could see the small fires that the grooms kept burning all night to give the stables a degree of warmth.

Rhiannon closed her eyes and took in a huge breath of frigid air. The cold was so refreshing after the overpowering heat of the room. Her mind drifted to her father, and she wondered how he kept warm. "Hold on Daddy, I'm coming for you," she whispered. Suddenly she felt a burst of cold air and heard the sharp fluttering of wings and quickly opened her eyes. Shocked, she reactively stepped back and gasped. The large raven that she had seen days before had flown in and perched on the windowsill. It opened its golden eyes wide and fluffed its oily black wings. Intrigued, she took a few steps closer. To her surprise, it opened its beak and started to sing in a low, quiet tone—this was not the voice of a raven.

Compelled, she moved even closer as the song got louder. It called out to her, and she was unable to stop from answering it. Slowly she reached out to touch the glossy black feathers. She no longer felt the cold of the night or the heat of the room, all she could feel was the need to touch the bird. It seemed her breath had stopped and she could feel her pulse no more. The room began to spin until she could make nothing out but the raven and her outstretched arm.

Suddenly, a dark hand shot out from under a glossy wing and grabbed Rhiannon's arm. The grip was solid and uncompromising as it pulled her toward the window. She tried to resist, but the bird was too strong.

From the back of her mind, she could hear a voice, soft and safe. It echoed through her body and in her ears, but she could not make out the words. Further and further she was being dragged closer to the cold night. Finally, she could make out the words: "Fight, my daughter! Fight!"

With one last bit of strength, Rhiannon pulled her arm back as hard as she could, grunting with effort and concentration. She felt fingernails cut through skin as the raven lost its grip on her arm. She fell back hard on the floor with a thud. Before she could get her bearings, Luna and Poeso were at the window snarling at the angry raven. Rhiannon blinked, trying to process what was happening. Finally, her vision steadied, and she saw the pax leap onto the sill, teeth, and claws bared. The cat screamed and swiped at the raven as it took flight and disappeared into the darkness. Rhiannon jumped up and slammed the shutter closed and quickly closed the iron latch.

She looked down at her arm as small rivulets of blood trickled down her arm from four scratches running the length of her forearm. The cuts tingled and began to sting. The room started to dim, and her arm burned as if being consumed by fire. She took two unsteady steps towards her bed and then collapsed as her world went dark.

CHAPTER FOUR

"The Emissary Class are special Goyors who speak for their gods, especially Pom 'Ni, to their people. They are said to be chosen because of their level of devotion and skill in reading the Temmer Tree leaves. Theirs is a lifetime appointment that can last hundreds of years."
—The Forest Folk: Goyor; Sarah Unell

The air rushed around her like water deafening her ears to all but the sound of her own mind racing with the wind. The air was sweet and warm like tasting the dew of the passionflower itself. Freedom coursed through her veins and melted away the constraints of a body. She was energy, pure and fiery as the sun. Had she turned into the Sun Goddess Tec 'Lo? No, she was as she had always been, but somehow more. She had all the energy and heat of a raging fire ready to consume all in her path, but she also had the cold, hard, unquenchable power of a storm whipped ocean. Strength and exuberance fed her white-hot soul.

The darkness receded and blended with many colors too bright to see at first, but then the colors faded into the Ventran countryside. She could see the three-palace compound of Màrrach in the distance growing ever smaller as she raced on towards the giant mountain range that split the two kingdoms. As she passed over the jagged, rough mountain, she saw a pair of great winged cats drifting below her locked in an aerial dance of need and rebirth.

She raced onward as though time and distance were nothing but meaningless words. From the clouds a large tree came into view, towering above the other trees nearby. Its trunk was thick and dark, and its branches were like arms stretched up to the heavens frozen in obeisance to the gods and goddesses. Gouged from the unnatural trunk was a blacked, hollow gateway to a world she could no longer remember.

Soon Sona Tuath came into view. Its gleaming white walls soared above the grassy plains and rocky shores, protecting the busy city within. The castle rose out of the stables, and a dusty marketplace with its whitewashed stone walls gleaming like a polished diamond.

All was not well in the city. Opposing forces came together, clashing and writhing like an angered sea. She could hear the shouts of the conquerors and the screams of the dying. The smell of death hung heavy in the air. The muddy ground ran red with wasted blood.

Along the north wall, she caught sight of the figures of a man and woman hastily retreating from the castle heading into a wooded area. She followed them for a short distance. Their faces were etched with fright and urgency. Quickly, they made their way down a small dirt path.

From behind she could see three mounted soldiers bearing down on the fleeing couple. Desperate, they tried to hide amongst the sparse fall bushes. However, blond hair and light skin did nothing to hide them in their earthy toned world.

Knowing they would be discovered, the man suddenly took a ring from his finger and gently handed it to the woman. With a moment spared for a whispered word and tender embrace, he leaped from the bushes with his sword drawn. Just before the riders converged on them, the woman ran into a stand of large oaks, not stopping to look back when she heard the clashing of steel.

Curious, she moved closer to the woman and saw she was carrying a heavily wrapped bundle. The woman took a ring from her slender finger, and with the ring the man had given her, she slipped them both deep into the folds of the bundle. Lovingly the woman drew back some of the wrapping revealing a tiny sleeping newborn. With tears streaming down her face, the woman tenderly kissed the babe, then covered it up again and carefully placed her infant within the hollow of a large tree. After a quick prayer, the woman pulled a dagger from her skirts and went back towards her husband who now lay close to death.

With a sense of sadness, she turned away from the babe and its doomed parents and began her journey home. Before she left Beaynid all together, though, she came upon a small village. One quite different from any other she had ever seen, for this one was hidden. Tucked away amongst huge trees, thick bushes and dense shrubberies, lay a village that could not be seen with the eyes of mortals. Only the gods and goddesses and the Goyors themselves knew what slept along the forest floor.

From under a moss-covered branch appeared a woman in a long white robe. Her dark skin was quite a contrast to the cool sharpness of her robe. She descended lower to look closer at the woman who seemed to be calling her down from the clouds. The woman's graying hair was thick and bushy as it formed a halo around her head. Bright, golden combs clung proudly to thick hair encircled with broad, green leaves.

She was hesitant to come closer, but the woman motioned to her, giving her a kind smile. Standing before this woman, she suddenly felt small and unimportant and was humbled in the most intimate way.

"It is alright, Rhiannon Kossi. Come closer, my child," the woman urged. Cautiously, she approached. "I have been calling you for so long that I had thought you would never come."

"I couldn't hear you," she replied.

"No, I suppose you could not when you were beyond our reach," she shook her head then smiled again. "However, you have come home and have finally heard my cries."

"Who are you and why do you call for me?"

The woman smiled kindly. "I am Journey-Of-The-Moon, of the Goyor, or Forest Folk. I am very glad to finally meet you, Empress Kossi." She made a slow, elegant bow. "There is something that I need to give to you. Something of great importance that will help you fulfill that which you have been called home to do."

"Do you mean the prophecy?"

The woman did not answer, but held out her hand. Slowly she reached for what the woman was offering. The older woman opened her hand, and a small string of brown beads fell into Rhiannon's palm.

"When you are ready to displace Baobh come back here to Ghroc, and I will give you what you need to face her."

"What do I use these for?" she asked, holding up the beaded necklace.

"That is so your eyes will be opened, and you will be able to find us again."

"Will I defeat her?" she asked, hesitantly.

"Do not ask questions about things for which you do not want to know the truth."

Her eyes widened, and fear began to eat at her heart. "Do you mean that I won't be able to beat Baobh?"

"You need to keep your heart pure and your mind focused on what must be done."

"But what about the prophecy?"

"If you are to prevail, Rhiannon, you will need the help of many. Now, return to your slumber, chosen one. Heal and learn the ways of your people, for soon you will have to face a very dangerous and evil adversary."

From somewhere behind her, the sound of once trickling water grew louder until its roar drowned out all other sound. She turned to see what manner of water could make such a racket but saw nothing. When she turned back, the woman and the village were gone!

Suddenly, water began rushing into her mouth and nose. She moved her arms to push the choking liquid away, but felt nothing but warm air. Her breath was cut off, and panic overtook her senses as she began to choke.

Painful spasms wracked her body as she tried to take in a life-giving breath. Lost in the darkness, she cracked one of her eyes open only to be shocked by a light that seemed brighter than the sun. She quickly shut her eye, but pain blossomed in her head and pulsed with the racing rhythm of her heart. She could feel cool wetness dripping from her chin and running down her chest. Her mind felt as though it was stumbling through thick mud that threatened to swallow her whole. She could not remember where she was or the last thing that had happened to her. Desperate, she tried to make sense of her surroundings. Finally, the choking subsided, and she was able to breathe again. Her temples throbbed, muscle and joints ached, and she burned with fever.

She tried to lift her right arm to rub at her sore temples, but it would not move. She concentrated harder, but still, the limb would not budge. She slowly lifted her left arm and tried to reach her head again, but exhausted she let it drop. Panic bloomed, and her stomach clenched. She could hardly move and was lost in a world of warm gray and blistering pain. She lay motionless except the rise and fall of her breath. She started to fade away into the darkness, surrendering to the pain and searing heat.

CHAPTER FIVE

"The Emissary Class are special Goyors who speak for their gods, especially Pom 'Ni, to their people. They are said to be chosen because of their level of devotion and skill in reading the Temmer Tree leaves. Theirs is a lifetime appointment that can last hundreds of years."
—The Forest Folk: Goyor; Sarah Unell

The air rushed around her like water deafening her ears to all but the sound of her own mind racing with the wind. The air was sweet and warm like tasting the dew of the passionflower itself. Freedom coursed through her veins and melted away the constraints of a body. She was energy, pure and fiery as the sun. Had she turned into the Sun Goddess Tec 'Lo? No, she was as she had always been, but somehow more. She had all the energy and heat of a raging fire ready to consume all in her path, but she also had the cold, hard, unquenchable power of a storm whipped ocean. Strength and exuberance fed her white-hot soul.

The darkness receded and blended with many colors too bright to see at first, but then the colors faded into the Ventran countryside. She could see the three-palace compound of Màrrach in the distance growing ever smaller as she raced on towards the giant mountain range that split the two kingdoms. As she passed over the jagged, rough mountain, she saw a pair of great winged cats drifting below her locked in an aerial dance of need and rebirth.

She raced onward as though time and distance were nothing but meaningless words. From the clouds a large tree came into view, towering above the other trees nearby. Its trunk was thick and dark, and its branches were like arms stretched up to the heavens frozen in obeisance to the gods and goddesses. Gouged from the unnatural trunk was a blacked, hollow gateway to a world she could no longer remember.

Soon Sona Tuath came into view. Its gleaming white walls soared above the grassy plains and rocky shores, protecting the busy city within. The castle rose out of the stables, and a dusty marketplace with its whitewashed stone walls gleaming like a polished diamond.

All was not well in the city. Opposing forces came together, clashing and writhing like an angered sea. She could hear the shouts of the conquerors and the screams of the dying. The smell of death hung heavy in the air. The muddy ground ran red with wasted blood.

Along the north wall, she caught sight of the figures of a man and woman hastily retreating from the castle heading into a wooded area. She followed them for a short distance. Their faces were etched with fright and urgency. Quickly, they made their way down a small dirt path.

From behind she could see three mounted soldiers bearing down on the fleeing couple. Desperate, they tried to hide amongst the sparse fall bushes. However, blond hair and light skin did nothing to hide them in their earthy toned world.

Knowing they would be discovered, the man suddenly took a ring from his finger and gently handed it to the woman. With a moment spared for a whispered word and tender embrace, he leaped from the bushes with his sword drawn. Just before the riders converged on them, the woman ran into a stand of large oaks, not stopping to look back when she heard the clashing of steel.

Curious, she moved closer to the woman and saw she was carrying a heavily wrapped bundle. The woman took a ring from her slender finger, and with the ring the man had given her, she slipped them both deep into the folds of the bundle. Lovingly the woman drew back some of the wrapping revealing a tiny sleeping newborn. With tears streaming down her face, the woman tenderly kissed the babe, then covered it up again and carefully placed her infant within the hollow of a large tree. After a quick prayer, the woman pulled a dagger from her skirts and went back towards her husband who now lay close to death.

With a sense of sadness, she turned away from the babe and its doomed parents and began her journey home. Before she left Beaynid all together, though, she came upon a small village. One quite different from any other she had ever seen, for this one was hidden. Tucked away amongst huge trees, thick bushes and dense shrubberies, lay a village that could not be seen with the eyes of mortals. Only the gods and goddesses and the Goyors themselves knew what slept along the forest floor.

From under a moss-covered branch appeared a woman in a long white robe. Her dark skin was quite a contrast to the cool sharpness of her robe. She descended lower to look closer at the woman who seemed to be calling her down from the clouds. The woman's graying hair was thick and bushy as it formed a halo around her head. Bright, golden combs clung proudly to thick hair encircled with broad, green leaves.

She was hesitant to come closer, but the woman motioned to her, giving her a kind smile. Standing before this woman, she suddenly felt small and unimportant and was humbled in the most intimate way.

"It is alright, Rhiannon Kossi. Come closer, my child," the woman urged. Cautiously, she approached. "I have been calling you for so long that I had thought you would never come."

"I couldn't hear you," she replied.

"No, I suppose you could not when you were beyond our reach," she shook her head then smiled again. "However, you have come home and have finally heard my cries."

"Who are you and why do you call for me?"

The woman smiled kindly. "I am Journey-Of-The-Moon, of the Goyor, or Forest Folk. I am very glad to finally meet you, Empress Kossi." She made a slow, elegant bow. "There is something that I need to give to you. Something of great importance that will help you fulfill that which you have been called home to do."

"Do you mean the prophecy?"

The woman did not answer, but held out her hand. Slowly she reached for what the woman was offering. The older woman opened her hand, and a small string of brown beads fell into Rhiannon's palm.

"When you are ready to displace Baobh come back here to Ghroc, and I will give you what you need to face her."

"What do I use these for?" she asked, holding up the beaded necklace.

"That is so your eyes will be opened, and you will be able to find us again."

"Will I defeat her?" she asked, hesitantly.

"Do not ask questions about things for which you do not want to know the truth."

Her eyes widened, and fear began to eat at her heart. "Do you mean that I won't be able to beat Baobh?"

"You need to keep your heart pure and your mind focused on what must be done."

"But what about the prophecy?"

"If you are to prevail, Rhiannon, you will need the help of many. Now, return to your slumber, chosen one. Heal and learn the ways of your people, for soon you will have to face a very dangerous and evil adversary."

From somewhere behind her, the sound of once trickling water grew louder until its roar drowned out all other sound. She turned to see what manner of water could make such a racket but saw nothing. When she turned back, the woman and the village were gone!

Suddenly, water began rushing into her mouth and nose. She moved her arms to push the choking liquid away, but felt nothing but warm air. Her breath was cut off, and panic overtook her senses as she began to choke.

Painful spasms wracked her body as she tried to take in a life-giving breath. Lost in the darkness, she cracked one of her eyes open only to be shocked by a light that seemed brighter than the sun. She quickly shut her eye, but pain blossomed in her head and pulsed with the racing rhythm of her heart. She could feel cool wetness dripping from her chin and running down her chest. Her mind felt as though it was stumbling through thick mud that threatened to swallow her whole. She could not remember where she was or the last thing that had happened to her. Desperate, she tried to make sense of her surroundings. Finally, the choking subsided, and she was able to breathe again. Her temples throbbed, muscle and joints ached, and she burned with fever.

She tried to lift her right arm to rub at her sore temples, but it would not move. She concentrated harder, but still, the limb would not budge. She slowly lifted her left arm and tried to reach her head again, but exhausted she let it drop. Panic bloomed, and her stomach clenched. She could hardly move and was lost in a world of warm gray and blistering pain. She lay motionless except the rise and fall of her breath. She started to fade away into the darkness, surrendering to the pain and searing heat.

CHAPTER SIX

"There are many remedies one can use to bring down fever; willow bark, catnip, and peppermint, but I have found something even better! It grows in this harsh, northern land of the Archigos: something I call fentern. If the patient cannot drink a tea, grind it into a paste and make a tincture. Rub across the forehead where the pulse beats and at the wrists. The patient's fever will break within the hour."
—Herbs of Ventra and Their Uses; unpublished writings of Tess

The snow kept falling day and night blanketing Ventra in an icy shroud. The sparkling crystals of Ventrian snow shone like diamonds under the weak, winter sun. When it finally let up, all of Ventra was under a thick layer of snow. But finally, the sun agreed to come out and warm frozen souls.

Tim reined in his mount and turned the animal down a now familiar path lined with a deep rut that had been worn by friends and those anxious over the health of their empress. He had wanted to stay with Rhiannon when they brought her to the healer woman, but the old crone shooed him out her door with a broom in hand. So every day he was forced to make the journey from Màrrach to her cabin, a good hour's ride away. Most of the last two weeks he had to ride in snow and freezing temperatures, but he made the journey still. Kyia had been the only one allowed to stay with Rhiannon and the old woman—except the she-wolf and pax, of course.

The sun was warm on his face as he tilted his head up and shut his eyes. All around him, he could hear the delicate sound of ice melting from branches and pine needles. The air was crisp and filled with the scent of pine and mountain sage. A bitter breeze blew through the tall trees sounding like a thousand whispers from ancient gods. A pair of blue jays called to each other from the tops of tall oaks.

The old healer woman's great, two-story home came into view. The entire downstairs had been set aside to nurse the sick. Tim's horse picked up the pace, excited that he would soon be in a warm barn. As Tim rode up, a small servant took his horse and led it off to be taken care of. Four warriors stood quietly talking in the courtyard. Shankee had insisted that the warriors stay, no matter what the old healer woman said.

The cottage was dark and smelled like fire and herbs. Empty beds stood amongst dark, carved wooden cabinets holding clean linen, bandages and other such things. Porcelain washbasins stood empty, but ever-ready. Lanterns and candles were placed at bedsides and hung from huge, log beams. Rhiannon, however, was the only sick one there. Suddenly Luna darted out of a dark corner and hurled her one-hundred-and-fifty-pound body at him. Tim was thrown back and landed with a thud on the floor. The she-wolf happily took the opportunity to bathe his face in canine spit.

"Okay, good Luna," Tim pushed the massive she-wolf off his chest and got up off the floor. "You are a good beastie, you are." He affectionately patted Luna's head and wiped his face. With Luna's daily greetings taken care of, Tim walked over to where Rhiannon lay sleeping and sat down beside her. The pax lay curled, purring loudly at the foot of her large oak bed. Etâhpe'o-poeso opened one eye as Tim walked up, but then lazily closed it again and resumed her catnap.

"How was the ride this morning?" Kyia asked as she walked in holding a tray full of herbs and bandages.

"A little warmer today, thank you," Tim answered politely as Luna ran off to the kitchen to beg for a treat from the servants.

"Has Shih 'Ni returned?"

"No, they are still gone," Tim solemnly answered

"It has been two weeks, what could be keeping them? I thought surely they would be back by now." Kyia wrinkled her forehead and then turned her attention to Rhiannon.

"Maybe they have found her." Tim removed his coat and set it on an empty chair.

"I'm sure they would have brought Baobh back if they'd found her." Kyia gently removed the bandages that were wrapped around Rhiannon's arm.

"He was in a rage. Maybe he rode all the way into Sona Tuath?"

"Shih 'Ni can be hotheaded, but he's not stupid, young Tim."

"How long should it take to search Ventra anyway?"

"Ventra is a big place," she replied as she worked. "It

could take months to scour every inch of our land. But I think he'll be back before then." Kyia carefully washed the deep, infected scars torn into Rhiannon's flesh. The cuts were red and smelled like death. Puss and dried blood washed away with warm water.

"She has not awakened at all?" Tim asked, looking down at Rhiannon.

"No, but her fever finally broke last night." Kyia started to gently apply warm bandages covered with a poultice of strong smelling herbs onto the cuts, then carefully wrapped her arm in clean white strips of linen. "She choked on some water I was trying to give her, and I thought I saw her open an eye, but she's been sleeping ever since."

"What are those beads in her hand?" Tim pointed to her left hand.

"I'm not sure. They were there last night when I checked on her. Do you recognize them?"

"No. I have never seen them before. It looks like they have some kind of writing on them."

"I was going to ask Tess about them but forgot. Maybe she had them when we brought her here." Kyia shrugged.

"Where is Tess, anyway?"

"She left early this morning in search of more herbs."

"Maybe if you let some light in here, Rhiannon would wake up," Tim suggested.

Kyia laughed. "Tess likes it hot and dark in here. I think she'd kill me if she came home and found the draperies pulled open."

Suddenly remembering what he carried, he smiled and fumbled with his over tunic. "Well, when Rhiannon does wake up, she will be happy to see this." Tim pulled a dirty envelope from a small purse he carried strapped across his chest. The name "Rhiannon" was carefully scrolled across one side and was sealed with plain, hardened wax on the other side. "'Tis from Flath," Tim announced, happily.

"The Seun?" Kyia asked cautiously.

"The leader of the rebellion," Tim answered, proudly.

Kyia looked away, deep in thought. "Does he love her?" she asked, after a while.

Tim looked at Rhiannon, then back at Kyia. "Yes, Kyia, he does."

She sighed as she looked across the room at the roaring fire. "This'll cause her great trouble." Calmly she picked up the tray and dirty bandages and left.

Tim sat in silence, staring at the envelope, thinking about what Kyia had said. It was true that their relationship would not be easy, in fact maybe even impossible. He knew Seuns hated the Archigos and from the few months that he had spent in Màrrach, he knew the feeling was mutual.

He sighed and looked into the dancing orange flames of the fire. It would be better for them both to just forget each other and go on with their lives. Rhiannon would be empress of Ventra and, because of his role in the rebellion, Tim was sure Flath would get bestowed upon him a high-ranking position within the infrastructure of the new Beaynidan government. Miles of harsh terrain and a perilous mountain range would separate them. But, even more treacherous, they would be separated by an unbridgeable gulf of hatred.

The fire crackled and cast long golden shadows across

the dark room. Tim thought about throwing the letter in the fire. Luna came back from the kitchen and curled up on the bear pelt rug at Tim's feet. The chair creaked as he sat back contemplatively watching the flames. In a different situation, they would have been happy. He looked down at the worn envelope with her name lovingly scrolled across the mud-streaked paper. Carefully, he turned it over to reveal the wax that sealed the letter inside. It was a plain seal of red wax—the same seal that Flath always used. Gypsies did not have a family name, so they had no real origins and thus did not have a crest or clan symbol to stamp into the wax seal. To Tim, though, the plainness of Flath's seal was more powerful than the royal seal of Sona Tuath itself. No, he would not throw the letter into the fire.

"Tim," Rhiannon weakly whispered.

Quickly he stuffed the letter back into his purse and knelt by her side. "I am here milady." He took her hand in his, careful not to disturb her bandaged arm. She slowly rolled her head from side to side, keeping her eyes closed tightly. "I am here, Rhiannon," Tim whispered again.

"Baobh," she breathed. Luna started whining and sat up, putting her front paws on Rhiannon's bed.

"You are going to be alright now," Tim comforted her.

"Is she waking?" Kyia rushed into the room, pushing Luna down from the bed.

"Yes," Tim answered. Kyia grabbed a clean strip of linen and dipped it into a basin of water then carefully mopped Rhiannon's brow.

"A baby…"

"You're going to be alright, just rest now," Kyia encouraged.

"A baby, in the forest…" Rhiannon's voice was hardly more than a whisper.

Anxiously Tim looked up at Kyia. "What is she talking about?"

"She's delirious. It's because she's had such a high fever for so long. She'll be alright though."

From behind him, Tim could hear the rustling of bags and clomping of boots coming near. "Is she finally coming around?" a husky voice called out.

"Yes, Tess. She's trying to talk," Kyia replied to the old woman.

A plump, rosy-skinned woman appeared at Rhiannon's bed, holding a bag brimming with roots and tree bark. Her auburn hair was heavily streaked with gray and was falling out of her fur cap in long, ruddy strands. She stared down at Rhiannon with bright blue eyes. Her face was weathered and lined but spoke of legendary beauty, now long forgotten. Her round frame was quite a bit shorter than the Archigos but not nearly as short as the Oread. She wore a long, woolen tunic the color of saffron and black leggings.

"Very good, she'll be awake by dinnertime." Thick lips curled into a warm smile, and then she walked away. Rhiannon quieted down and fell back into a deep sleep. Tim returned to his chair, and Kyia left to help Tess with tea and poultice recipes.

Dinnertime had come and gone, but still, Rhiannon slept. This time, however, Tim refused to be dismissed after the evening meal. Everyone had retired for the night, so the house was deathly quiet. Outside, Tim could hear the wind howling through naked branches and pine trees protesting in the harshness of the storm. Tim sat on a low chair at Rhiannon's side, gently holding her hand. He spotted the strange strand of beads still gripped in her left hand. He had forgotten to mention them to Tess and evidently, she had not seen them. He speculated that maybe Shih 'Ni had given them to her.

The wine he drank with dinner and the overpowering heat of the room started to run through his veins and take over his thoughts so that soon he was fast asleep, his head gently resting on Rhiannon's bed, still clasping her hand.

He dreamt of invading armies, clashing swords and the screams of the dying. He dreamt of gleaming whitewashed walls and a pristine castle overlooking the sea. He dreamed of a powerful, kind man and an equally powerful, and generous woman ruling over two kingdoms and bringing much happiness and contentment to everyone.

"Tim," a woman's voice whispered. "Tim," she called again through dense, sticky fog. A cool wetness lapped at his face as he tried to get away. "Timmmm." He heard Rhiannon call to him. Tim blinked his eyes a few times trying to remember where he was. His eyes focused on Luna, who was gently licking his face. Then he saw Rhiannon, anxiously staring back at him.

"Milady, you are awake." Tim rubbed tired eyes and sat up straight.

"Where are we?" Rhiannon looked around suspiciously.

"We are at a healer's cottage not far from Màrrach."

"Are you ill?" She tried to sit up to get a better look at Tim but winced and lay back down.

"No, I am fine. 'Tis you who have been injured."

"Yes, now I remember," She hissed through gritted teeth. "It was a raven. A huge raven with golden eyes."

"'T'was Baobh." Tim squeezed her hand in reassurance, as much for himself, as for her. "We are safe here. There are warriors posted outside."

"I'm safe nowhere. She's hunting for me like she did my mother." Rhiannon clamped her eyes shut tight, and tears ran down her sunken face. "I might as well just walk into Sona Tuath and hand myself over to her. She's too powerful to fight, and I'm tired of hiding." The tears flowed down her face as though a mighty river were just let loose from its banks.

Tim carefully lay down next to her and gently took her in his arms. "It will be alright, milady. You are safe here, and when you are well, we will all go and put an end to Baobh's wickedness." He spoke softly into her dark, unbound hair and tenderly kissed her forehead. "As you are my sister, Rhiannon, I will march with you. As you are their empress, they will all march with you, Empress Kossi, and we will bring her down. Of that, you can be assured."

CHAPTER SEVEN

"Dreams have long been used by the goddesses of the Archigos to communicate with their empresses. There have been some strange dreams indeed that have haunted our empresses of the past. In later generations, it seems dreams have been a way for our empresses (and in one case, the son of an empress) to find their mates. Most of these dreams have been accredited to Verna, though there have been dreams recorded which were reported to have been sent from other goddesses."
—Gods and Goddesses of the Archigos; Ykellen Gunn

At dawn, Rhiannon woke with a jolt—the burning in her forearm traveled up to her shoulder and made her whole body throb in pain. She reached for her arm and realized that she held something in her hand. Through a haze of pain, she sat up and looked closely at the beaded necklace wrapped through her fingers.

They were brown and green and had strange writing on each bead. They were so familiar, yet she could not remember where she had seen them. She closed her eyes and tried to remember. She sucked in a deep breath as she recalled flying high above the land. Her pulse quickened, and her stomach tightened as she felt the cool clouds slip by.

Tim finally awoke still lying next to her. "Where did you get those?" he asked. "I do not remember ever seeing them before." Rhiannon was staring at the strand of beads intertwined in her long fingers as he sat up rubbing his eyes.

"At first I wasn't sure. But now I remember." She looked over at him. "Remember that dream I had when I knew that Flath had been captured?"

"Yes," Tim answered warily.

"I had another dream like that. Only it didn't have anything to do with the pax this time."

Alarmingly, Tim looked over at Poeso who had walked into the room and jumped up onto the bed. "I had a dream, and in my dream, I saw the baby!"

"Milady—," Rhiannon put her finger to his mouth and cut his words off.

"Rhiannon, okay?"

"But it would not be right for me to forget your place, milady."

Rhiannon dropped the beads on her lap, and before Tim could react, she grabbed a small knife that lay on a table beside her bed. Carefully, she made a cut across the palm of her right hand. Blood welled at the cut and pooled in her hand. Tim gasped and tried to grab the knife away from her, but she held it tight. "What are you doing?"

"Your turn!" she ordered. Tim was speechless, his mouth gaping and his eyes widened. "You cut your palm now."

Tim shut his mouth and loyally did as she bid him to, a small trickle of blood dripped from his hand. They embraced hands, blood mingling and dripping as one.

"You are now blood of my blood. We are brother and sister now, and there's nothing you can do about it. As so, address me as you would your sister, okay?"

Tim swallowed, then looked up at Rhiannon as a tear slipped from his eye. "As you wish, sister."

"It is as I wish." She held out her left arm asking for an embrace of which Tim happily obliged. "I don't know what I would do without you, Tim. I am so grateful you stayed with me," she whispered.

"How could I have left my sister to fend for herself in a land full of savages?" He smiled at her, and then lovingly tied a cloth bandage around her hand. "Tell me about your dream."

"I saw the baby!" She stated excitedly.

"What baby?" Tim asked as he crawled out of bed.

"The baby you told me about. High Prince Eric and Princess Lorena's infant. The one that no one was even sure existed. I saw her hide the baby in a hollowed-out tree!" Rhiannon's eyes were huge and insistent. "All we have to do now is find that baby, and we'll have a king for Beaynid."

Tim grabbed a clean piece of cloth and tied it around his hand. "Do we even know if this infant is a boy or a girl? That would make a difference."

She stopped and thought for a while. "I don't know." Rhiannon shrugged her shoulders.

"Well, okay. That narrows it down," he said with a tinge of sarcasm.

"You don't believe me, do you?" Rhiannon arched a brow in question.

"You've had these dreams before, mi—," he stopped himself, and then started again, this time calling her by her name, "...Rhiannon, so you could have had another one, I suppose." Tim looked down at his feet.

"But..." Rhiannon prodded.

"Kyia told me that you were hallucinating because of having such a high fever for so long," Tim sighed

Slowly and very deliberately, Rhiannon picked up the discarded beads that lay in her lap and held them up to Tim. "Then what are these?"

Tim shrugged. "What are they?"

"In my vision, I went to Ghroc."

"Ghroc?" Tim's eyes grew wide with astonishment. "No one has ever seen Ghroc."

"I have." Rhiannon smiled smugly. "It's a hidden village, and I know about where it is. Journey-Of-The-Moon gave me these beads so that I could see the village when I return."

"Who is Journey-Of-The-Moon?" Tim reached out and touched the smooth, cool beads.

"I'm not sure, but she said she was of the Goyor or Forest Folk."

"That is where Baobh is from."

"She's a Goyor?" Rhiannon whispered.

Tim nodded stoically. "Well, half Goyor, perhaps. She claims that her father was of Seun royalty."

"Royalty?" Rhiannon asked skeptically.

"Yes. That is why she feels she has a right to the throne of Sona Tuath."

"Interesting…," Rhiannon replied, but her mind wandered back to the dark-skinned woman in the forest. "Journey-Of-The-Moon told me to come back when I am ready to go up against Baobh. She said she would give me what I needed to beat her."

"Did she say what it was?"

"Unfortunately, no." Carefully Rhiannon slipped the beads over her head. "But I guess we'll find out soon enough."

Tim sighed again. "I wish you did not have to go. I mean, why can you not just send your warriors. 'Tis too dangerous for you go, Rhiannon."

She smiled and took Tim's bandaged hand in hers. "Don't worry so much for me, Tim. Remember the prophecy?" Rhiannon's stomach growled very loudly, making Tim laugh and temporarily forget his worries. "It's hard to tell which hurts worse, my throbbing arm or my empty stomach."

"I will have the servants bring you something to break your fast." Tim got up and quickly disappeared into the kitchen.

Rhiannon sat in her warm bed and began to think about the baby. He—or she for that matter—would be about twenty-four now. His or her father was a Seun, but his mother, although fair, had a little different look about her. She sighed, knowing it would be a hard task to find the rightful ruler in this huge land.

"Rhiannon, I forgot to give you this." Tim appeared before her holding Flath's letter. "It is a letter for you."

"Is it from Flath?" Rhiannon smiled broadly and grabbed the letter. "Oh, thank you, Tim!" She studied the way her name was scrolled across the parchment, then tenderly turned it over and ran her fingers over the wax seal. She looked up, but Tim was gone. Carefully, she separated the hardened wax from the parchment and opened the envelope. She removed the neatly folded paper but could not bring herself to open it.

Her hand began to tremble as her stomach tightened. Taking a deep breath, she finally unfolded the letter and read it:

My dearest Rhiannon,

I was so happy to receive your missive. I was not aware that you would be able to send or receive correspondence under the circumstances, however, am delighted to hear from you.

I gave Teo your greetings and well wishes, and he sends his back to you and young Tim.

The fighting here is sporadic and at times seems worthless, as we have suffered such great loss as to not give much of a resistance. Supplies are low, as are the men's morale, but still, we carry on. The end of winter will come, as it does every year, and we all look forward to that time.

I pray this missive finds you well. I hope you are becoming accustomed to the ways of your people. That is if they can put up with your strong-willed defiance and sharp tongue. I hope you are not giving them as hard of a time as you gave me, Greannmhor. If so, I expect they will pay me dearly to take you back, in which case I will have plenty of coin to keep the rebellion going, at least until I am old and gray.

However, I am sure your people are grateful to have you back with them, for you will be a great empress someday, Rhiannon. You will lead your people to victory in all things.

Stay safe, Greannmhor.

May the sun shine upon your face,

Flath

Slowly she folded the letter up and stuck it under her blankets. She was overwhelmed with a sadness that made it hard to breathe. She looked over to the roaring fire as it consumed a few huge logs. After a while, she pulled Flath's letter from under her blankets and read over each word again. She knew as sure as the sun would continue to rise, she would continue to love him for the rest of her life. After all, he was the man that had haunted her dreams for so long.

"**D**o you know what these are, dear?" Tess asked later that day and held up the small brown and green beads to the candlelight, gripping them carefully in her thick, dry hands.

"They're Goyor beads," Rhiannon replied suspiciously looking from Tess to Tim, then back to the old woman.

"They aren't just any Goyor beads, girl, these are Emissary beads."

"What are Emissaries?" Tim asked, moving closer.

Tess turned the small beads in her hands, carefully inspecting each tiny drawing and symbol. "The Emissary are the class who speak for their gods." She handed the necklace back to Rhiannon who returned them to her neck. "They are the special chosen ones who converse with Pom-Ni, and their other gods." Tess tucked an errant wisp of ruddy hair behind a pudgy ear.

Kyia walked into the room holding a tray with hot tea. Curls of steam rose from an earthenware cup and disappeared into the dark room. "Time for your tea, milady." Rhiannon wrinkled her nose, but carefully sipped the bitter tea, nonetheless.

Tess carefully started changing the bandages on Rhiannon's arm. "So, it was in a vision that you were given those beads, then?"

"It was in a dream, really," Rhiannon remembered how it felt to fly over the mountains and on to Sona Tuath. "It was like I was really there, though. I could feel the cool air and smell the forest."

Tess chuckled, "That's the way of visions, my dear." She continued to dress Rhiannon's wounds. "Your mother had visions also."

"You knew my mother?" she asked with surprise. Kyia looked over at Tess, and an expression passed between them that Rhiannon could not read

"Yes, I knew your mother well," Tess answered.

After a long pause, she said, "Tell me about my mother, please."

Kyia turned and headed for the kitchen. "Tim, could you please help me with getting supper ready?" Tim dutifully followed her to the kitchen. Luna, anticipating the possibility of getting some scraps, jumped up and followed.

Tess finished bandaging Rhiannon's arm. "Well, what is it that you want to know?" She sat back in her ornately carved rocking chair.

"What kind of a woman was she?" Rhiannon asked quietly.

Tess smiled and started to rhythmically rock back and forth. She took a worn, tobacco-stained pipe from her pocket and methodically stuffed it with dried leaves. She lit a small stick from a burning candle, then held the flame over the tobacco and slowly drew it into her lungs. She stared off into the fire as if in a different time. "You look very much like her. Nothing of your father in you, you know."

"You know my father too?" Rhiannon leaned closer as if willing her to speak quicker. But the old woman was lost in reminiscence.

"I knew your father too, my dear."

Rhiannon wanted to correct Tess' past tense reference to her father, as if he were dead, but could not interrupt the healer's musing.

"Like I said, you have nothing of your father's looks, but that's the way it is with the Archigos. If you ask, they'll tell you they're strong enough to keep the blood of outlanders from entering into a child of their loins" Tess got a humorous look in her eyes, and then looked at Rhiannon. "It was the same with your mother. She took nothing from her mother, but was a mirror image of her father, your grandfather."

"My grandmother wasn't an Archigos?" Rhiannon asked, surprised.

"No, child. It seems the Kossi's have a weakness for outlanders." Tess chuckled, and then looked back towards the fire.

"But I thought the throne was only passed down through women?" Rhiannon asked between sips of bitter, hot tea. Poeso stirred and then resumed her rough melody.

"Normally, yes, but it was your mother who was born with the Kiss of Verna and not one of her cousins." Tess' eyes smiled as old memories danced before her. "It created quite a scandal, you see. Your grandfather, Lu 'Oun, was the youngest of three children and the only male. After his eldest sister, Tammrah took the throne everyone just expected that the line would continue through her." Tess snickered again in a low rumbling rhythm. "But after the birth of her seventh son, everyone started looking to the youngest sister to produce an heir. She had already birthed two sons by that time—no daughters to speak of.

An empress had never resulted from the offspring of a Kossi son, so your grandfather wasn't too concerned about taking a wife and producing an heir. He busied himself with refining his skills as one of the best warriors the Archigos ever produced."

Rhiannon finished her tea and lay back on a pile of soft pillows, enjoying the soothing rhythm of Tess' rough voice. The warm crackling fire and hot tea melted into her bones, relaxing her and taking away the pain of a mending arm. Poeso's purring gently sawed through the large room. The dry smoke from Tess' pipe swirled above her head, giving her a feeling of being in a small, safe sanctuary.

"Exhausted after the birth of three more sons," Tess

continued, "Tammrah finally gave up her quest to produce an empress. The responsibility of continuing the Kossi line fell to Juji, the younger sister. The poor thing was almost hysterical when she gave birth to her fifth son. Great fires reached to the heavens with sacrifices to Ceres, the goddess of motherhood, and Aubo, Baubo, Min, Hathor and all the other goddesses of children and childbirth and girls. They were in fear that they somehow had offended the goddesses, so they kept the sacrifices burning day and night".

"About that time your grandfather started having disturbing dreams of which no manner of medicines could cure". Tess leaned closer to Rhiannon, the old woman's face peering out of gray smoke. "The dreams increased in detail and seduction until he was powerless to resist its call."

Rhiannon's eyes widened. "I had dreams too. Dreams that eventually brought me here," she said softly.

A faraway twinkle in Tess' eye and the motion of a slight nod was the only acknowledgment that Tess had heard Rhiannon at all. The old woman relaxed back in her rocking chair and continued, "The mightiest of Ventra's warriors became obsessed with the reoccurring dream, thus adding to the woes of the whole Kossi clan, for they thought he was going mad!

But for your grandfather, the only thing that existed was the woman in his dreams. Eventually, after suffering for almost a year, he finally set out to find the woman in his dreams. Most thought he would never return, and no one even took notice on the day that Lu 'Oun left, for Juji had died in the early morning hours as she birthed her sixth son."

"Did he find her? The woman in his dreams?" Rhiannon sat up and asked excitedly.

"Oh yes!" Tess smiled and took a deep hit from her glowing pipe. Satisfied, like a child at the end of a fairy tale, Rhiannon leaned back on her pillows gently adjusting her bandaged arm. "He boarded a ship heading to a faraway place called Assuria and found his mate amongst the River Folk. By the time he returned to Ventra his new wife was heavy with child. Everyone was happy that he had returned but suspicious of his new mate. Up until then, no Archigos had taken a mate of a different race. But after a while, they grew bored with the outlander and resumed lamenting their missing heir.

"Your grandmother grew as huge as a horse and could barely walk when her time finally came. With only a tiny slip of a birthing maiden and your nervous grandfather pacing the floor, your grandmother gave birth to three tiny infants."

"She had triplets?" Rhiannon asked, incredulously.

Tess nodded and continued, "As each moist, squalling babe came into the world your grandfather grabbed each one and held it to his chest. He held a daughter in one arm and a son in the other and then the smallest of babies slipped from its warm cocoon. The birthing maiden gasped and held the little girl up for your grandfather to see. This insignificant little babe bore the red Kiss of Verna on her tiny pink chest. They all stared at the next Empress of Ventra…your mother."

"That must have created quite a surprise," Rhiannon whispered in awe.

"Oh yes! Your father was quite perplexed about what to do with the child. He wasn't expecting to be drawn into the crazed frenzy that now surrounded the throne. He had left the Grand Palace with his pregnant wife and built a home amongst the trees where he planned to raise his family. Practically no one had even noticed they were gone, for they were all too preoccupied with the lack of a new empress. Why, out of desperation, Tammrah chose her eighth mate and became pregnant yet again."

"She had more than one husband?" Rhiannon raised a brow.

Tess laughed, small puffs of smoke rose from her mouth and nose. "After the birth of her fourth son, she excused her first mate and took a new one trying to produce that all-important female infant. Desperate to produce an heir, she took a new mate after each new son was born. It was quite common amongst past empresses who had trouble producing a daughter, though none had taken so many mates, nor birthed so many babes. The Archigos had thought they had somehow displeased Verna and they increased their sacrifices so that the valley was always bathed in gray smoke for years."

"So, what happened when they found out about my mother?"

"Well, when your grandparents laid your mother in the bulging lap of the now aging—and very pregnant—empress, she began to weep. No one was sure of just what to do, but Tammrah just held on tightly to your mother and wept hysterically. Whispers and shocked gasps filled the room and warriors ran in and out trying to get a glimpse of the infant. Finally, as the setting sun cast golden beams that slashed across Tammrah's drawn, tired face, she announced there would be the celebration to end all celebrations to introduce the next Empress of Ventra."

"That's quite a story." Rhiannon sighed. She tried to picture her mother as a child. She looked over at the old woman who was slowly rocking in her chair and contentedly sucking on her pipe. Her worn face was relaxed, and her watery eyes were lost in another time. "What was my mother like when she was little?"

Tess looked over to Rhiannon, almost surprised that she was still there. She smiled warmly. "Sernia was a kind-hearted, gentle girl, patient and thoughtful beyond her years. She was always the child who never got into too much trouble or told a lie or fought with her brother and sister. Sernia was always the first to go to someone who was sad or hurt." Tess took another long draw on her pipe. "She understood the complexities of life and emotion. She was very close to her parents and Empress Tammrah. She was almost everything that an empress could ever wish to be."

"*Almost* everything?" Rhiannon questioned.

Tess continued, "She was the smallest of the three children and even as she grew, she wasn't the powerful, ruthless warrioress that so many past empresses had been. Some, who were still upset that the new empress didn't come from Tammrah even said Sernia wasn't a good enough warrioress to lead the Archigos. Her sister and brother, Vehura and Laquent, excelled in their skills as warriors."

Tess looked down at Rhiannon. "Sernia, however, was pure poetry on the back of her big, black horse. She was the best horsewoman you've ever seen. Oh, my dear, when she got onto the back of that horse it was like they were one; unyielding, strong and as fast as the northern wind. Hair and mane, feet and hooves, all melted together as though there was nothing else on earth but Sernia and her horse. Anyone who saw Sernia ride would have their breath taken away, she was sheer beauty and grace, the very whisper of Verna herself." A tear slipped down Tess' wrinkled cheek, and her voice died on the crackle of the fire.

Rhiannon looked down at the string of brown beads. They were smooth and cool in her hand. After a while, she took a deep breath and said Tess, "Tell me about my mother's necklace." She had been afraid to ask anyone about the necklace since her arrival in Ventra. She doubted her ability to wield its power even though she had used the stone to heal both Flath and Luna. Self-doubt ate away at her as she waited for the old woman to answer, not even knowing if she knew anything about the necklace.

Tess took another suck off her pipe and slowly blew out the dry smoke that took its place wreathed about her ruddy head. "What do you want to know?" she asked nonchalantly.

"I want to know how it works."

"You used the stone to heal your man and your wolf. You know how it works."

"Just because I remembered a song from my childhood, words that I don't even understand, by the way, doesn't mean I understand how it works." Rhiannon sharpened her gaze upon the old healer.

Tess rocked back and forth in her chair for a while, not answering. Rhiannon thought perhaps she did not mean to answer her at all. Finally, she said, "The necklace is blessed by the goddess, Verna. She makes it work." The older woman's voice was dry and crackly from her pipe smoke. Tess' green eyes rose to Rhiannon's black ones. "Verna, and the intent *you* infuse into the stones."

"You're not an Archigos. You can't tell me you believe that."

"You don't?" Tess shot back at her.

"No," Rhiannon replied quickly and then wondered if she had answered too hastily. She peered around into the shadowed room expecting someone to jump out and challenge her words.

She looked back over at Tess who slowly took another long drag from her pipe and let the smoke slip from between her lips as they curled into a smile. "You are your father's daughter."

"My father wasn't a convert, I guess?"

Tess' head rolled back, and she let out a barking laugh. "Hardly. But he didn't voice it around, mind you."

"No, I guess he couldn't."

"But you don't believe either?"

"I don't know what I believe right now. Up until a few months ago, I was living on a cattle ranch in Montana until I was sucked through some mysterious tree by some guys that looked like they had escaped from a Renaissance fair somewhere." Rhiannon thought her words sounded petulant.

Tess took a deep breath as if deciding upon something. "The stones react to the sound of certain people's voices. No one knows why they will have a reaction to some voices and not others. Perhaps it is because no one but the Empresses of Ventra has ever tried to get them to work…that is until Baobh."

"So, you don't believe they are some kind of magical relic left to us mortals from the gods?" The fire popped, and Rhiannon jumped, once again sure that her faithlessness had been discovered.

"Those rocks were taken from of the Del 'Nort mine, like all the other gems the Oread pull from the mountain."

"So, they're not special." Rhiannon felt almost disappointed.

"I did not say that, dear. I said that's where they came from. There has been no other stone like those found in the mine since then, in all the hundreds of years since they were found."

"Three red rocks, in all these long years?"

"Those three gemstones were once one big piece!" Rhiannon raised her brows but didn't interrupt the healer. "It's said that they were found in one big piece, but when the miner tried to extract the stones something happened, and he fell dead as the stone fell away from the wall of the cave they were working in. When the stone hit the floor of the mine, it broke into three pieces. No one would touch it for days. Finally, the empress, at the time, came to the mine to see what all the ruckus was about. She went in there and fearlessly took up those stones and took them back to Màrrach." Tess took a break from her story to toke on her pipe. Rhiannon waited, trying to be patient.

After a while, she began again. "It was weeks later, after the stones had been captured in that elaborate silver necklace, that the word began to spread that the empress had stumbled upon the fact that the stone came to life when she sang. Longer still it took to discover that the stones could both hurt and heal. Of course, the Archigos said that it was in a vision from the goddess Verna that the empress was told of how to use the stones and that they were a gift to Ventra."

"But you don't believe the official story?"

Tess barked in laughter again. "If you want the truth of the matter, ask an Oread, dear." Rhiannon shelved that information for later use. "The Oread legends say that the stones just have some makeup that causes them to vibrate—to react—to a specific pitch in certain voices, giving that person the power to heal or fight."

"Strange..." Rhiannon's mind was racing. As a teenager, Rhiannon had known an old lady who kept a metaphysical shop in town who swore crystals contained powers of healing. At the time she thought the crone was a kook, but now she wondered if the woman had it right all along.

"I suppose it isn't so strange, really. Ancient legend says the Archigos came from a place far away and were once a part of a race of Forest Folk who were expert alchemists who worked with gems and stones. Perhaps the Archigos retained a bit of that skill over the ages."

Rhiannon looked down at her open palms as they lay on her blanketed legs, the Emissary beads softly glowing in the wavering light of the fire. She wondered if she had that skill —that ancient skill to wield the power of those strange, bipolar stones that could either save or kill so extremely. She took a deep breath and let it out slowly. Were she and the whole of the mighty Archigos army enough to defeat Baobh and those legendary gemstones this time?

CHAPTER EIGHT

"Indomitable and powerful; noble son of the Archigos
Stoic and serious; warrior of Ventra
Lethal and obstinate; man of the North
As a child gave his heart to the little girl with a diamond on
her chest
Mourned her loss when she was gone
Returned, she did, and took his heart again
Proud and protective; will she give you the idol and
a Nikah?"
—Oread Poems of Love; Creta O'mun

Rhiannon stood in the paddock gently stroking Zellan's muzzle. Tim had brought him up from Màrrach a few days before. It was a beautifully clear late February morning. A cold chill hung in the air gripping the land in its cold fingers. Zellan's breath left his nostrils in wispy clouds. Luna ran around the stables sniffing anything that seemed interesting, while Poeso sat in a shaft of impotent sunlight twitching her tail to and fro.

The months had passed very slowly, but her arm had finally healed enough to no longer require bandages. She was still weak in that arm, but the infection was gone, and the open wound had finally knitted together leaving only tender, red scars. The poison had left her system, but the damage had been done, and Tess did not know if she would ever recover the strength in her right arm. She twisted her arm around and squeezed her fist flexing sleepy muscles with only the dullest of pain. She was restless and ready to get back to Màrrach to continue her training.

Tim and Kyia had ridden off to Màrrach earlier in the day. Tim was to request another one of Rhiannon's letters to be delivered to Flath by way of Xev's older brother again. Kyia was to deliver a report of Rhiannon's progress to Shankee. She asked Tim to bring her sword back when he returned.

She wondered how Shih 'Ni was fairing. He had been gone for almost two months now, and there were whispers that he surely must be dead. She bit her lip then looked up into the blue sky offering up a small prayer to Verna that Shih 'Ni would soon return. She was not sure if she believed in the Archigos goddess but offered her prayer just in case.

"How are you feeling today, Lady Kossi?" A young, gangly warrior walked up to her.

"Much better, thank you." She smiled sweetly.

"Your color is good, milady. Your health must be returning." The young man smiled, sheepishly.

"Yes, it is, and I'm anxious to get back to Màrrach." Poeso rubbed up against Rhiannon and almost pushed her into the warrior.

"In such a hurry to leave my care?" A rough voice inquired from behind.

Rhiannon spun around. "Not really, I just need to get

back and continue my training. It's not easy learning to become an empress, you know."

"All in good time, my dear." Tess handed Rhiannon a basket. I would like you to help me gather some herbs. It's not far. We won't need the horses, come along." Tess turned and headed for a small path into the trees.

They walked quietly through the dim forest. Old, packed snow lined the well-traveled path. It had not snowed in quite some time, but the forest was still blanketed in white. Rhiannon wondered what kind of herbs they would find under three feet of snow but said nothing.

Several paces behind them a group of warriors talked quietly, though always vigilant. The forest was damp and very cold. The smell of pine filled the air. Thousands of tiny drips of melting snow sparkled in the sunshine. Small finches darted in and out of bushes and trees, happily chirping a forest melody. A cold wind rushed through the trees and Rhiannon yanked her cap lower over her ears and pulled her coat tightly around her body. They stopped at a large pine tree, half of which was covered by green clumps of moss. "Could you get that spot of moss up there for me?" Tess pointed up to a large mass.

Rhiannon rose onto her toes and carefully pulled the moss away from the damp bark. It smelt like mud and felt fuzzy, almost like a small animal. She half expected it to squeak and quickly threw it into the basket. "What kind of medicine do you make out of that?"

"Oh, I don't make anything medicinal from that." She chuckled. "It would most likely produce poison. I grind it up and use it to patch holes in the walls of my house."

"Oh." Rhiannon looked suspiciously at the mound of green in her basket and quickly rubbed her hands on her coat.

"How did you come to live here in Ventra?" Rhiannon asked.

"I was once married to an Archigos. After he died, I decided to stay here. My homeland is too far for an old woman to travel." When Rhiannon did not respond, she continued, "The Archigos don't mind, and in fact are quite helpful. That's not the usual, mind you." Tess stopped and looked up at Rhiannon. "Usually the outlander mate of an Archigos is forced to leave after their mate dies. I'm a healer though, so they need me." Tess laughed and then continued down the path.

"Why do they make them leave?" Rhiannon's curiosity was piqued.

"Well, this land was given to them by Verna—so they say—and no one else. They are quite greedy when it comes to Ventra. Empress Shankee is warm and generous to those she invites to visit, but quite cold to those who trespass."

"No one else but Archigos live in Ventra?"

"Except the Oread, no one else lives here. Off to the far west, there is a rather large peninsula that sticks out into the sea like a stubby 'ol finger. They've allowed it to be settled by seafaring people 'cause of all the goods they can get in trade."

"That's interesting," Rhiannon commented sardonically.

"The Archigos are proud, arrogant people, but they aren't stupid." Tess delicately scraped off a large piece of bark from a tall evergreen then quickly slipped it into a worn leather pouch that hung from her waist.

"Do you know how my mother and father met? Is he from here…or from the tree?"

"The tree?" Tess stopped again and looked up at Rhiannon.

"The Tree of Jur."

"Oh, that tree."

Tess sighed and looked as if she wanted to say something but thought better of it. Finally, she started speaking again. "Your mother started suffering from unrelenting night terrors—just like her father before her." Tess wound her arm through Rhiannon's and slowly pulled her down the forest path. "Her nights were haunted by bright dreams of wars, villains, and a single man." Rhiannon's arm tightened, and Tess slowed her walk ever so slightly. "After suffering for months," she continued, "Your mother realized the man in her dreams was not of this place but must be from the Tree of Jur. She sought the counsel of the Priests of Jur to find out what was on the other side of the tree. Vehura thought her sister had finally gone mad, but your grandfather spoke on her behalf."

Tess stopped short and plucked a small plant out from its hiding place under a taller bush. She smelt it and then threw it into the basket that Rhiannon was holding and looked up at her. She continued down the path in front of Rhiannon. "Your mother sent out a handful of warriors to look for the traveling priests of Jur. After a while, they returned with a small group of four priests and priestesses. She begged them to tell her the secrets of the tree.

Hesitantly they told her no one had come through the tree in a very long time. She pushed them for answers on how the tree worked, but for a long time, they would not tell her. They stayed in Màrrach for over two months before Sernia finally learned the secrets that they held." Tess motioned for Rhiannon to follow her down the path again. "In the spring Sernia and a few of her closest warrioress' traveled to the tree and waited for it to open."

Rhiannon tripped over a root that snaked across the path and almost landed in a small puddle of mud but righted herself at the last minute. Tess spun around at the sound of her thundering footsteps. "I'm alright!" She laughed. "Go on."

Tess wrinkled her forehead, turned around and then continued. "Well, that big tree started spewing mist and light until it filled the ground, and everyone started wondering if they would be killed by the mysterious thing. But in the middle of the darkest part of the giant hollow a man's hand appeared, then the rest of him melted out of the eerie glow and mist. He looked a might disoriented, but after he saw your mother, he knew just why he'd been summoned." They came to a fork in the road and stopped. "Oh yes, it's this way, c'mon." They started down the path to the left, Poeso following along quietly with four men dutifully tagging along a little further down the path.

"Your mother ordered a spectacular marriage celebration and feast. It lasted for a week, at least! Your parents were quite happy, and Verna herself seemed pleased with the union. After a short while, you came along." Tess turned and looked at Rhiannon. She smiled so warm and proudly that she made Rhiannon feel awkward.

Rhiannon broke away from her gaze and looked down at the damp earth. She had a tingling sensation at the base of her spine that quickly spread through her body and ended at her heart. With sudden realization, she looked up at the old woman. "Tess, are you—,"

"Ah, here we are." She interrupted. "Follow me!" She motioned with her hand and disappeared down a small embankment following the faintest of trails. They stopped in front of a huge willow tree. The snow thinned as it got close and then was gone all together around the huge, weeping tree. Sun shone down upon the tree bathing it in golden light. Long, sinuous branches were covered with tiny pink blossoms that filled the air with a sweet honey-like aroma. Small daisies and posies grew in white and lavender drifts along with green grass and patches of clover. A small stream of blue water bubbled up from the base of the tree and flowed back toward Tess' cabin, widening as it flowed away. It was spring in the middle of a winter forest!

Rhiannon slowly approached the lazy, flowing branches. She reached out and touched the soft leaves and tiny flowers that felt like the softest cotton and left the sweet smell of honey between her fingers. "It's so beautiful," she whispered.

Tess came to stand next to her. "That's just what your mother said the first time I brought her here. This was her favorite spot in all of Ventra."

Rhiannon looked down at the plump, ruddy, old woman. Her scarf was on askew, and her coat was stained with the remains of herbs and medicines. Tess slowly turned and looked up at Rhiannon—neither woman spoke. Rhiannon stared back into eyes that held a faint resemblance in shape to her own. The tip of her nose and the fall of her lips were like faint footsteps that Tess had left on Rhiannon from generations past. "Are you…" her words trailed off into the cool afternoon.

"Yes, my dear. I am your grandmother." Tess confessed.

Rhiannon dropped her basket and wrapped Tess in her arms. Tears streaked down her cheeks as she squeezed harder. "Why didn't you tell me," she whispered when she was finally able to speak.

"Well, the Archigos don't put any importance on family that involves the outlanders, you see. I didn't want to cloud your mind. You have so much to think about as it is…" her words died on the soft spring-like breeze. Finally, Rhiannon let the old woman go and straightened up. "Everyone needs to know where they come from," she whispered and wiped an itchy tear from her chin.

Tess reached up and tenderly touched her leathery hand to Rhiannon's cheek. "So much like your mother, you are." She smiled warmly. "She would've been so proud."

"Grandfather is dead, then?" Rhiannon asked.

"Oh yes. He's been dead for some time now. He died with many others when they marched against Baobh."

"Shankee's mother, Vehura …" Rhiannon asked.

"Yes." Tess nodded. "Maybe you can see why Shankee is so hesitant to wage a war she might not win."

"But Baobh must be stopped. Someone has to stop her!"

"She is an evil far greater than any this land has ever

seen. She is the unspoken evil that took my husband, all my children and all but three of my grandchildren."

"She's stolen so many lives. It has to end, Tess!"

"Yes, it does, and it will. I've heard the prophecy, and I believe it! You will stop her." She sighed and then smiled.

They sat beneath the shady willow amongst the clover and said nothing but listened to the breeze. Finally, Rhiannon spoke, "You mentioned another grandchild besides me and Shankee. Who is it?" Tess hesitated. "Who is it, Tess?" Rhiannon persisted.

"She isn't going to be happy I told you. She wanted to be the one to tell you, if the question ever came up."

Rhiannon wrinkled her forehead. "Well, then I will keep it a secret until she tells me."

Tess looked at Rhiannon with doubt but told her anyway. "My son, Laquent, took a woman of Beaynid as a mate."

"A Seun?" Rhiannon asked in shock.

"Oh no! This woman is from the port town of Tel' Rhea on the western coast. Anyway, she was with child when Laquent left Màrrach with the other warriors to go after Baobh," her voice grew sad. "He never laid eyes upon his daughter."

Rhiannon looked over at the bubbling stream, so alive in a land that has seen so much death. Finally, she looked back over at Tess. "Who is she?"

"Kyia."

"Kyia is my cousin?" Rhiannon asked in disbelief. "Why didn't she just tell me?"

"Don't be cross with her, child. She is not like most

Archigos—in fact, she's like your mother in some ways—she is quite shy and humble." Tess shook her head. "She wanted to be your confidant first, your cousin later, if you so choose."

Rhiannon crossed her ankles and plucked at the clover. "There's subterfuge everywhere," Rhiannon whispered.

"Not subterfuge, The Tree of Eternal Spring," Tess chuckled—changing the subject. "It's supposed to bring luck, prosperity and even fertility to those who drink from the spring and sit beneath its branches."

Rhiannon studied the ancient tree and all its features—graceful, flowing branches covered in aromatic flowers, rough bark wrapped around a large, twisted trunk that curled into snake-like roots that gave birth to a blue, bubbling stream of life. It seemed so out of place in the middle of a dark, damp forest caught in the middle of winter, though she could not picture this extraordinary tree anywhere else.

She was brought out of her thoughts by loud footfall on the path behind her. She turned to see Shih 'Ni run into the clearing. Whips of his black hair were hanging out of the remains of a messy braid. He was unshaven, and his clothes were filthy. She was stunned to see him in such disarray. "Rhiannon!" he yelled and pulled her up from the grass. "I thought you were dead," he breathed into her hair.

"I'm fine," she replied, though her voice was muffled by his coat.

"I didn't think I would see you again!"

"Uh, well I'm fine…but I think you might kill me if you don't let go."

Quickly Shih 'Ni released her. "The last night I saw you, I knew you were already dead. That's why I've stayed away for so long. I couldn't think of coming back here with only your memory."

"Well, I think I have enough herbs. I'll meet you two back home." Tess picked up the basket and quickly left the clearing.

Rhiannon smiled at Shih 'Ni. "I appreciate your friendship more than you'll ever know. I was worried when you didn't return."

He kissed her forehead and gently touched her arm. "Thank Verna you're still alive. She has heard my prayers!" Shih 'Ni took a step back and looked at Rhiannon for a long while. "I have to say something to you, Rhiannon, so please let me speak." Rhiannon arched a brow in question, but soon became very uneasy when she saw trepidation in his eyes.

Shih 'Ni gently touched Rhiannon's cheek. His fingers were warm and moist and felt good on her face. "I was afraid I wouldn't be able to go on when I thought I had lost you again." He looked deeply into her eyes. "I prayed to Verna when I saw you lying there on the floor of your bedchamber. I knew you were dead, but I prayed anyway. These long months have passed so very slowly. I even prayed again to Verna, but this time I asked her to take my life because I could not go on without you." A tear welled in his eye then rolled down his face.

"Shih 'Ni, I—."

"No, wait. I must get this out before I lose my nerve. I have always loved you, Rhiannon. Even when we were little children, I knew that I would be your mate. When your parents took you away, I didn't eat for a week and was brought here, to Tess, for remedies, but nothing could ease the pain of a broken heart. When you returned to Màrrach last fall it was as if you had returned to me." Rhiannon wanted to look away, but the emotion that burned in his eyes and his poignant speech made it impossible. "I love you, Rhiannon. I know you think you love that gypsy, but he's not one of us. He has no knowledge of our people and our ways. He can't help you rule Ventra. If you just give me a chance, I'll prove to you that I am the best mate for you."

The forest was silent as if listening to an intimate conversation. "Shih 'Ni you are my very best friend. You and I have a long history together...," her words trailed off. She was unsure of what to say. "You're a good man, Shih 'Ni," she finally spoke again. "But I have already given my heart to another man."

Shih 'Ni looked down at the green clumps of grass that covered the ground. He was silent for a long time studying the old tree and following the deep, blue water that bubbled forth from its heart and flowed away to Màrrach. Rhiannon could see the pain plainly brushed across his dark features. Her stomach clenched, and she felt sick for being the one to cause him such hurt.

Shih 'Ni sighed then spoke again. "Have you really thought this out, Rhiannon? The Archigos will never accept a Seun as your mate."

"They won't have a choice. Who I choose is up to me." Her words sounded infantile even to her ears.

"Rhiannon, please think about what is best for Ventra and for her people. You must start thinking like a leader. A Seun will never be accepted here. What kind of life will that be for him? Have you thought of that?" Shih 'Ni tried to reason.

Rhiannon had not thought about that. How welcome would Flath feel here? The Archigos would go out of their way to make sure he did not feel welcome, ever. Could she ask that of Flath? For the first time, she felt unsure of her future plans with the man she loved.

That moment of indecision must have shown on her face because it emboldened Shih 'Ni to go on. "I can see that you're starting to realize that this might not be the best place for your gypsy."

"My mother took an outlander as a mate, as did my grandfather and my aunt and uncle. Having a foreigner as a mate is not new to Kossis. Even Shankee's husband is an outlander." Rhiannon tried to reason with herself as much as with Shih 'Ni.

"But none were Seun," he said quietly.

Rhiannon took a deep breath and folded her arms across her chest. "Shih 'Ni, I know you don't approve, and I know it will be hard, but I've made my decision. I don't want to lose you as a friend. Please accept my choice. My heart belongs to another man." She unfolded her arms and held them out in a pleading expression. It was breaking her heart to treat Shih 'Ni in such a way.

Finally, he replied, "You have spoken, then, Rhiannon. You have made your choice, and I have lost you. But when things do not turn out for you and your gypsy, I'll be waiting for you." He bent down, tenderly kissed Rhiannon's lips and slowly walked away.

She absently touched her lips, hating herself for hurting him so. She prayed that he would forgive her some day and they could once again be close friends. She was empty inside and already felt lonely. She felt a piece of herself die as she watched him retreat down the snow-covered forest path.

CHAPTER NINE

"The Archigos War Horse is a terrible thing to behold,
especially if one is meeting it in battle. They are a sleek,
strong embodiment of their riders: Warriors of Fame."
—Customs of Exotics; Lorn VacLell

W ind and motion. Freedom and ability. Speed and talent. Past and present collided in a dance as poetic as the moon herself, yet as deadly as the fiery sun. An undulating sea of blackness: flowing mane, cutting hooves, flexing muscle and the pull of sinew.

Zellan charged towards his target. His black eyes were wide with excitement, his mouth dry with anticipation. His dull coat of molting season was now lathered in exertion. Rhiannon pushed him hard, careening towards their victim. Slowly she raised her sword, its steel tip glistening in the spring sun. She raised her face to the sky and shouted out a battle cry to Verna.

Her voice rose on the wind and was swiftly carried to her opponent's ears. She jerked Zellan's reins as they rounded their mounted assailant. Steel clashed and sung out across the grassy meadow. Rhiannon came down hard across the woman's sword, causing her to groan with effort as she pushed the blow off her blade. Their horses danced around cutting steel with only the slightest nudge of heel or toe or a quick verbal command to know their next step.

Grunts of exertion peppered the air as sharp hooves cut deep into the damp earth, trampling the green turf. The deep thud of blade against blade vibrated through muscle and bone. As the fight continued neither missed a strike nor made a mistake. Their breathing was heavy and labored; sweat ran into burning eyes and blurred their vision. Horses stepped, turned and leaped in time as huge eyes rolled and nostrils flared.

Exhaustion crept through body and mind causing both to slow slightly. The familiar burning radiated from the old wound on Rhiannon's right forearm and began to crawl up her arm, sending sharp stabbing pains shooting through her body. Just as she had over the last three months, Rhiannon gritted her teeth and pushed the pain from her mind. She concentrated on nothing but the fall of her sword and her next move.

Finally, Rhiannon saw her opening. She pushed her blade down hard on the woman's sword, causing her to lose her balance. Rhiannon stood higher in her saddle using her full weight to push the woman from her horse. She fell with a thud and lost her grip on the sword that tumbled away when she hit the grass.

Rhiannon jumped from Zellan and was quickly on top of the woman before she could re-arm herself. Gracefully Rhiannon held her sword up above her head then carefully drove it deep into the soft dirt just inches from the woman's head.

"I won. Now you have to take me!" Rhiannon stated between huge breaths of warm air.

"Were you trying to kill me, or did you just miss that last stab?" Kyia asked, eyeing Rhiannon's blade that was thrust into the earth.

"You're just a sore loser," Rhiannon chuckled as she hoisted Kyia up on her feet.

"Very impressive!" Shih 'Ni called from a group of warriors that had gathered to watch the match.

Rhiannon took a bow. "You're next!" she yelled over to him. She could hear some of the male warriors taunting Shih 'Ni with some rather crude remarks.

"So, when are we leaving?" Rhiannon turned her attention back to Kyia.

"Shankee will have my head," Kyia protested.

"By the time she realizes that I'm gone, we'll be too far away for her to do anything about it and by the time we return, she'll be cooled off enough not to want to kill us both."

"You're the empress, I'm dispensable," Kyia quipped.

"Too bad! You lost, and now you have to live up to your word." Rhiannon pulled her sword from the ground, wiped the dirt from the blade then quickly sheathed it. "Don't worry, Kyia. I'll handle Shankee when we get back."

"When you get back? Where are you going?" Shih 'Ni asked as he walked up.

"Kyia promised me that Tim and I could come with her and the rest of the trading party when they leave for Tel' Rhia next month."

"Shankee will not allow that!"

"Shankee won't know, Shih 'Ni," Rhiannon stated forcefully.

Shih 'Ni folded his arms across his chest and looked down his nose at Rhiannon. "Don't look at me that way! Kyia promised, and there's nothing you can do about it."

"I can tell Shankee!" Shih 'Ni protested.

"You could, but you won't." Rhiannon smiled confidently.

"You two sound like a couple of children. I lost the fight thus losing the bet, and I'll have to take them with me now. She'll be fine. We always travel well protected."

"Then I'll accompany you." Shih 'Ni announced, matter-of-factly.

"What?" Rhiannon and Kyia asked, at the same time.

"Won't that look suspicious? The Master of Arms accompanying a trading party?"

"Well, I don't suppose she's going to march right out in broad daylight." Shih 'Ni pointed his thumb at Rhiannon. "I'll sneak out with her and Tim."

"Oh, now that's the adult thing to do." Kyia rolled her eyes. "Shankee is going to kill me!"

"Leave Shankee to me." Rhiannon climbed up into her saddle. "She can no more bend my will then harness the wind!" she called out as she galloped off towards the stables.

It was still a few hours before dawn as the trading party left the supply houses. Six wagons and two dozen warriors clamored into the darkness. They towed eight ill-tempered Venturien horses behind the last wagon. The wagons were filled with sparkling gems, intricate jewelry and other things such as skins and leather clothing made by Oread artisans. The Oread were also talented sculptors and painters, and the Archigos found the art went for a good sum of gold.

The sky grew from deep black to gray and then a faint pink as morning threatened the frail darkness. They made their way out of Màrrach and down into Laoch Valley. Stout horses pulling the heavy wagons splashed through the icy waters of the East Fork River toward the Vel' Kur Mountains. They had slipped past the guards at the supply houses and the patrols that roamed Màrrach. Within another hour or so they would start their ascent of Vel' Kur.

Rhiannon sat on the seat of the second wagon while Tim was hidden under leather tarps among the goods of Ventra. Luna lay sleeping next to Tim content to be out of the cold. Shih 'Ni rode alongside the line of wagons upon Zellan's back—his red diamond cleverly hidden under intricate leather throngs and the bright blankets often worn by the horses of Ventra. In the dark, neither horse nor rider was recognizable.

"Will you meet up with the Seun?" Kyia asked.

"He has a name, you know." The cold March morning lay across the land like a sheet of ice. Spring equinox was but a week away however winter was not easily loosening his grip on Ventra.

"Will you see Flath on our journey, or are you just excited to be getting away from Màrrach and Shankee?"

"I sent word to Flath that I will meet him in Bell." Rhiannon looked over to a group of warriors that were approaching. "But I'm equally happy to be rid of Shankee for a while, too."

"A trading party leaving so early in the season?" called out one of the approaching warriors.

"It's been a long winter, and we're anxious for the warmth of the south," answered a warrior in the first wagon as he pulled his horses to a stop. Rhiannon looked back at Shih 'Ni, who had doubled back and melted into a group of warriors on horseback.

"The sun will be up soon, we need to get out of here before it's light enough for them to see us," Rhiannon whispered as the sky grew yellow and sunlight started peeking over the eastern hills.

"You'll miss the Spring Rites!"

"Ah well, I'm getting too old to do the mating dance, my friend."

The younger man laughed. "You will never be too old to watch," he chided, then changed the subject. "What are you carrying this time?"

"The usual," the wagon driver answered. Rhiannon looked back at Shih 'Ni as the sun slowly rose above the hills throwing the valley into golden light.

"Bring back some of that dark beer!" The conversation

continued. "And plenty of silk, the women like that stuff, you know."

"Oh, we'll be bringing back plenty of sweet mead and beer and ale," the wagon driver chuckled. "And the Empress has requested silk and some other fashion trinkets as well."

One of the warriors looked over towards Rhiannon and started approaching. Quickly she looked around, but there was nowhere to hide. She could hear the man approaching but avoided looking straight at him. "What do I do?" she hissed at Kyia.

Suddenly Shih 'Ni rode up and blocked the man's view. "Enough of all this talk. Let's get moving again!" he shouted.

"Master Shih 'Ni!" the warrior pulled his horse to a stop. "What are you doing accompanying the trading party?" Rhiannon peeked around Shih 'Ni and saw the man looking at Zellan suspiciously but knew he would not question Shih 'Ni about it.

"We've received word of highwaymen roving about the countryside of Beaynid, so I have been asked to accompany the trading party. We must be on our way so that I may return as quickly as possible."

"Please forgive me for delaying you, Master Shih 'Ni. May the sun smile upon your face and have a safe journey." The warrior gave his farewell, and a quick nod of his head and his party of warriors started to leave. Shih 'Ni rode to the front of the caravan barking orders to start moving again. The retreating warrior curiously looked back at the wagon but saw no one but Kyia as the party started moving once again.

As the trading party started up the path to the Vel' Kur Mountains, Rhiannon and Tim climbed from the back of the wagon. She looked back at the valley now bathed in golden light. A melancholy feeling started to seep through her as she was taken by a strong yearning to look upon the shimmering domes of Màrrach just one more time.

CHAPTER TEN

"The soft, vibrantly colored sheep of Ppie are said to have been given to Beaynid from The One God, Ak. Unlike their more docile cousins, Ppie sheep are obstinate and have a penchant to escape their low, stone fences and strike out on their own. Because of their bright colors, however, they are quickly taken by predators who favor the tender and piquant taste."
—*Field Guide of Beaynid; Myrin Zantroc*

The dying sunlight cast long shadows across the wooden playing board. Carved pieces of ivory in shapes of various animals stood tall in the small circles of inlaid maple. Teo took the carved form of a giant bear and knocked over the smaller statuette of a wolf.

"I've won ye thrice in a row! 'Tis no challenge, play'n wi ye." Teo sat back in his chair and appraised Flath with a critical eye.

Flath scrubbed a calloused hand across the stubble on his chin. "I guess I am just not concentrating on the game." He got up and walked over to the window and watched as the sun edged nearer to the treetops.

A thin, gray-haired man walked into the room. "Your

horses are ready. Are you sure you will not stay just one more night?" He approached Flath and clasped the bigger man's shoulder.

"I must get back to my men, William." Flath smiled warmly at his old friend. "I have waited here for three nights now, and am grateful for your warm hospitality, but we must be on our way."

"Surely they are just running late. Will you not stay just one more night?" William wore a hopeful expression. "I am sure the Archigos will be here by morning."

Flath looked over at Teo who had interlocked his thick fingers across his belly, shut his eyes and looked as if he had drifted off to sleep. He looked back over to William apologetically. "I am sorry. We really must be on our way."

"Well, if you must, then please take some food with you." William turned and called into a small back room that served as a kitchen. "Lana, please bring the packs in here, will you?"

Almost immediately, William's twelve-year-old niece appeared at Flath's elbow holding two large knapsacks, which Flath quickly took from her.

"Thank you," he said.

She stared up at him with a besotted expression. Huge, glossy green eyes begging him to notice her. She was just blossoming into a woman, yet clearly still a child. Her carefully combed strawberry blonde hair fell in straight ribbons down her back. Small, dainty hands wrung the skirt of her frilly, white apron.

"Are you leaving already?" Her voice was just above a whisper.

Flath turned back toward her and sat the knapsacks down. "I am afraid so, Lana. Teo and I thank you for helping your uncle clean up after us and for cooking us such delicious meals." Gently, he placed a quick kiss upon her forehead which sent her running from the room several shades redder than when she had entered.

"She is sweet on you, Captain." William smiled at his niece.

"She will get over it five minutes after we leave," Flath chuckled. He picked the knapsacks up and headed for the door. "Come on Teo. We still have about an hour of daylight left if we hurry."

After the knapsacks had been secured, both men embraced William and bid him goodbye. They mounted their horses and turned down the dirt path leading out of town. The men rode along in silence as the sun's late spring rays turned from hot light to a cool, golden glow. White smoke from cooking fires rose from brick chimneys smudging the landscape and filling the air with the tantalizing aroma of cooking meat.

"I've never seen ye in such a hurry to get away from a comfortable place," Teo finally commented.

"I worry how the men fare. We have been gone too long already," Flath replied, tight-lipped, staring up ahead of them.

"Is that it, old friend?"

Flath looked over at the red man and raised an eyebrow in question. Teo laughed and then raised his canteen, full of ale, to his lips as a few drops ran from the corners of his mouth escaping into his fiery beard. After a few swigs, he lowered it, running the back of his thick hand across his face.

"I've known ye long enough laddie to know when things aren't aright with ye."

When Flath did not reply, he went on. "Yer nervous about see'n her again."

"She was supposed to be here three days ago!" he stated forcefully, still not looking at Teo.

"Adam has things fully under control. There's no need to be rush'n back." Teo pulled his horse a little closer to Flath's mount.

"The lass will be here an will make things aright with ye."

"You sound like an old woman. Are you going soft on me, old man?" Teo bristled, and Flath laughed.

"Rhiannon has traveled a long distance an under great threat from Baobh, just ta see ye. And ye leave before ye even get a chance ta see her again?"

Flath took a deep breath. "They are three days late! We do not even know if they are still on their way. Maybe she was not able to leave Màrrach. Or maybe they had to turn around for some reason…"

"Mayhap they'll arrive just after we've gone from Bell!"

"Well, I cannot waste any more time waiting for them!"

The horse's hooves clomped loudly as they crossed the gently arched bridge that took them from Bell. A board creaked under their weight, and Teo nervously looked down, kneeing his horse to move quicker across the bridge. They left the bridge, turned at a fork in the road and headed into the cover of the trees and a less worn path heading southeast.

Flath took one more look behind him at the path that carried travelers from the north into Bell. The bright sun shone in his eyes making them water so that he could not see clearly, and then they were in the cover of the wood, the path not visible any longer. His heart lay heavy in his chest as each step took him further from Bell.

With the late afternoon sunshine flooding her eyes, Shih 'Ni's back was lost in a world of golden light. From behind her, she could hear the first of the wagons start over the bridge that brought them into Bell. Wooden planks creaked as the horses thudded across. She shielded her eyes and looked over at Tim.

"Are you happy to be home?"

"It does not seem like home any longer," he stated softly.

"Home isn't always the place where you happen to be living at the moment, Tim. But it's a place you can always come back to and be happy and welcome." Rhiannon tried to cheer him up.

Tim looked over and smiled. "I am glad to be home and happy that you will finally meet my father."

Rhiannon reached over and patted Tim's arm. "I don't know what I would have done without you, Tim."

"Oh, you would have been fine. You would have just

had to learn Venn a lot quicker," he chuckled, shifting back into his usual good mood.

Shih 'Ni slowed and reined his mount back around next to Tim. "Are you sure we're traveling in the right direction?" he asked guardedly.

"Of course I am. My father's house is right down this path," he answered gingerly then squeezed his mount into a run.

"I think he's happy to be home," Rhiannon laughed as she watched Tim disappear down the path.

Kyia road up from behind them. Her spirited paint mare, no less energetic as on the day they left. "I'm going to take the party to the inn and meet up with you three later." Then she turned her mount and headed off toward the middle of town.

The sun finally sunk below the treetops allowing Rhiannon the freedom to study Shih 'Ni's face. Dark eyes darted around the path and in between the trees. His muscles were bunched and taut; always on the edge of a silent war.

"Are you anxious to see your man?" he asked, nonchalantly. Since that talk they had under the Tree of Eternal Spring last winter, he had been cool to her, though still friendly-ish.

"Yes." Rhiannon looked around wondering where Luna had run off to. The last time she had seen the she-wolf was just before they started over that bridge and Poeso had flown off earlier in search of food.

"Maybe after this encounter you'll change your mind about trying to persuade your warriors to accept the Seun."

He had a disgusted look on his face as he spoke. His lips carefully forming the word Seun like it was a foul word.

"Well, this is a good opportunity for some of you, at least, to get to know the man—Seun or not."

"They won't accept him, Rhiannon," Shih 'Ni stated forcefully.

Rhiannon looked over at him quietly studying the mighty warrior. His long, black hair was braided as was the custom. The tattoos of his rank scrolled out from under his sleeveless tunic. Weapons were stashed in every conceivable place upon his body. To all who did not know him, they would only see the hard, lethal exterior. Rhiannon, however, knew he was quite vulnerable. "Will you accept him?" she quietly asked. His silence was answer enough for her to know that he would not.

A warm, sweet smelling breeze came up from the south, toying with Rhiannon's long, onyx hair that she wore loose on this day. Kyia had braided a small portion of Rhiannon's hair placing a few jeweled beads into the braid and even fastening two small feathers from Poeso's wing. The feathers fluttered in the breeze making the ruby beads wink in the sunlight. She shifted in her saddle wishing she could just rush ahead like Tim had done. Shih 'Ni settled into a sulking silence.

When they reached Tim's house, Tim and William were standing near the entrance of the house. Lana stood on the doorstep quietly watching Rhiannon and Shih 'Ni ride up. As they approached Tim solemnly walked up to Rhiannon. "I am sorry. Father said Flath has left," he stated, in Ska.

Though not as fluent in Ska as in Venn she understood what he had said.

Shih 'Ni said something rude in Venn and slid off his horse, leading it to a small water-filled trough near a large barn. Chickens scattered in all directions as Shih 'Ni made his way across the yard.

The color drained from Rhiannon's face as her stomach knotted. "Left?"

William walked over to them. "It seems he could not wait any longer, milady. He and Teo left here no more than a half of an hour ago." William spoke in Venn as a gesture of respect for Rhiannon.

Rhiannon quickly jerked the reins and spun Zellan around and galloped back down the path toward the bridge. She could hear Shih 'Ni shouting at her to stop, but she kneed Zellan on quicker. She had seen the path that led off into the forest. It was the only other path than the one they were traveling. If Flath and Teo stuck to that path, she would find them. Daylight slowly faded as she crossed over the bridge and headed down the path that took her into the forest.

"If we make good time we can make it back to camp by sundown tomorrow." Flath dug his heels into the sides of his mount.

"If we turn around now we can make it back to William's by supper time," Teo replied. The forest was quickly becoming dark, the thick canopy smothering out all but dappled light. Flath road on, his heart ached with every step. He made the hasty decision that Rhiannon had changed her mind about coming to Bell. He surmised that she finally realized a Seun was not good enough for an Archigos Empress—let alone a gypsy.

Flath gripped his reins so tightly that he could no longer feel his fingers. His surroundings started melting away as he stared down the narrow path they followed. Trees sped by and melted into darkness. Even Teo seemed to disappear into an unexplained blankness.

From the corner of his mind, he heard a horse scream out. Suddenly he was aware that his horse had stopped and was nervously stomping at the dirt and snorting in anger. Just as he was becoming aware of his surroundings again, his horse screamed and reared up. Not paying attention, Flath fell back and was abruptly deposited onto the dirt path. Teo reined in his horse just in time to keep the gelding from stepping on Flath's head.

"Crazy horse! What has gotten into the beast?" Flath jumped to his feet and dusted himself off.

"A wolf!" Teo yelled, unsheathing his sword.

Flath looked across the path where a single beam of dying sunlight broke free from the trees and shown down on a large, silver she-wolf standing on top of a rock at the head of the path. Flath instinctively gripped the hilt of his sword, but then quickly let go.

"Luna!" he called smiling, running up to the wolf. Luna leaped from the rock and loped towards Flath. She jumped into his arms knocking him to the mossy ground. Flath gave her a squeeze and ran his fingers through her thick, soft fur. "What a good wolf you are!"

Teo sheathed his sword and dismounted. He quickly gathered up Flath's horse, and then tied them both to a nearby tree. He approached the man and beast as they rolled around on the damp, spongy forest floor.

"Well, well, it is the beastie," Teo said as he patted the wolf on her head. "And look, the cat too."

Flath followed Teo's gaze to see the pax sauntering out from behind a large bush. She walked over to Teo and rubbed up against him, her loud, coarse purring echoing off the trees. "She's a might bigger than the last time we saw her," Teo observed.

"Yes, a full-grown cat now." Flath scratched Poeso's large head, her huge eyes closing in contentment. The urgent thunder of hooves echoed off the trees signaling a rider was quickly approaching. Teo gripped his sword hilt as Flath stood up and did the same.

From out of the shady corner of the forest, rode a horse as dark as night itself, his bright red diamond blazing across a muscled chest. His rider shrouded with equally deep, black hair flowing out from her head, wreathed by a golden circlet, rubies, and diamonds glinting in the weak sunlight across her forehead, two tawny feathers floating softly in her hair.

She pulled Zellan to an abrupt stop. The huge stallion's hooves cut deeply into soft forest dirt. He snorted his disapproval, but if Rhiannon noticed she did not show it. She jumped from Zellan's back and quickly walked up to them; she was the very embodiment of an Archigos

Warrioress. Her sleeveless leather tunic was studded with tiny gems and intricate stitch work suggesting royalty. From behind her left shoulder, a Venturien sword hilt gleamed in a stray shaft of dusty light. Her slippered feet made no sound as she came closer. He knew at that moment she was the most dangerous woman he would ever meet, and it had nothing to do with her skill as a warrioress.

She walked up to him, and he swallowed trying to find words, but he could not speak. She gently laid a hand on his chest. He fought not to fold at her touch. "I thought I might not find you," she breathed in the eloquent, twisty words of Ska.

"You found me," he quietly replied, then took her into his arms, weapons and all, and kissed her deeply. They parted when Shih 'Ni pulled his mount to a stop and slid from his horse, sword drawn, looking for blood. Before Flath could arm himself Shih 'Ni had his sword to Flath's throat.

"Shih 'Ni!" Rhiannon shouted as Teo drew his sword and slowly approached.

The two men were of the same height and while their physique differed—Flath's thick, brawny might, to Shih 'Ni's sleek, quick, skillful preciseness—both men were equally deadly and equally proud. "Who are you to take such liberties with my empress?" Shih 'Ni hissed from behind clenched teeth.

"The one that will hasten your death, Archigos," Flath answered in Venn with a sneer.

"I hardly think so, gypsy!" Shih 'Ni spat.

"Enough!" Rhiannon screamed and pushed Shih 'Ni back.

"Milady, you shouldn't be out here by yourself," Shih 'Ni started to reprimand.

"Flath!" Tim rode up to the group quickly, slid from his horse and ran up to the older man.

"Tim! You have grown a foot, for sure!" They embraced. "Look at you! You have changed into an Archigos warrior." Flath smiled down at Tim noting his Archigos clothes and weapons. He noted, too, the scars left on his young face from the beating he endured in what seemed such a long time ago. "I see you have taken good care of our empress." Flath looked over to Rhiannon and smiled warmly at her.

"Tim looked down at his feet and did not say a word.

Shih 'Ni snorted, sheathed his sword and watched the proceedings with disgust.

"Will you come back with us to my father's house?" Tim asked, hopefully.

Rhiannon walked back up to Flath and took his hand in hers. "Please," she whispered, and he could not refuse her request.

A full moon shone down upon the pasture as colorful Ppie sheep slept peacefully. Ever vigilant sheepdogs roamed the pasture to keep predators out. With a soft touch, Flath traced the scar left by the poisonous gashes Baobh had carved into Rhiannon's forearm. "I should have been there to protect you," he whispered.

"I had the entire nation of Ventra to protect me. There would have been nothing you could've done."

"I would not have let you out of my sight—even to sleep!"

She looked up at him. "You were hundreds of miles away, where you should have been—with your men." Rhiannon placed her finger to his lips. "It's over now. We'll deal with her when the time comes." She smiled at him then looked out over the dark hills. A night bird sang in time to the swaying of pepper trees. Passionflower bloomed all over the countryside turning the air into invisible honey. Rhiannon leaned back and rested her head on Flath's shoulder.

"At times I get so tired of fighting a war that never seems to end," Flath lamented. "I want to leave this land and live a normal life."

Rhiannon laughed. "A normal life, for you? I don't think you would be happy living a mundane, boring existence."

"Maybe not, but I would like the opportunity to try, at least."

"Could you really leave this? I mean, leave the rebellion before it's finished?"

Flath was silent for a moment. "Nay, I could not," he admitted. "When I see villagers so impoverished by Baobh's demand for coin that they are left with no money to buy seed for crops or livestock to raise, then I am reminded of why I am here. Baobh has bled the land dry in her hunger for money. She lives in luxury while her people starve."

"She'll cause irreversible damage if she's not stopped," Rhiannon said soberly.

"Aye! The land is on the brink of a famine."

"Is it that bad?" Her brow furrowed in concerned.

"Here in Bell, and villages further west, there is still relative security, and they are able to feed themselves, barely. But that is only because Baobh has not gotten this far yet. I see her hardened faced soldiers slowly creeping further west with every passing month."

He shook his head in disgust. "The closer you get to Sona Tuath, the poorer the people are, and soon all of the lands of Beaynid will suffer."

"Then we must stop her as soon as we can, Flath."

"You have changed, Greannmhor," Flath whispered into her hair.

"I'm still the same."

"You were but a confused, argumentative woman when I last saw you. Now you are a determined Archigos Empress," Flath observed.

"Not an empress quite yet, Flath. But soon, I promise." Rhiannon pushed a lock of hair from her face. "I'm planning on forcing Shankee to give me Ventra as soon as we return from Tel 'Rhia."

"Are you sure you are ready, Greannmhor?"

"I am ready, Flath." She sat up and looked at him. "I am ready to bring my warriors into Beaynid and help you take Sona Tuath and free my father."

"Will they follow you?" Flath was solemn.

"I'll make them see it's necessary to remove Baobh and put a king or queen on the throne that will be favorable towards Ventra."

Flath laughed a humorless chuckle. "A Seun king who is favorable towards the Archigos?" he asked, sarcastically. "Or are you planning on putting an Archigos on the throne of Sona Tuath?"

"Well, something almost as good." Rhiannon smiled. Flath arched brows in question. "When I was sick with poison, I had a dream." Rhiannon held his gaze.

"A dream?" Flath asked.

"There's a baby, Flath. A successor to the throne of Sona Tuath."

"A baby?" he echoed her again, his interest piqued.

"Well, not a baby anymore. I saw High Prince Eric and Princess Lorena's child."

"It was just a rumor that they had a child, Greannmhor."

"No! There really was a baby. I saw Princess Lorena hide it in a tree stump just before she and High Prince Eric were killed. She stuck two signet rings down into the baby's blankets and put him into a hollow in an oak tree."

"Oh, well mayhap she stuck it in the Tree of Jur, and now it is gone forever," Flath chuckled.

"Flath, I'm serious!" Rhiannon insisted. "It wasn't the Tree of Jur. It was a tree not far from the north wall of Sona Tuath, on a bluff overlooking the castle. You must believe me. I know what I saw, and I know there is an heir to the throne. All we have to do is find him or her."

Flath sighed. "Okay, let us say there is an heir. How are

we going to find this fellow? And we are not even sure whether it was a man or a woman?"

"Well, I'm not really sure if the baby was a boy or a girl. But it will obviously be a Seun."

"Well that narrows it down, Greannmhor," Flath said sarcastically. "And how do we know that it did not just die in that tree? Maybe Baobh's men found and killed it."

"I was given the dream for a reason, Flath. Why would I dream of a dead heir? Of what good would it be to us then?"

Flath took in a deep breath and let it out slowly. "How old was the babe that you saw?"

"An infant, maybe three or four months old," Rhiannon answered excitedly.

"Okay, so he or she would be around four-and-twenty. There has got to be hundreds of thousands of people in Beaynid that would fit this description. How will we ever find this person, and actually prove that he or she is the heir? Besides, Baobh was the first woman that has ever ruled Beaynid, and I do not think that after she is gone, they will be too keen on letting a woman rule again."

"Well if it's a woman that is the heir, then she can marry and give the chauvinistic pigs their king," Rhiannon replied flippantly.

Flath laughed. "Still the same old Greannmhor that I love."

"Anyway, the one who possesses those rings will be the rightful heir to the throne."

Flath smiled at her. "Everything is so simple with you."

"After we kill Baobh, we will search for this person,

and when we find him or her, we will put them on the throne. What's so hard about that?" She smiled at him, and then placed a warm kiss on his cheek. "Then you can come with me to Ventra and help me rule," she whispered into his ear. They lay back in the soft grass, and he took her into his arms holding her tightly. She rested her head against his chest and listened to his heartbeat, dreaming of the day she would bring him to Ventra.

She had not noticed until now the huge empty gulf he had left in her heart that day he left her in Ventra. But now, laying on his chest listening to his heartbeat, she felt whole again. She was full of hope for the future. The Archigos would eventually accept him, she would make sure of that, for she could not imagine a future without him.

"Must you really leave? Why don't you ride with us to Tel 'Rhia, we are only a week away?" she asked the next morning.

"Greannmhor I must get back," Flath said as he held Rhiannon in his arms. "We will see each other soon enough." He kissed her tenderly.

"Look for me at the end of the thirteenth week. Look for me, and all my warriors." She turned and opened her saddle pouch and pulled out two large, leather purses and handed them to Flath. "They are full of gold coin and gems. Use it as you see fit."

Flath's eyes grew large when he felt the weight of the

pouches. "Where did you get this much gold, Greannmhor?"

Rhiannon looked down at her feet. "I took it from Màrrach's coffers." She quickly looked up again. "I am the empress, I have a right," she defended.

"Shankee is going to be livid." Flath put the pouches down, took her right arm and softly ran his fingertips across the jagged scars left by Baobh. "Be careful, Rhiannon. I do not know what I would do if I lost you." He tenderly kissed her open palm. "I curse myself for not being there to protect you."

"I will not be safe until she is dead—no matter how many I have at my side," Rhiannon said flatly.

"Milady, we must be on our way!" Kyia called from atop her horse.

Rhiannon turned to see the trading party waiting to move on to Tel 'Rhia. She turned back to Flath, leaned in and whispered, "Start putting the word out that the Archigos will be marching with the rebellion in the near future. We want as many defections from the Beaynidan army as we can get. They will be frightened when they hear we are coming. Buy their loyalty if you must. There should be enough coin and jewels there to do that."

His brows rose in question. "What about Yellow Island's army? What prevents them from returning?"

"I've already taken care of that, my love," she smiled. "I wrote King Umar a rather stern letter warning him not to interfere or he would have the wrath of twenty-thousand Archigos warriors on his soil in a matter of weeks."

Flath laughed quite loudly. "I cannot believe you act with such outlandishness!"

"Believe it, Captain. You won't have any more trouble with them. I also assured him that whoever we place on the throne will be indebted to Yellow Island."

"Such a diplomat, Greannmhor," he said softly and kissed her forehead.

"I will always love you, Flath. Please don't ever doubt that."

"I will hold you to your word, milady," he said then mounted his horse.

With tears in her eyes, she watched him ride away and sighed. She must make her plans a reality. Her future with Flath depended on all her plans working out just so. And so much depended on her warriors following her into battle. She turned to see Shih Ni watching her closely with a look that was both disgusted and hurt. Suddenly she was not so sure of herself.

CHAPTER ELEVEN

*"The errant empress finally arrived back in Màrrach today.
Empress Shankee has been low and angry since she
discovered her cousin had slipped away from Ventra. We
have been forced to endure her foul mood and wrath from
too much drink. We hope that her loathsome temperament
will now improve, back to her usual haughty aloofness."
—Unpublished diary of servants; Lama Mann; personal
servant of Shankee Kossi*

The weary trading party road into Màrrach on a warm, early June morning, the sky was bright and clear, the Oread working hard in the fields all around them. Rhiannon had an overwhelming feeling of being home. A home that she had grown to love despite all that she feared. She sighed and looked over at the sparring areas and then out over the horse training fields and pastures. Her warriors were as they always had been—feverishly preparing for some unseen war in a far-off land. Though now they trained for a battle that was very close, even if it was unknown to them.

"She is going to be quite angry, is she not?" Tim asked as they rode up to the courtyard and slipped from their horses.

"Are you re-thinking your decision to come back with me instead of staying at home with your father?"

"No! I will never leave your side, Rhiannon." She put her arm around the boy and kissed the top of his head. The cool, mild temperature in the palace welcomed them as they entered. Birds sang and squawked in an endless display of brightly colored feathers as they did every day. Flowers always spilled from the fertile ground, and the cool, clean, life-giving water continued to be irrigated straight from the roots of the Tree of Eternal Spring, as it sat deep in the forest.

In Shankee's study, dark cloak-like drapes shut out all but a few dusty rays of sunshine. Oread servants quickly closed the doors behind Tim and Rhiannon, and the room was heavy with silence and a cool hostility that hung thickly in the air like smoke.

"Did you have fun on your irresponsible sojourn to meet the gypsy?" Shankee's voice crackled like dry fire.

"Actually, cousin, I did. Thank you for asking," Rhiannon replied in Venn.

Shankee slowly walked up to the pair. She looked haggard and much older than when Rhiannon had seen her last. Her clothes were of plain linen, and she wore no jewelry except the customary diamond stud in her nose—even the crown of Ventra was missing from her head. She looked defeated, but not so conquered as to lose her usual sharp indignation.

The proxy empress took a deep breath and let it out ever so slowly, almost whistling through her teeth. "You have been here for a year," she finally stated, "And you still have not chosen a tjaty and produced an heir."

"I have chosen a mate Shankee and as soon as Baobh is dealt with he will be accompanying me back here to Màrrach."

"You talk of the Seun?"

"Yes."

Shankee rubbed her eyes and sighed again. "I can't keep you from doing foolish things that might end in your death before you produced an heir to rule in your absence. This burden of rule must be removed from my shoulders, I have grown too weary under this load." Shankee paused a long moment before continuing. "When your mother was killed, the responsibility of Ventra's rule fell upon Tess' next daughter: my mother. She never expected to have to take on the role of proxy empress, especially since your mother had already produced an heir. But when you were taken away, my mother had no choice." Shankee's dark eyes looked through Rhiannon to a distant time shrouded in shadow and sadness.

She started speaking again, "A few months later she gathered the warriors and marched against Baobh for the murder of her sister. When her body was brought home, I was chosen as the next proxy empress. A responsibility I did not want and, in fact, have grown to resent greatly over the years. Now that you have returned, Rhiannon, daughter of Sernia, it's time for you to take your place on the throne."

Rhiannon looked over at Tim, who gave her a

reassuring smile, and then back up to Shankee. "I'm ready, Shankee. I'm ready to be the Empress of Ventra."

"I pray to the goddesses you are, cousin."

From the folds in her tunic, she produced a small box and handed it to Rhiannon. "I received this from Sona Tuath shortly after you left. I have seen the contents and suspect you will want to ready your warriors as soon as possible," she stated without emotion.

Rhiannon took a deep breath and removed the small, square lid. Inside was a severed finger; a silver and turquoise ring still encircling the appendage. Rhiannon gasped and dropped the box. Tears gathered and spilled down her cheeks.

"I made my father that ring when I was ten!" she cried.

"I suspect your father is still alive, or at least he was when they took his finger," Shankee said softly, with sudden empathy.

She walked over and put her hand on Rhiannon's shoulder. "I am truly sorry, Rhiannon. I have made preparations for the Fiann rituals to begin tonight. Kyia, myself and my oldest daughter, Li, will attend you. We will start at sundown." Shankee quietly walked from the room, leaving Tim to comfort Rhiannon.

Jasmine scented candles guttered as a hot breeze blew in through the open windows later that afternoon. Rhiannon could taste wax in her mouth as she tried to calm her nerves. The sun was just setting outside the ceremonial chamber. From the window, she heard thousands of voices solemnly chanting in a harsh cadence that soothed Rhiannon's heart. They sang in the ancient tongue of the Archigos. A language much older than Venn and from a time much earlier than their life in Ventra: back before the age of the gods and goddesses began.

Unlike the anxious fervor outside, everything was calm and methodical in Rhiannon's dressing chamber. Kyia had gone over exactly what the Fiann entailed and what the meanings were behind the symbols. She informed Rhiannon what was to be expected of her and what her attendants would be doing as well.

Kyia approached and carefully sat the ceremonial headdress atop Rhiannon's glossy hair. As she looked at Rhiannon, she cocked her head, first one way and then to the next, making sure the headdress was absolutely perfect.

"Are you nervous?" She smiled at Rhiannon.

"Does it make me less of a ruler if I say yes?" Rhiannon whispered.

"It makes you more of a ruler, milady."

Rhiannon pulled at the white robe she was wearing, trying to make it straight. The neckline was low cut, clearly slowing the bright, red diamond mark of the empress on the top of her left breast. The long hem of the robe fell to her ankles. The robe was sleeveless and tied up at both shoulders. It was made of fine, soft silk and was free from any color or embellishment.

Shankee's twenty-one-year-old daughter Li, walked up to Rhiannon and gently slipped two, intricately woven, willow branch bracelets upon her wrists. These were to symbolize the delicate, yet unbreakable power that an Archigos empress possessed in the rule of her hands.

Rhiannon stared into the large, full-length mirror. Who she saw looking back at her was someone foreign to her, yet someone she always knew was there, deep inside a confined soul. Gone was the woman who led an empty life on a ranch in Montana. Now, stood a woman who was about to become the Empress of Ventra.

She gently ran her fingers over the elaborate headdress that had been worn by generations of Archigos Empress' before her, the last being her mother. Seven snow white feathers of the Giant Owl symbolized wisdom. Seven claws of a tigress stood for ferocity. Making up the crown of the headdress was two, pure ivory tusks of a mature mountain boar, which fit snugly around Rhiannon's head. The large tusks symbolize the tenacity a successful empress must possess. The strong, stringy white bark from the Lion Tree, which served as weaving, signified oneness with the earth.

One large white feather stuck up from the center of the headdress, then three on one side, and three on the other side. One giant tigress claw emerged from the center; its sharp point rested between her eyes at the base of the bridge of her nose. Three more claws, on each side of the headdress, thrust out from the feather and bark, lying across the skin from cheek to jaw. White strips of bark held together the feathers, tusks, and claws, leaving long, curly strips hanging from the last tigress claw near her ears. Around her neck still hung the Emissary Beads that she was given by Journey-Of-The-Moon in her clandestine dream along with a torque of gold studded with large diamonds for the goddess Verna.

Shankee quietly placed slippers on Rhiannon's feet that were made from the hide of an albino Venturien Stag to symbolize speed and agility. Shankee's motions were slow and deliberate, trance-like. Li was working in much the same way. Mother and daughter had not spoken once since the preparations began. Different gems hanging from golden chains were wrapped around ankles and wrists and her neck. Every gem venerated some god or goddess, responsible for everything from war and harvest to the sweet waters from the Tree of Eternal Spring.

"It's time, Rhiannon," Shankee called from the doorway.

Suddenly afraid, Rhiannon looked over at Kyia who smiled encouragingly. "When we return from liberating Sona Tuath, we will have the biggest Fiann celebration there has ever been!"

Rhiannon smiled. "Yes, after we return victorious."

"It's time to make you an empress, Rhiannon." Rhiannon nodded and turned to leave, but Kyia grabbed her arm. "I must tell you something before you go." She was quiet but held Rhiannon's eyes.

"Go on," Rhiannon urged.

"I've wanted to tell you this for a long time but couldn't ever find the right time." She took a deep breath. "Of course, I've never told you because it means little, really. You are royalty, and the extended family relation is oft overlooked. But most of all, I didn't want to cause our friendship to end." Kyia lowered her eyes.

"Our friendship is one of the most precious things that we have. What could possibly separate my love for you?" Rhiannon took Kyia's face into her hands and pulled the younger woman's gaze up to meet hers once again. Her throat tightened, for she knew what Kyia was about to admit. Rhiannon had often wondered when she would finally mention their relation, though not sure she ever would at all.

Finally, Kyia spoke again. Her voice was quiet and unsure, like a small child's. "I'm the daughter of Sernia's brother, Laquent. I'm your cousin, Rhiannon." Kyia let out a long breath. Rhiannon thought of Tess' revelation, but said nothing, just as she had promised.

"Why didn't you tell me this before?"

"I didn't feel the time was right," she whispered.

"And the time is right, now?" Rhiannon smiled.

"I didn't want you to leave for your journey with this lie between us like an evil monster, ready to gobble me up."

Rhiannon smiled and wiped a tear from Kyia's face and embraced her. "Cousin or no, you're still my friend and confidant. But I'm glad you're my cousin too."

"You don't look surprised," Kyia said suspiciously as she pulled from the embrace. "Did Shih 'Ni speak of this to you?" she asked angrily.

Rhiannon smiled and shook her head, "No."

"It was Tess, wasn't it!" she accused.

Rhiannon couldn't lie to her and finally nodded in defeat. "But I promised her that I wouldn't tell you, so you can't say anything to her."

Kyia smiled softly, suddenly looking like a small child. "So, it matters not that we are kin?"

"Yes. I mean no." Rhiannon shook her head, and Kyia arched an eyebrow. "What I'm trying to say is that our friendship is strong, not because we are cousins. I mean, Shankee's our cousin, and I find it hard to even tolerate her," she whispered under her breath and winked. "But I'm still happy that we're related. Except for my father, I had no family growing up, so family is important to me." Rhiannon smiled.

"We must go now Rhiannon," Shankee called out again from the open door. Rhiannon gave Kyia a quick hug and then turned and walked from the chamber. Slowly she walked down the long, marble hallway that led to the inside courtyard, and then out of the palace where her warriors waited for a glimpse of their new empress, en' Fiann.

Please help me; mother Rhiannon begged as she walked out onto the steps of the Grand Palace. At that very moment, all fell silent. Thousands of faces turned to look at the woman who stood before them. Her stomach tightened as doubts flooded through her like a swollen springtime stream. She searched for Shih 'Ni and found him standing next to the lodge that she would soon be entering. He watched her, but his face was expressionless and almost hard. Finally, though, his eyes slanted, and his wide lips started curling into a small, private smile. Bashfully, she smiled and looked away, thanking Verna for her friends.

Rhiannon took a deep breath and slowly descended the soft pink, sandstone stairs. Before her, a sea of warriors opened to form a narrow path between them, leading to a small lodge near the edge of the trees.

The sky was ablaze in brilliant red with deep orange slashes reaching to the heavens. The sun had sunk below the western hills before they had left the room and was now nothing more than a pool of orange-red blood. Only the distant whinny of a horse or the call of a bird was audible as their future empress disappeared into the crowd. Suddenly a dark chanting rose into the approaching evening—loud and full of mournful expression. Tears fell from her face as she followed the long path to the lodge that lay ahead.

When Rhiannon and her attendants reached their destination, she hesitated and turned again looking out over her warriors. *Can I send all these people to their possible deaths?* She clamped her eyes shut and pushed the thought from her mind. Some would die, she knew that. But would their deaths be for a cause that they could feel proud of? Or would they loathe their new ruler for her murderous decision to lead them into war?

"Milady?" Shankee's voice called from beside her. Rhiannon took a deep breath, then turned and entered the low-roofed lodge bereft of any windows.

Inside it was smoky and hot. Oil lamps and candles burned, providing the only light in the room. In the center of the lodge was a large fire, the smoke creeping up and out through a hole in the ceiling. Clay jars filled with spices and herbs were sitting on the floor. Large bear skins were laid out around the fire. A very ancient looking woman was sitting on a white bear pelt nearest the fire. Kyia had told her that this woman was the Archigos Ceremony Keeper and was almost never seen outside of ceremonies or festivals. She told her that the woman was the oldest living Archigos in Ventra—one hundred-and-eighty-two years old, so the old woman claimed.

Standing in the four corners of the lodge, lost in the smoky shadows, were four of the woman's female descendants. These young women were not warriors but were chosen by the woman to be her apprentices and to be the next generation of Ceremony Keepers.

Rhiannon took her place near the fire, sitting across from the old woman. Kyia, Shankee, and Li sat on the pelts next to her. The Ceremony Keeper's face was so wrinkled; her small eyes were barely visible. She too wore a robe of white and a smaller, less ostentatious headdress made of red feathers and a beaver pelt. She was covered with red and blue tattoos from head to toe. Even her wrinkled cheeks had blue splotches across them.

The old woman pulled a cork from one of the jars and took a pinch of the dark red powder inside. She threw it into the fire with a large sweep of her thin arm. The fire immediately flared up so that the flames licked the blackened ceiling, and then quickly died down. A sweet odor filled the room. Rhiannon choked but forced herself to take a deep breath.

From out of the darkened corner of the room, one of the young apprentices walked up to the old woman. She held a large, ornate dagger made of polished silver and carved with the figures of gods and goddesses. The gemstone-studded hilt winked in the firelight. Carefully, she handed it to her great-great-great-grandmother. The old woman slowly rose from the soft bear pelt and walked around behind Rhiannon with a soft chanting trailing from her mouth: she was ready to perform the *Mottai Addithal*. Rhiannon could feel the sharp blade cutting away at her dark blanket of hair, then a cool light feeling as the fringe of it tickled her shoulders.

The old woman hobbled back to her spot before the fire, handed the dagger back to her apprentices and carefully lowered herself onto the pelt, Rhiannon's long hair trailing from her bony hand. Meticulously she laid out the long strands of Rhiannon's hair onto the fire. The acrid smell of burning hair filled the lodge quickly as fire consumed the hair. The old woman's small eyes grew large and round as she watched the fire flare and burn.

"The gods and goddesses have accepted your sacrifice!" she stated, happily.

"Now your journey begins, Rhiannon, daughter of Sernia," the old woman sang in a crackly, dry voice. "Clear your mind of all things and ready yourself for your journey."

The old woman took a few more pinches from the other jars and tossed them into the fire, their musky aroma filling the lodge completely, making it hard to focus on the other's faces.

She heard the old woman's voice call out from the blanket of smoke and a cup was suddenly put into Rhiannon's hand. Carefully, she drank the cool, sweet liquid and set the cup down. The old woman started chanting, her voice melting out from the smoke as if coming from nowhere.

The corners of Rhiannon's mind started to fuzz as a deep warmth ran through her body. She closed her eyes and slowed her breathing and tried to push all thought from her mind. The nervousness had passed and a content, relaxed feeling caressed her soul. Her father's face flashed across her mind. He was happy and smiling down at a young Rhiannon. Then the beautiful face of her mother came into focus. She smiled and nodded at her daughter as if to say, everything is going to be alright.

Slowly, Rhiannon began to feel herself being carried out of the lodge and up into the sky over Ventra. The trees, valleys, meadows, and streams were all visible to her as she drifted by a cloud. Up high on a rocky mass, she finally stopped so that she could overlook the whole of Ventra.

Rhiannon's heart beat with the rhythm of the wind, her blood flowing with the rivers of her home. Her soul was one with the land and with her people. She was the life and breath of Ventra, its heart, and soul; life-giving waters flowed from her very spirit.

"Rhiannon, daughter of Sernia," a soft voice sounding like trickling water sung to her from the wind.

"It is you who I have chosen to lead your people. It is you who must defend Ventra, the birthplace of your ancestors."

An eagle flew up to the rocky ledge and stood before Rhiannon; one large eye, holding her in the blackness of its glossy pupil. Suddenly the bird melted into the shape of a woman.

Ice blue eyes looked back at her. The woman's skin was the color of cream; her golden hair flowed out around her like sunshine. She wore a simple pink robe; her skirt danced in the breeze.

"It is you who must lead the Archigos now. They will listen to your voice, Rhiannon Kossi. You are a part of a prophecy that must be fulfilled in order for Ventra to have peace. Your journey is long and fraught with much heartache and loss. You will grow weary but do not give up, for the future of the dual kingdoms of Ventra and Beaynid lay at your feet!"

The woman slowly opened one golden hand and softly blew into her palm. Glowing dust carried on the wind of her lips sparkled in the sunlight and whirred around Rhiannon caressing her skin like feathers.

The woman smiled, her form slowly shifting into feather and claw. She turned to look one more time at Rhiannon and then jumped from the ledge; a warm breeze carrying her away.

"March your warriors on Sona Tuath," a whisper echoed in her head.

The wind turned cold, the sky dark. A frigid rain started to fall on Ventra, falling in sheets, obstructing her view. She began to shiver as the wind blew the rain towards her. Sharp, cutting drops of water soaked her in seconds. She looked down trying to shield her eyes. Red blood ran down her legs and arms, dripping like rain, pooling on the rocky floor until it was covered in blood. Everywhere she looked was covered in wet, bright red blood as it flowed from her body.

She began to choke, gagging on the smell of flowing blood. Someone grabbed the short strands of her hair and started to pull her away from the ledge. She tried to yield to the force and back away from the cutting rain, but her feet would not move. Her hair started to tear and snap from her scalp, but she could not move her heavy limbs. Her fingers and toes grew numb as the corners of her consciousness began to fade into blackness.

Suddenly she was surrounded by a deep blanket of silence. It seemed as if she had been pulled through a hole too small for her body to fit through. Her body ached and was wet with sweat or blood—or both. Her throat was dry and scratchy, and she could smell fire. Behind her closed lids, she was lost in a world of shadows.

A biting pain stabbed at her nose, causing her to gasp. She heard the snap of cartilage, and then tasted the blood as it trickled down the back of her throat. As pain seared into her mind, the silence dissipated and Rhiannon could hear the scratchy chanting of the old woman again.

Rhiannon opened her eyes to the dim, smoky room. Her nose burned and the skin across her chest and shoulders throbbed. She could barely make out the wooden ceiling of the lodge through the thick smoke. She was lying across the bear pelt with the old woman's wrinkled face looking down at her.

"How was your journey, Rhiannon?" she asked.

"I feel like I've been hit by a bus," she murmured in response.

Rhiannon's robe had been untied at the shoulders and folded down to her navel. The ceremonial tattoos—announcing her a warrioress as well as the ruling empress—had been etched across her chest, their scrolling tentacles reaching across her shoulders where it ended. The left side of her nose had been pierced in true Archigos fashion, the tiny diamond speckled with her own blood.

Two of the old woman's great-great-great-granddaughter apprentices gently cleaned the wounds of her carved flesh, and then slowly rubbed a foul-smelling salve into her skin.

After they had retied her robe, they helped her sit up to face the old woman's leathery face. She smiled a toothless grin at the younger woman. Rhiannon was relieved the ceremony had drawn to a close.

"Now you must journey into the forest and seek the guidance of the gods and goddesses," she proclaimed. "They will have the final say as to whether you are to take the throne of Ventra or not. If they let you live, you are approved. However, if you perish in the forest alone, that is your punishment for waking them needlessly!" Her small voice suddenly boomed with dread and proclamation.

Carefully Rhiannon stood, her head spinning. She filled her lungs with sweet, dry smoke trying to clear her head. Finally, she turned to Shankee who had appeared out of the darkness.

"Ready my warriors. We march as soon as I return," she stated with new found confidence.

"As you wish, my Empress." Shankee dipped into a low bow.

Rhiannon heard the old woman's cackling laughter as she left the lodge and melted into the dark forest.

Thankful to be free from the stifling confines of the smoke-filled lodge, Rhiannon filled her lungs with cool night air as she ran through the large trees. She felt like she was flying through the dense forest. Her neck was unexpectedly cool as the short strands of her hair floated out behind her. She did not know where she was headed, nor what might happen, but she was free! It would only be a matter of time until her father was also freed from Sona Tuath. Soon all Beaynid would be free from the rule of that evil, power-hungry woman.

Rhiannon followed the light of a full moon as she ran deeper into the dark forest. Her muscles started to throb, and her lungs burned, but she continued to run. A large screech owl flew above her as if guiding her towards some prize.

Finally, just before dawn, she collapsed onto the soft, fern covered forest floor. Lying on her back, she breathed in deeply, tasting pine, fern pollen and clover. The once dark sky was slowly slipping into a cool pink hue. The distant screech of an owl was carried on a gentle summer wind through the tall trees. Unable to stay awake any longer she drifted off into a fitful sleep under the soft feathers of forest ferns.

Suddenly aware that someone was watching her, Rhiannon slowly opened her eyes to see the shiny black hoof of a horse. She sat up and was met by a pair of deep black eyes. It was not a horse at all! She jumped to her feet in astonishment. What stood before her was a glossy black equine, a long horn protruding from its forehead! Its thick onyx mane flowed down solid muscled shoulders and chest. A long, silken tail pooled on a carpet of green clover. It circled her three times, watching her intently. Finally, it used its moist, warm muzzle to gently nudge her toward its back.

Rhiannon awkwardly climbed on the horned animal's back. Nervous fingers dug into thick mane as they galloped off through the trees. Soon they reached the Tree of Eternal Spring. A shaft of golden sunlight bathed the tree in a warm light. Rhiannon slid from the creature's back and walked towards the tree. The long wisps of its branches swayed in the warm, summer breeze.

Rhiannon turned back around to see if the creature remained but, in its place, stood her mother! She gasped and stepped back in shock trying to hide herself in the willow branches.

"Don't be afraid, my daughter," Sernia said, walking closer to Rhiannon.

"Mother," Rhiannon whispered.

"You have grown into a fine, strong woman, Rhiannon." Sernia smiled warmly. "I am so sorry that I missed all of those long years." Her face turned hollow and sad.

Rhiannon stepped out from the willow branches wiping away tears. "You left me!" she said angrily as a torrent of tears spilled from her eyes.

Sernia walked up to her daughter and took her into her arms. "I never left you completely, my love. I watched over you while you were growing up in the land of your father."

Rhiannon looked up at her mother. "Why didn't he tell me?"

"It was for your protection. He had to keep you hidden until the time came for you to be called." Sernia spoke softly.

"The nightmares?"

"Yes, Rhiannon. Whenever anything of any importance must be undertaken, we are called by unrelenting dreams." Sernia smiled reflectively. "When the time came, I dreamed of your father, and he, of me. It was our dreams that led us to each other, yet worlds apart."

"Is he still alive, mother?" Rhiannon asked urgently.

"He is, my daughter. But you must hurry if he is to be saved, for he is fading into darkness." A single, gleaming tear spilled from Sernia's eye.

Rhiannon sighed. "I don't know if I can defeat Baobh."

"You must defeat her, Rhiannon, or all will be lost. The fate of not only Beaynid but also Ventra depends on it."

"I am not strong enough." Rhiannon's voice faltered.

"You are strong enough to slay a thousand beasts with only your heart, dear one. You have only to find the power within you and use it."

"Come with me,' Rhiannon urged.

Sernia smiled and shook her head. "I cannot, my daughter, for Verna has called me to her. I must go back now."

"No, don't leave me again," Rhiannon cried.

Sernia kissed Rhiannon's forehead. "I will never be far off from you, Rhiannon."

"Nooo!" Rhiannon protested.

"You must sleep now, my love," Sernia whispered, then touched Rhiannon's forehead. She yawned and rubbed her eyes trying to stay awake, but the call to sleep was too great to fight. She looked one last time at her mother then slumped to the spongy forest ground and fell fast asleep.

CHAPTER TWELVE

Her call is loud, though undisciplined, but she calls to us
anyway
Will we answer the Call of the Empress?
To take us from Ventra she would; the Goyor she would slay
She implores us to heed her heart's request
A land to the south—people, their hair so bright; she wants
to take us away
Will we answer the Call of the Empress?
Hard it is to leave the land of our birth—the land of Ventra;
what will we say?
She implores us to heed her heart's request

The Dark Queen has danced in Archigos blood, so red
Will we answer the Call of the Empress?
Off to Beaynid did our old ruler, us led
She implores us to heed her heart's request
The battle was great, but upon Archigos blood the Goyor
Queen fed
Will we answer the Call of the Empress?
With fields of our brothers and sisters dead, in dishonor,
we fled
She implores us to heed her heart's request

Now, again the decision lay at our feet

Will we answer the Call of the Empress?
Will we have success this time; can this evil we now beat?
She implores us to heed her heart's request
Can we hope to win or are we doomed to defeat?
Will we answer the Call of the Empress?
Rhiannon asks, and we must answer; this story must now be
complete
She implores us to heed her heart's request
— The Call of the Empress; Ju 'Blm

Bright sunlight flooded in the windows of her throne room as morning called the land awake. Luna sat on a cold marble step beside Rhiannon's throne watching over the group with disinterest. Etâhpe'o-poeso lazily lay at her feet quietly napping.

Your warriors are angry, milady. They don't wish to fight side by side with the enemy."

Rhiannon looked at the tall man standing before her as she stood on the dais. His long dark hair was graying, his skin creased with age and the Venturien sun. His body though was still honed like a mighty weapon not yet softened by age.

Rhiannon scanned the room, but still, there was no Shankee. She had not seen her since she had walked back into Màrrach the morning before, the Fiann rituals complete. Rhiannon took a deep breath. She certainly did not need Shankee any longer; Ventra did not need Shankee any longer.

Rhiannon was now empress and Ventra was her responsibility now. Still, she had wished Shankee had been there. If for nothing else, just to show her support, especially now.

She craned her neck and looked back around at Shih 'Ni, her eyes pleading for help, though knowing he could offer none. A faint smile crossed his lips, and he gently placed a reassuring hand on her shoulder.

She sighed and looked back out over the large group of two hundred and fifty War Party leaders. They were among the strongest and most skilled of her warriors, each given the responsibility of leading a band of fifty or so warriors. She had to convince them to march against Baobh before she could convince the whole of her army.

"This is a very decisive time for Ventra and her warriors," she started, her mouth suddenly dry. "I understand the animosity between us and Beaynid. I fully acknowledge my warrior's feelings in this matter." She looked over at Kyia, and Tim, who were standing quietly in the corner of the Throne Room then looked back at the warriors who stood before her. "But we must act against Baobh now before she once again has the chance to kill another of Ventra's empresses." Rhiannon took a deep breath. "Baobh's army has been weakened by the rebellion and now is the opportune time to march against her. I have the assurance of King Umar from Yellow Island that he will not interfere."

"Then why not just let the rebellion finish off her army?" A warrioress asked, black eyes staring out from a frown.

"The rebellion has suffered a great loss and doesn't have the power to do so," Rhiannon answered.

"Why fight alongside that sorry band of rebels at all? Why not just take Sona Tuath for ourselves and put an Archigos on their throne? That would really wound their misplaced Seun pride!" The woman spoke with poison on her tongue as the group erupted in laughter.

"The rebellion will offer us a familiarity with foreign terrain and even the castle itself," Rhiannon stated without humor when the laughter died down. "And, though all will rejoice when Baobh is gone, taking Sona Tuath will still be a delicate situation."

"Delicate?" the warrioress spat. "They seethe with hatred for us!"

"Yes, you're correct. There's no love lost between our people and theirs, but our goal is not to make friends—it's to rid the land of Baobh." She watched the faces of her warriors, trying to read their thoughts. She knew they were still unconvinced and she sighed inwardly. "I also plan on installing a king who is favorable to the Archigos," she started again.

"What do we care how their king feels about us?" a warrior shouted from the back of the room.

"Beaynid could be a powerful ally," she stated as exasperated and angry noises erupted from the crowd. She shook her head and began again. "You might not be concerned about who rules Beaynid now, or in the future, but as your empress, I have to be! Once Baobh is overthrown, it will be to our advantage to have a benevolent king on the throne of Sona Tuath." The men and women looked around at each other and started talking amongst themselves. She hoped that she had finally appealed to their better senses.

Shih 'Ni laid his hand on her shoulder again, trying to calm her nerves. "Baobh will not stop until I am dead. I must kill her or be killed by her. Our immediate future wholly depends on the destruction of Baobh, and our continued peace depends on who takes her place."

"Are you forgetting the massacre that happened the last time we marched on Sona Tuath?" another warrior asked. "What's to prevent another bloodbath? I've heard Baobh has the entire Necklace of Verna Now."

The room fell silent. "That's true; she has my mother's necklace. It's also been said she is aided by Lord Rull." She looked into the eyes of each of her war party leaders. "But are we not blessed by the goddess Verna? Are we not deadly warriors capable of destroying Baobh? The prophecy foretold we will be victorious!" She had their attention. "It is our destiny to march against Sona Tuath. It is my destiny to destroy Baobh!" She stood.

No one spoke. The room was silent except for the busy sounds of an army preparing for battle far below. Finally, she said, "I must stop Baobh before she causes further harm to my people. Are you with me... or are you against your empress?"

Finally, one by one, each warrior took their sword from the sheath they wore strapped to their backs, lay it on the marbled floor before her, then kneel down and bow dark heads in a poetic dance of loyalty and savage pride. From behind her, she heard Shih Ni's steel blade ring out as he removed his sword also from its sheath. He came around in front of her and laid his sword at her feet. "We are with you, Rhiannon Kossi, Empress of Ventra." He knelt quietly below her as a tear slipped down her cheek.

Her hair, too short for a braid, ruffled around her shoulders in the cool morning breeze as she pushed her cloak's hood from her head. Dawn shrouded clouds of red and pink were painted across the eastern sky. Bright, newborn rays of a pre-birthed sun backlit the eastern tail of the mountain range that separated Ventra from Beaynid. Poeso soared above them leading the way as the nation of Ventra left Màrrach.

This was the culmination of over a year's worth of hard work and excruciating physical training for both her and Zellan. She reached down and patted Zellan's sleek, black neck. He was an Archigos Warhorse like no other. They were as one, each predicting the others moves, flowing together like a dangerous river swallowing all in their path. She thought back to their life before they had come into this world and how unpredictable and unruly he was. A reflective smile formed on her full lips. He was so different, so controlled and proud, a lethal warrior, just as she now was.

She looked over to Shih Ni who had been watching her intently. She smiled, and he answered with a warm smile of his own. He had been so angry about Flath during the trading trip west, but by the time they had finally reached

Tel 'Rhia, Flath was forgotten, and he was himself again. Always serious and consumed with male bravado, but always at Rhiannon's side, ready to offer any support she might need.

The June dawn was chilly and damp, the rising sun offering no warmth. The land seemed to gently coax the sun to rise turning everything it touched to a golden hue. As they set out for the foothills, two dark riders approached, their Archigos War Horses easily identifiable.

"I didn't think you'd be coming," Rhiannon called out as they reined in next to her.

Shankee smiled and nodded toward her oldest child, Li, who was now in quiet conversation with Kyia. "You are our Empress," she said. "We will follow you."

"Thank you, Shankee."

The former proxy empress waved dismissively. "I never thought it was wise to march against Baobh again, but perhaps it's the only way." She shrugged and looked off into the distance, watching the newborn sun slide out from behind the mountains; then she looked back over to Rhiannon. "It was a long, bloody fight that none can forget whether they were there or were at home to receive their dead." She sighed. "I hope you can understand my reluctance to follow in my mother's footsteps."

Rhiannon nodded in acknowledgment. "I hope you can understand my reluctance to follow in my mother's footsteps as well."

Shankee took a deep breath, then let it out slowly. "Our mothers: both powerful Archigos warrioress, both dead by the same hand." Her mouth twisted into a humorless smile. "The evil woman will not stop until one of you lay dead."

"I know," Rhiannon said quietly and rode on in silence.

Slowly they made their way towards the mountain pass. Rhiannon twisted in her low Archigos saddle to watch Ventra disappear as they headed up into the jagged mountain range.

"These supplies should last us until the Archigos arrive." Flath sat atop his horse happily chewing on a large piece of jerky.

"Another week, aye?" Teo asked, swatting at a bee.

"Aye. She said by the end of the thirteenth week." Flath answered.

"So ye will go back with her, then?"

"I will," he nodded in agreement, his mouth hooking into a satisfied smile.

"A Seun boy, rule'n with an Archigos Empress, ha!" Teo slapped Flath on the back again. "Well done, lad, well done."

"We will see how long it will take before the first warrior tries to kill me," Flath said jokingly. "I will bet their Master-at-Arms...what's-his-name...oh aye, Shih 'Ni...I am sure he will be the first to try."

Suddenly, something small darted out from the brush. Flath and Teo yanked their mounts to an abrupt stop. "Gods, 'tis a child!" Teo shouted and quickly dismounted.

"Are you hurt?" Flath asked anxiously as he looked

down at the child's delicate, filth smudged face. The girl could not have been more than five or six years old.

Large wet tears started to fall from her eyes, carving a path in the dirt as it slipped down her cheeks. Teo scooped the child up in his arms, careful of any unseen injuries. "'Tis a'right wee lass, we will'na hurt ye."

Flath looked around for her parents but saw no one except Jon and Bleen who had stopped the wagon and were looking back at the commotion. "Where are your parents, child?" Flath asked quietly.

"Lost," she was finally able to say between sobs.

"Gypsy?" Flath asked.

The girl's eyes grew wide with fear, and her hands and arms flew up in defense as if she expected to be beaten. "'Tis a'right, lass. No one will strike ye while ye are with Teo." He tenderly wrapped the child in his arms and stroked her hair.

Flath turned to Jon and Bleen and waved them on. "Go ahead! We are going to take the child back to her parents."

"Do you wish us to wait?" Jon called out.

"Nay. We will be along as soon as we can." Flath answered, then Jon waved and slapped the reins across broad rumps sending the horses on down the path again. "Well, let us find this young lady her parents," he said.

"Do ye wish ta ride the horsy wi' Teo?" The burly, red-haired man asked in a playful voice as he carefully sat the small girl up onto the back of his horse. She laughed, tears forgotten, as they rode off into the trees in the direction of where she had come.

"What is your name, lass?"

"Caroline," she happily sang.

"'Tisn't that yer mother's name, lad?" Teo looked over at Flath.

"Aye," he said, curtly, and coaxed his horse into a quicker pace.

As the sun finally set on a long summer day, dappled sunshine became cool shadows in the forest. Caroline and Teo were happily singing from behind Flath. He remained silent, stoically cutting a path in the direction that Caroline had said she had come from.

As the shadows became deeper, Teo finally reined in his horse and stopped. "Do ye smell that, laddie?" he asked, hopeful.

Flath stopped and took a deep breath. "Food cooking," he answered as the frantic calls of worried family drifted on a warm breeze.

"Grammy!" Caroline screamed so loud that Teo jumped. "That's my grammy!"

They slid from their horses and melted further into the forest following the desperate calls. Caroline pulled away from Teo and darted past a large bush and into a clearing.

Flath walked on ahead as Teo pulled his stubborn horse past prickly bushes. As Flath stepped into the clearing, he stopped short. His heartbeat quickened, and his throat tightened. Teo stumbled into the clearing, pulling his obstinate mount behind.

"This is uncle Teo!" Caroline announced. "But that's just Flath." She pointed over to Flath with a sour look on her face. "He doesn't talk much," she chirped.

An old man walked over to Teo and bowed to the red

man. "Thank you for bringing my granddaughter back. We have been mighty worried."

Teo slapped the older man on the back and smiled at him. "'Tis the least we could do fer such a sweet, wee lass."

The man let out a breath he had been holding and visibly relaxed. "Thank you for not leaving her to perish in the wood."

"Ack! Only a monster could do that ta a barrin."

The man stooped to pick up his granddaughter. "We are gypsies, and most would see us dead."

"'Tis a'right auld man, we are not most." Teo smiled. "I am Teo Jass, son of Holt of Perth, at your service, kind sir."

Teo turned to Flath and pointed. "And this is—"

"I know who this is," an older woman standing next to the man replied, while not taking her eyes off Flath. "This is my son."

The campfire burned hot—much too hot for a warm summer night. Oil lamps burned from low branches around the small camp. Children laughed and played as they ran around the bushes trying to catch fireflies. Flath looked over to Teo across the campfire. Caroline sat happily in his lap as several other children sat around him listening to him tell an animated story of monsters and beautiful princesses.

Teo had excitedly accepted their invitation to stay for supper and to share their camp for the night. Flath scowled and looked into the fire. He was actually surprised that they had let him eat and pass the time with them. The last time he had seen his family, he was being banished from the clan, never to return.

Flath sighed and looked out over the camp. It had

grown since last he had seen it. His father had told him that his sister Ruby had married a man she had met in Nabb while at a fair and then had sailed away with him. She had always been a wild one, Flath reminisced, not being able to keep the smile from his face when he pictured his beautiful dark-haired sister.

A young man walked over and put several more logs on the fire. He shyly smiled at Flath through the flames. Flath smiled back. His brother's boy had grown from a small child to a young man while Flath had been gone. Flath looked over at his brother and his wife. His brother Jack was bent over his lute, strumming a familiar tune. His shoulder-length brown hair, now with a touch of gray, was held tightly back in a queue. His chubby, sweet-tempered wife and youngest child, now a young woman, sang along cheerfully.

He looked over to Caroline again, so resembling his sister and mother both. Caroline was his sister Donna's youngest child. Dark ringlets curled all over her head. Huge brown eyes stared at him through the fire, and then timidly she smiled. He smiled back, not being able to help himself. Flath was the youngest of four children. He was once just as much a part of this clan as was any of his family. Now, however, he was an outsider.

"'Tis nice to see you again, brother." His sister Donna walked up and handed him a flask of ale. "We have all missed you."

Small lines creased Donna's face that was, as always, framed with her dark curls. She looked so much older than when he saw her last. He smiled, not knowing what to say.

She walked back over to Caroline and took her from Teo's lap, the story now ended.

Finally, free from the children, Teo walked over and sat next to Flath. "Children, wee devils, not happy till they get a good story," he chided.

"You are not happy until you can tell a good story, old friend," Flath took a long drink from the shiny flask, then handed it to Teo.

"'Tis good ta be back wi' yer family?"

"Quite unsettling, actually. The last time I saw any of these people I was being run off and admonished never to return."

"Things change, me boy. They've heard that ye have been lead'n the rebellion. They're mighty proud of ye!"

Flath laughed bitterly. "I am the same man they accused of stealing and ran off like a criminal from the only family I knew. The same, yet so different," he finished reflectively.

"They made a mistake, lad. Forgive them for their ignorance. Look how much ye have accomplished that ye would not have if ye had stayed."

Flath snorted. "What, exactly, have I accomplished?"

Teo clamped a wide hand on his friend's shoulder. "Ye lead a dedicated group of men who, all of them to a one, would lay down his life for ye. Ye have found and returned ta the Archigos their missin' empress, and now ye will rule with her over a mighty nation of warriors. What haven't ye accomplished, me boy? If ye would have stayed, ye would have done like your father and his father before him. Ye would have led a good life, though ye would have not made a difference. There would have been no rebellion. The

Archigos empress mayhap would have never been returned to Ventra. And the prophecy would have never been fulfilled!" Flath grunted as he quietly watched the camp prepare for slumber. Mothers tucked their children in, fathers dimmed lamps, and everything started to quiet. Nothing had really changed at all since he had left.

Finally, Flath's parents came and sat down next him and Teo. He could clearly read guilt in their weathered eyes and felt satisfied at seeing the pain on their faces. His father's once blonde hair, now gray, was awash in the orange firelight. His fair, Seun skin was now withered by too much sun and too much time.

Flath thought of the last time he saw his father. He recalled the older man's stern, hard expression as he told him to leave and never return. "I did not think I would ever see you again," his father said quietly.

"You told me never to come back. How would our paths ever cross again?"

Flath's parents looked at each other. Their expressions were dark, almost haunted. "'Twas something that had to be done, son." His father tried to explain.

"You knew I stole nothing!" Flath shouted, waking some of the clan, who quickly turned over, pretending not to have heard. "Yet you still sent me away. Why?"

His mother started to cry and reached out for him. "Please understand, we had to, Flath." Her hand was cold and withered with age.

"Why, mother? I was still a child. How could you have sent me away from my family?"

Her hand recoiled, and she buried her face in her hands,

sobbing. His father wrapped her in his arms and whispered softly to her. Flath refused to feel badly and looked away. Teo put his hand on Flath's shoulder, silently lending support.

After a few moments, his father scooted across the dirt a little closer to him. "After I tell you this, you will understand why we had to do what we did," his father's voice was morbid.

He took a small cloth from under his tunic and handed it to Flath. The fabric was tightly woven and soft to the touch. The color was now faded, and it was stained and dirty. Flath carefully unfolded it, studying it from behind wary eyes.

"A babe's blanket?" he questioned, spitefully.

His father took a deep breath. "That was your baby blanket."

"You sent me away, and now you offer me a filthy blanket as repentance?" Flath was indignant.

His father reached into a small pouch and pulled something out and slowly handed it to his son. "We found these with you when you were a babe."

The firelight sputtered in a cool wind causing deep shadows to dance across Flath's open palm where two rings lay unimportantly winking in the ochre glow. Two rings: a man's and a woman's. The rings were tarnished with age and neglect, but he could clearly see the engraved images of the banner of Sona Tuath—the crest of Basilias. He looked up at his parents, unable to speak.

"We had to send you away. You were meant for much greater things than to live with gypsies," his mother's voice was soft as lamb's wool.

Flath gripped the blanket in one hand and the rings in the other. "What is this babble? Do not speak in riddles!" Flath's vision was like a pinpoint of light on his father's face.

With tears spilling down his creased face, he spoke, "We heard the squalling of an infant, so we followed the cries. We found you hidden in the trunk of a dead tree, wrapped in that blanket with those rings tucked inside," he said, pointing to the rings.

Flath went numb and could barely hear over the rush of his blood and wild pounding of his heart. His mouth was so dry he could not speak. Rhiannon's words played through his mind as if they were sitting beside each other once again.

His father went on. "We found the bodies of your mother and father lying beside the road not far from where we found you," his voice trailed off.

"Who were they?" Flath finally asked, though he already knew the answer.

The old man looked over at his wife who nodded in encouragement. "They were the High Prince and Princess of Sona Tuath, Flath. Your grandfather was King Basilias."

Flath's stomach started to bubble, and he began to tremble. He jumped up and ran off into the brush where he lost his supper. He wiped his mouth with the soft baby blanket, the weight of the rings was still heavy in his grip. They lay burning like a coal squeezed tightly in the palm of his hand. He stood trembling, staring out into the suffocating darkness of the thick wood. He heard someone approaching and felt his father's frail touch—or at least the man he had always believed to be his father.

"Please forgive us," he said weakly. "We are simple folk with little means. We did the best we could for you, and when you had grown enough, we thought it best to send you out into the world, for you to make your own way, whatever that way may be." He walked in front of Flath and looked into his eyes. "With Baobh still ruling it was too dangerous for us to tell you who you were. But now, with her demise on the threshold, you need to know."

"I understand now," he said so quietly that he was not sure his father had heard. "You will always be my father." He pointed to the sleeping camp, "This will always be my clan." He took his father into his arms. "For what you have done, I owe you everything... Beaynid owes you even more."

CHAPTER THIRTEEN

"Before humans roamed the earth, there were Protectors placed within the womb of the forest. These Folk were the Wards of the Land and cared for every living creature within. It was not until humans began to spread from the places of their origins out into the land that the numbers of the Protectors began to dwindle."
—*Tales of the Ancients; Burnk Lau*

D on't look so worried," Rhiannon chided.

"We should have brought more warriors," Shih 'Ni replied, tightly.

"We'll find it soon," Rhiannon said, unconcerned, pushing a branch out of her way as they entered a particularly dense part of the forest. "We'll be fine." She ducked under a low branch, and then crawled over a downed tree with Luna by her side, as always. The brush was thick, forcing all to go single file. Shih 'Ni took the lead, followed by Rhiannon, Kyia and then Tim. The forest's vegetation grew swollen and seemed to bar their passage as they tried to continue. The air was hot and humid and thick with the smell of pine, clover, and moist dirt.

Rhiannon heard the ring of steel and looked up quickly. Shih 'Ni had unsheathed his sword and was holding it above his dark head, ready to hack his way through the barrier of vegetation. "Shih 'Ni, no!" she warned.

"I can't move any further," he answered in frustration. "I need to cut through this cursed shrubbery."

Rhiannon peered around Shih 'Ni to see a huge bush bristling with an explosion of thorns. "I don't think it would be wise to do that," she said, thoughtfully.

Angrily, Shih 'Ni shoved his sword back into its sheath. "Then this is as far as we may go, milady." Rhiannon sighed as she bent down to try and remove a thorny vine from around her ankle. Branches full of green leaves and unruly vines obstructed her view, so she carefully tried to unwind the thorny tentacle. "Ouch!" She pricked her finger and pulled her hand away just as a bead of bright red blood welled, then dropped to the ground.

As soon as the tiny drop of blood hit the forest floor the tangled mass of vegetation suddenly melted away and faded into a small woodland village. Instinctively Tim moved close to Rhiannon. His green eyes were huge with wonder. Rhiannon put her hand on his shoulder. "Welcome to Ghroc, Tim." She smiled warmly at him. "I bet you never thought you'd see this."

"Nay," he breathed, looking around at the small cottages that seemed to be a part of the forest its self.

A worn, pinecone lined woodland path lead up to each of the lichen covered cottages that looked like they had grown right out of the soil. The roofs were thatched with pine needle, moss, and grass. Small round, glassless windows were cut in the side of the cottages providing air and a little sunlight. In a few of the cottages, vividly colored bluebirds had made their nests right in the roofs of the dwellings, while large, fuzzy, red squirrels scampered about the cottages and trees. Brilliantly painted flowers grew effortlessly in front of each cottage perfuming the air with sweet smells. Spongy mushrooms and frilly ferns carpeted the forest floor.

Slowly a handful of small dark-skinned children appeared from between the trees and bushes. Curious, they carefully started creeping closer to Rhiannon and her small group.

Rhiannon squatted down and motioned them over with her hand. "Come here, it's okay," she called.

They approached slowly while warily watching Shih 'Ni. Rhiannon looked over at him and almost laughed at his expression. He looked almost frightened! "Mighty Archigos Warrior terrified by a bunch of small children."

He snorted and folded his arms across his broad chest. "Mighty Archigos Empress completely becharmed by a gang of brats," he huffed.

Kyia walked up and nimbly sat on the ground next to Rhiannon. "They're so adorable, milady."

Shih 'Ni clicked his tongue in disgust. "Women!" he said and shook his head.

"Come on, come closer, we won't hurt you," Rhiannon persuaded, opening her arms.

The children were dressed in fine linen dyed the colors of the forest: deep green, browns, grays, oranges and yellows. Tiny white flowers were stuck in their bushy, dark hair. Their cocoa colored skin was completely flawless and pure. Their tiny ears were pointed and their features fine and soft. Brown eyes, large and ringed with thick, raven colored lashes peered up at them, and tiny plump lips curled into innocent smiles. "I've never seen anything as beautiful or poetic," Rhiannon said quietly, taking a young girl in her lap.

"What's your name?" she asked the child.

"My name is Singing Brook," she proudly replied. "And that is my brother, Fox." She pointed to the small boy in Kyia's lap.

"Those are beautiful names." Rhiannon smiled down at the child. The girl giggled, and then clenched her tiny fist and closed her eyes as if concentrating. She turned her fist over and slowly uncurled her pudgy fingers revealing a delicate red flower in the palm of her small hand. "This is for you," she said cheerfully and placed the flower in Rhiannon's hair.

"Thank you, Singing Brook. It's beautiful." She kissed the child on her warm forehead.

"Are you an Archigos Warrior?" a little boy craned his neck back and looked up at Shih 'Ni.

He looked down at the child whose eyes were round with awe. "I am," Shih 'Ni replied, cautiously.

"I've never seen one!" the boy breathed. "Is it true that you are strong enough to pick up a whole mountain and move it?" Rhiannon laughed, and Shih 'Ni cast her an annoyed glance.

"That's Bear Paw. He always talks about Archigos Warriors," Singing Brook giggled.

"Is that your sword?" Bear Paw asked.

"Yes," Shih 'Ni replied shortly.

"Can I hold it?"

"No!" The look on Shih 'Ni's face was hilariously alarmed.

"Come over here Bear Paw." Rhiannon motioned him over, and after giving Shih 'Ni one more pleading glance, he obeyed Rhiannon. "How old are you Bear Paw?" she asked with a smile.

"I am three, milady."

"Shih 'Ni is very strong, but I haven't seen him lift any mountains lately. If he does though, I'll be sure and tell you." Rhiannon smiled, and Shih 'Ni snorted.

"I see you have met the children of our village," a tranquil voice called out.

Rhiannon removed Singing Brook from her lap and stood up. Journey-Of-The-Moon stood at the mouth of the path not far from where they were gathered. She slowly stroked Etâhpe'o-poeso's head who was contentedly sitting at her feet.

"Welcome to Ghroc," Journey-Of-The-Moon smiled at the warriors.

Rhiannon walked up to the Goyor Emissary. "It's so nice to see you again."

"As it is to see you, Empress Kossi."

She looked much the same as Rhiannon remembered her from her dream. Her bushy black hair was lightly painted with strands of silver. Two gleaming combs of gold sparkled in the sunlight as they lay, nestled in her hair. A band of green Temmer Tree leaves was wrapped around her head, worn by all the Emissary Class, as were the brown and green Earth Beads around her neck—very similar to the ones that Rhiannon now wore. Her face was kindly; brown eyes shined with love and wisdom. She wore the customary long, white robes that all the priestesses wore.

"I see you have already met Poeso," Rhiannon said and looked down at the cat.

"Oh yes. I sent the pax to you, my dear. There is much danger in this land, and she volunteered to go to you and serve as one of your protectors." Rhiannon looked at Journey-Of-The-Moon with wide eyes. "Do not look so surprised, Rhiannon, for I also sent the she-wolf to you. It was necessary for you to stay safe until you could fulfill your portion of the prophecy, my dear."

"Thank you," she finally said when she had found her tongue. Journey-Of-The-Moon simply smiled at her.

"And now I must give you this," she continued. She pulled a small vial out of a pocket hidden in her robes. She held it up to Rhiannon, its clear liquid sparkled in the sunlight, sending sharp rainbow-colored shards of light reaching across the forest floor.

"This is the broth blood from the roots of the Temmer Tree. This is what will help you and your friends complete the task that lay before you." She looked passed Rhiannon to her companions, then back to the empress. "Keep it safe, Rhiannon, for you will not defeat her without it."

"What do I do with it?"

"You must pour the broth blood onto her. It will dim her powers. But be quick, Rhiannon, for it will only last a short time," she cautioned. "You must make haste if you are to defeat her." Journey-Of-The-Moon's delicate brows drew up in concern.

"But how can I be defeated? What about the prophecy?" Rhiannon asked quietly.

"You must consider your task very seriously, for prophecies can be put to rest, lying unfulfilled until a new generation, a stronger generation, heeds its call."

Rhiannon swallowed and slowly nodded her head. "I have no assurances that we will win, then?" It was a statement as much as a question.

"She is but days away from birthing an heir to the throne, Rhiannon. You and your friends must succeed, or Baobh will raise up a successor as evil as she." Journey-Of-The-Moon sighed deeply. "She was driven by revenge and seduced by the power it promised. She is dead to her traditions and people." Her words grew quiet and mournful as she looked down at the fertile earth that she and the rest of her kind worked to care for.

A soft, warm breeze slipped through the treetops sending dried pine needles falling slowly to the ground. Journey-Of-The-Moon lifted her head and tilted it slightly as if she was listening to the wind.

Suddenly she looked back at Rhiannon. "We must go now, for the wind brings the beast seeking to spy." Quickly she walked around Rhiannon towards the children. "Come children, quickly!" The children ran to Journey-Of-The-Moon, their tiny faces etched with fear. As they hurried past Rhiannon, the Goyor Emissary turned to her. "Do not fear, the beast will not see you, but be on your way." Rhiannon looked up at the clear sky and could see something riding on the warm air currents but even with her keen Archigos eyesight could not see exactly what the object was. "Finish your task, Empress Kossi, be at it urgently." Then she fled down the path.

She clenched her teeth as another pain wracked her body. It was close, she knew. The pain grew harder until it was unbearable; a strangled sound escaped from her lips. Not a woman's scream, but a cat's mighty roar of madness.

A listless tigress paced the forest floor. Trampled foliage cracked under her weight. As another pain burned through her body, she flopped onto the dirt and leaves. An eerie howling echoed off the mossy tree trunks. Her body wracked by pain, she got up again and continued to pace, her long tongue hanging from a dry mouth.

Nearby, lurking in the bushes was her mate, ever vigilant for an opportunistic predator who might be lured by the smell of blood. His eyes roved the forest floor, his keen sense of smell told him it was close.

Finally, she lay; her great bulk heaving on the ground. Hot blood started to spill, filling the air like an early morning mist. Panting so hard she could not breathe, her mind so crazed with pain, her concentration finally lost. One last heave; a cat's screech cut through the air, then crescendos into the shrill scream of a woman's voice as the cat's form blurred into a woman just as a baby passed from inside her taut belly out into the bright new world.

The woman propped herself up on one shaky elbow, bringing her baby up to rest on her naked body. Eagle emerged from the bushes and knelt beside her, gently running a finger over his son. He bent down and tenderly kissed the woman's forehead.

"You have done it, Baobh. You have given Pom-Ni a new son!" he said proudly. "Our son will serve Pom-Ni well."

"No!" Baobh howled. "He will not go back to Ghroc and tend the earth. He is the heir to the throne of Sona Tuath. He will be a mighty Goyor king!"

"That he will be, my Queen, but he will also know the kind and tender touch of Pom-Ni, for it is his heritage!"

Baobh bought the squalling infant up to softly suckle. "He is a Basilias, King of the Seuns," she stated a little more gently. "That is all the heritage he should be concerned with."

CHAPTER FOURTEEN

*With hair of gold and a heart so full, the Gypsy King led his
men so bold
A gypsy clan, he was from, but his was a greater destiny; a
story that must be told
For his parents told him a terrible tale and handed him, two
bands of gold
He was the son of the High Prince from the castle white
His heart was heavy, for he never had the throne in his sight
Between the woman he loved, and his people, he must
choose; so was the Gypsy King's plight
—The Gypsy King; Tamrah Jenn*

Hot sunshine slashed across the thick bands of gold.
The gems that were encrusted within the Basilias
crest through tiny fragments of light across his face. Flath
sighed and gripped the rings in his hand, wanting so badly
to throw them into a river, or off a high cliff, or maybe in
the Carnaid Sea itself!

He did not ask for this responsibility, nor did he want it.
Maybe he would find some hapless, ignorant man to give
them to and profess him the new King of Beaynid. He
roughly raked his hand through his hair and continued to
stare down at the small objects.

"Starin' at um won't make um go away, lad." Teo walked up from behind him and sat on a shady boulder.

"I think I shall give them away, Teo. No one would know."

"Ye would know."

"I do not care!" he quipped. "I do not want them. I do not want the responsibility. I am no king. I am naught but a gypsy!"

"'Tis the responsibility that bothers ye son, or yer Archigos empress?" When Flath did not answer, Teo went on. "A man can learn ta be a King. 'Tisn't that what ye told the lass? That she could learn ta be an empress even though she wasn't brought up with it?"

"I cannot have her, Teo."

Teo smiled. "Lad, ye are a king. Ye may have whatever ye may wish."

"You heard the men! Most of them said they will not even fight with the Archigos. How could Rhiannon and I come together amongst all this hate? I was far better off a gypsy," he said quietly.

"Ye are who ye are, me boy. She is who she is. There's naught ye can do about it. But if ye love the lass, ye will find a way."

"'Tis not that simple, Teo."

"Nay! Nothin' worth hav'n is easy ta get an even harder ta hold on ta." Teo looked into Flath's eyes. "Aye, old prejudices are hard ta squelch, but love will find a way." Teo, the romantic fool, Flath thought and smiled faintly.

"Captain!" a young man broke through the brush, sweat

pouring from his face. "Ambush, captain! The queen's men!" He shouted between puffs of air.

"How did they get past the sentries?" Flath asked.

"I do not know," the man answered truthfully.

Flath and Teo jumped up and drew their swords. As they descended, Flath could hear the sound of steel against steel and the grunts and cries of men dying. They rushed down the hill into the mayhem, swords swinging, slashing out at Baobh's men. He looked around and could see they were completely outnumbered. The soldiers wore tunics of royal purple, not the bright yellow and blue of the Sona Tuathan Royal Guard. These Beaynidan soldiers were less accomplished as killers and less loyal, for sure. However, no less deadly, especially outnumbered ten to one.

Flath ducked a blade that had been aimed for his head and stumbled backward into a startled Beaynidan soldier whom he quickly ran through. Pulling his sword from the man's body, he continued on, hacking his way through the waylay and chaos. The rebellion would once again suffer a great loss, perhaps this time, even suffering total obliteration.

Flath sidestepped a sword blade and brought his sword down on the soldier's blade, then twisted it up and out of the man's hands. Flath dispatched the man and quickly moved towards Teo.

Back to back, they fought the soldiers off—their arms weary with the effort. Man after man fell to their swords, yet many more continued to approach. Sweat and blood ran into Flath's eyes burning them and making it hard to see.

"We are outnumbered, old friend!" Flath shouted over the din of battle.

"'Twill'na end like this, lad," Teo wheezed between breaths. "Keep fight'n; they'll run out of men!"

Flath looked around and could not see any more of his men. They had all been swallowed by the masses of the Beaynidan Army. Rhiannon's face flashed through Flath's mind. It would be hard on her to find his body amongst this bloody heap. But maybe being separated in death would be better than living without her.

He faltered in concentration and let his opponent have an opening. A more skilled man would have run him through, but this man was not that skilled, nor that determined and he merely nicked Flath's side. He cursed himself for not wearing his mail. He could feel the hot stickiness of blood as it soaked through his tunic. Flath spun and cut the man down, but two men came in his place. Both battered away at his sword, looking for the slightest opportunity to end his life.

Suddenly, a savage war cry tore through the thick air. A multitude of arrows rained down from the treetops. As each arrow found its target, Flath saw half of the men fall! He looked up just in time to see hundreds of Archigos warriors dropping from the trees. More warriors melted out from the forest, their weapons drawn, and war paint streaked across their faces. They struck down the Beaynidan soldiers with ease and grace. A great she-wolf snarled and tore at flesh while a massive beast of the sky swooped down to extinguish surprised men.

Rhiannon appeared in the crowd, her sword drawn,

cutting a path towards Flath. He stopped, unable to move, and just watched her effortless, poetic movements as smooth as honey and as deadly as a viper. A gleaming torque of gold encircled her head. Gemstones sparkled in the light bathing her in a halo of multi-colored shimmers. The glint of a tiny diamond sparkled on her nose, red paint marked her cheeks, and large tawny feathers were woven into her raven colored hair that fluttered at her shoulders. Peeking out from under her sleeveless tunic he could see red and blue tattoos announcing her an Archigos Warrioress and Empress. He was aware of nothing at that moment except how much he wanted her.

When she finally made it to his side, she looked down at his bloodstained tunic and concern etched itself across her face. "Are you alright?"

"What happened to your hair?" Was all he could think to say.

"What? Oh, part of the Fiann," she replied between swings of her blade.

He did not even care what a Fiann was, all he cared about was having her with him. But he knew that that could never happen now.

After the last of the Beaynidan soldiers fell, the warriors quickly melted back into the forest and away from the taint of Seun blood drenching the ground. "Help them with their wounded!" Rhiannon barked.

Begrudgingly her warriors began to pull the wounded from the bloodied heaps. The air, once heavy with the scent of summer rosemary and mint, was now laden with the coppery smell of blood. Flath choked on the taste and thick smell of congealing body fluids. The ground was now saturated with red rivers under heaps of dead or dying bodies.

"Burn the dead!" she yelled out, and fires were started, and the stench of burning flesh replaced the smell of blood.

"Rhiannon, should we not at least, bury our dead," Flath asked as he looked around at the shocked expressions on the faces of the rebel fighters.

She turned to him. "No time. We must get rid of the bodies as quickly as we can. The quicker we finish here, the quicker we can start our advance on Sona Tuath while we still have the element of surprise. Have a ritual if you would like but be quick about it."

Flath sighed and turned to what was left of his men. "Okay, men. Burn the bodies!" Flath was aware of the keen look of betrayal on their faces. "She is right. We must push on to Sona Tuath!" he ordered, with more conviction. "We cannot help the dead now, but we can honor their memories by taking back Sona Tuath!"

"Go to Sona Tuath with those savages?" one of the men yelled out, pointing at Rhiannon.

As quick as lightning, an Archigos warrioress had her sword tip digging into the man's throat. "You weak, little man. Do you think you're worthy to even follow us to pick up our horse's dung?" she asked, with an iced tongue.

The man smirked and spat into her face. She pulled back with a howl and quickly buried her sword deep into the man's body. The rest of the rebel fighters gasped and jumped back as they watched their comrade's lifeless body fall to the ground.

The man's empty eyes stared out at Rhiannon; even in death, hate was still keen on his face. She looked at her warrioress in shock. Flath moved towards Rhiannon, but in an instant, Archigos swords were drawn and pointed preventing him from moving any closer. He looked over to Teo, who was staring at the scene in disbelief.

"What have you done?" Rhiannon wailed as she ran up to her warrioress. "What have you done?" she screamed again.

"But...I—," the warrioress sputtered.

"Because of your hatred, you have made a murderess out of me!" Rhiannon shouted in Jurian for all to hear.

She pulled her sword from its sheath strapped across her back and before her warrioress could say anything more Rhiannon ran her through. Her body fell on top of the rebel fighter, together, at least, in death.

She turned and pointed her sword at the sky. "Anyone else who can't quell their hatred will suffer the same fate—Archigos or Beaynidan alike!" she shouted, her roughened, dry voice reverberating across the trees. "We are here to fight a battle against Baobh, not each other!" She now turned to the warriors. "We are here to kill the woman that has killed so many of our kin!" she continued to shout. "Will you let yourselves be bested by emotions and let your skill be clouded? You are Archigos Warriors! You will conquer!"

She turned to Flath, tears sparkling in her dark eyes and ran into the cover of the forest. He turned to follow her, but sharpened Venturien swords bit into his flesh. "Lower your swords!" he snarled in Venn, but the warriors held their position. "Lower your swords!" he admonished again.

Shih 'Ni pushed his way through the crowd of warriors and rebel fighters and walked up to Flath. He stood for a long moment, staring at Flath as if wrestling with a decision. What Flath saw in the man's eyes, however, was not hatred but something even deeper. Could it be envy or jealousy? Flath knew this man was Ventra's Master-of-Arms, second only to Rhiannon. What could he possibly find in a Seun gypsy's situation that was more appealing?

"Lower your blades," he finally commanded, his dark eyes holding Flath's gaze. Finally, Shih 'Ni moved closer and leaned in towards him. "Go to her, she will need you now," he said, barely above a whisper. Suddenly Flath understood perfectly. When he had first seen the man in Bell, he shrugged off his hostility as nothing more than the usual prejudice—nothing new. However, now he realized that Shih 'Ni regarded Flath as a rival for Rhiannon's affections. Flath saw the look of defeat on Shih 'Ni's face, and his respect for the man grew.

"Thank you, Master Shih 'Ni," Flath replied in Venn with a bow of his head. He walked over to Teo, who was suspiciously quiet. "Burn the dead, old friend. We move when she is ready."

"Aye, Captain," he said meekly and walked off.

He found her sitting on a boulder in the deep shadow of huge redwood. He could almost hear her tears splattering forgotten on the ground. Quietly he walked up and sat on the boulder next to her. He thought her action against her warrioress had been harsh and more than a little erratic. But she had made her point at the end of her sword, proving she was willing to end even the life of one of her own to not only win this war but to show solidarity with Beaynid. He was not quite sure her warriors would agree with her methods, though.

"I should have known that this wouldn't work," she finally cried, slipping back into Jurian. "But I didn't listen."

"They are the fools, Greannmhor. Your heart is pure in its desires. You know what is best for both our people, whether they know it or not." He took her hand, still sprayed with the blood of her warrioress. "You will make this work," he said, trying to convince himself as much as Rhiannon.

"I can't!" she lamented. "I've taken the life of one of my own. I can't do this, Flath."

He took her into his arms and spoke softly into her hair. "You are their empress; none will challenge your decision to mete out punishment."

"Not to my face." She shook her head. "But they will surely see it as a betrayal on my part."

"Your people are savvy, if not diplomatic. I am sure they will see that, under the circumstance, your warrioress gave you no other choice."

"I'm sure it was harder on her than me!" She cried.

"She murdered a man in cold blood for nothing more than an assault on her pride." He took a deep breath. "It will not be the first time you will have to hand out punishment, Greannmhor. And it certainly will not be the last decision you make that you will later agonize over. 'Tis a part of being a ruler."

"It's only a matter of time before they will see that I can't rule! Especially a nation as strong-willed as Ventra."

"You do not have a choice. You have a responsibility that you cannot shirk. It was the same responsibility that was given to your mother and many generations of other Archigos women. All of their blood runs in your veins and now 'tis your turn to rule, Greannmhor."

"But what lay before me is too hard a thing for me to accomplish. I can no more dampen the fires of hatred than tell the sun not to rise tomorrow. I can't even get my warriors to forget their hate long enough to take Sona Tuath. Maybe I won't even be able to defeat Baobh at all, and I'll end up just like my mother."

He tightened his hold on her. "Be strong Greannmhor, and your warriors will follow your lead. Concentrate on finishing the battle that lay before you."

"The prophecy doesn't ensure our victory, Flath. We can still lose, especially if our people can't work together."

"You are right, but what other choice do we have except to try?" He knew the Archigos, and the Seuns would never come together as she had hoped. However, it was crucial that they come together enough, at least, to take Sona Tuath.

She sat up and smiled at him as he wiped the tears from her face, smudging the red streaks of Archigos war paint that were splashed across her cheeks. He looked at her and saw a powerful warrioress, yet so soft and vulnerable that only a few words from him could destroy her. How could he give her up? He opened his mouth to tell her what he had learned about his parentage, but no words came out. Tell her, you coward!

"Rhiannon, I must tell you something." Suddenly Shih 'Ni appeared standing in a dusty shaft of white sunlight. She looked away from Flath—the opportunity lost.

"I was just told that several Beaynidan soldiers escaped during the fighting and have fled towards Sona Tuath."

Rhiannon jumped up. "We must go after them before they warn Baobh and she has a chance to mount a defense!"

"I have four warriors ready to go after them."

"Take one of the rebels; he can help with navigation."

"I will send Ian," Flath offered. "He is one of our faster riders." Flath squeezed Rhiannon's hand and was gone.

After the bodies had been burned and the wounded tended to, Rhiannon asked Flath to dispatch the men he had left, one each assigned to an Archigos War Party, to aid them with the unfamiliar terrain. Both sides blanched at the request of course, but knowing they had no choice, finally acquiesced. Warriors and rebel fighters alike moved on through the night finally stopping at dawn within sight of the great walled city of Sona Tuath.

CHAPTER FIFTEEN

Into the castle, they crept under the moon
Suddenly bells rang out; there would be fighting soon
Blood ran in the streets; many met their doom
The empress and the Gypsy King fought the queen—a
terrible sight
The Archigos Empress' blood did spill, but the queen lost
more—a terrible fight
Rebels and Warriors fought alongside; so much loss and
death—a terrible night
Fight for Sona Tuath—Kyia Kossi

The cobbles were slick with a mist that had rolled in off the Carnaid Sea. Crumpled bodies of the Sona Tuathan Royal Guardsmen lay in the gray light of a shrouded moon. The city was surrounded by a mist so thick it looked as if it were the only place still left on the earth. Rhiannon wiped the wetness from her face and set her sword to the ready. A dark cloud sailed across the full moon shutting out its illumination once again. The keen eyes of the Archigos were rivaled only by those of the Forest Folk. Thousands of warriors swept into the sleeping city, making no sound. The night was at its most bitterly lonesome mark before the whispered promises of the day are heard.

Even the roar of the waves was silenced by the

tremendous walls of Sona Tuath. Quietness rolled like the mist, making silence a sound in itself. Every inhabitant of the city lay in slumber—unguarded, unprotected and vulnerable. They were not here for the people of Sona Tuath. However, they were here for their queen.

Suddenly, the deep guttering blast of a huge horn pounded out into the darkness; later shouts could be heard closer to the center of town. The sharp ring of steel sliced through the once peaceful air. Torches began to spark as residents scrambled to see what was happening in their city.

"Well, there goes our element of surprise," Rhiannon said sourly. She looked over and saw Shih 'Ni and his war-party disappear behind a building. She turned towards Flath. "It's finally started," she said quietly.

"'Twill be over soon Greannmhor." He smiled at her and pushed a lock of hair out of her eyes. Kyia, Tim, and Ian ran up from behind them, their swords ready. "You should have stayed on the bluff with the horses!" Rhiannon scolded Tim. Worry sat in the pit of her stomach like rancid food. "You go back up there!" She pointed out into the night at an unseen bluff.

"I will not leave you!" Tim yelled and straightened up to his full height as if to give him more respectability.

"It's too dangerous for you to be here, Tim. Please go back up to the horses," Rhiannon pleaded.

Flath placed a hand on Rhiannon's shoulder. "Let him fight, Rhiannon. He has just as much right as we all do."

"But he is too young," she protested.

"He is no longer a boy Greannmhor, but a man."

Tim pointed his ornate Ventrian sword into the dark

night. "You are my sister, and I will not leave you," he stated again. Her heart ached for the uncertainty of the situation, but it also swelled with pride for the boy she had seen grow into a man. "I will be honored to fight next to you Tim," she finally whispered.

"Come this way!" Ian waved them on and disappeared down a dark street.

They followed him and quickly moved towards the castle in a sea of armed warriors—Luna followed close behind. The horrified screams of women and angry shouts of still sleepy men filled the moist air. Some of the men had rushed out of their homes, swords swinging and quickly met their deaths. The smarter ones cautiously peeked through cracked shudders, admonishing their wives and children to keep quiet.

As they got closer to the castle, Rhiannon could hear the ringing of steel and much shouting as captains barked out orders to the frightened soldiers. Archigos warriors scaled nearby houses and businesses sending deadly arrows raining down upon guardsmen. Huge torches burned into the black night, illuminating the beauty of Castle Sona Tuath.

Suddenly a large group of guards sprung out from the shadows of a building shouting and swinging sharp blades. Steel clashed against steel singing an unforgettable song. Luna quickly lurched after an unsuspecting guard and took him down easily. A large guardsman swung hard, but Rhiannon dodged and came up fast with her weapon dispatching the man with little effort.

As she turned, she saw another man lift his sword ready

to come down on her head. Quickly she pulled her sword up just in time and thwarted his blow. She was thrown back into a stout brick wall and saw him once again ready his sword. She rolled out of the way just as his blade grated against the wall, sparks flying. She squatted and swung her blade low trying to cut away at a weak spot in his chain mail, but the man was fast and blocked her hit. She spun around and tried to plant her sword in his back, but he rolled with her and blocked yet another blow. She came down hard, aiming for his shoulder, but he jumped out of the way. Her sword, not finding its target, hit the stones and sent orange sparks into the air. Trying to recover too quickly she slipped on the wet stones and fell to the slick ground with a thud.

She rolled over and gripped her sword, knowing the man would be on her immediately. She looked up and saw him standing above her ready to end her life. From the corner of her eye, she saw a flash of steel and Tim had buried his sword in the man's gut, cutting straight through his mail.

She stared at him but could not talk. She filled her lungs with cool air that tasted of blood and sweat. "You need to be more careful, sister!" he said sweetly and gave her a goofy grin.

"This way!" Ian stood at the mouth of an alley motioning for them to follow. They hastened into the darkness after him. They made several sharp turns and came out next to the courtyard wall. Ian ran over to a large drain pipe. "This will lead us into the courtyard," he said importantly, pointing at the blackened entrance of the pipe.

"Are you sure?" Flath asked skeptically.

"Oh aye, Captain, I used to play in here as a child," Ian answered and then disappeared into the pipe. Flath shrugged and one by one they followed him into the pipe. Their feet splashed across the unseen water as they followed the light to the other end of the pipe. On the other side, they emerged into a shallow, water-filled ditch that smelled putrid. Rhiannon hurried out of the water and around the back of a small outbuilding.

From there they had a perfect view of the battle raging in the courtyard. Her warriors were fighting with deadly haste. The guardsmen, though skilled soldiers, were not only outnumbered, but out skilled as well, and they easily fell to Archigos sword, axe and arrow. Etâhpe'o-poeso dove from the black sky and proved herself a deadly warrioress also.

Suddenly a bright flash of lightning-sparked from the sky and electrified the courtyard. Agonizing screams of dying men and women rose above the clashing swords and the immediate boom of thunder. Soldiers and warriors alike fell to white-hot bolts of lightning as they rained down upon everyone in the courtyard.

Rhiannon wanted to run out to them, but as she made a move, Flath grabbed her arm. "Nay, Greannmhor!"

"What's happening?" she asked frantically.

"Look!" Tim shouted and pointed to Baobh standing high above on a huge balcony.

In the shadowy flutters of giant torches, she could see a woman standing erect and bathed in a deep red glow. Mist rolled out from between her fingers as she clasped the necklace at her throat with one hand and waved the other to and fro over the courtyard. Her warriors were bent down under an unseen weight—crushing them right before her eyes! As they were flattened to the ground Baobh's soldiers quickly cut them down with no opposition.

"It's the power of the stones," Kyia breathed, her eyes widened in fear. "Stones that were taken from the heart of the Venturien mines of Del Nort. Our very land betrays us and Verna herself has deafened her ears to her children's screams!" Rhiannon looked over at Kyia who was watching with horror as more warriors were crushed under the weight of the stones. Indecision and desperation ate away at her. Fear crept through her like the chill of a cold morning. Could they win against such a powerful foe?

"She uses her powers as a Goyor as well. She calls the very fire from the sky!" Tim shouted. Rhiannon turned back to see a huge hot bolt of lightning consume an entire war-party. Rhiannon searched the dark sky for the shadow of a beast and its Forest Folk rider but saw nothing. She whispered a quick prayer of thanks to Verna, as Baobh would prove to be enough of a challenge without the assistance of this mysterious Lord Rull.

Quickly she turned towards Ian, "You must get me in there!"

"We can go through the kitchens. I know the way!" he answered.

Rhiannon turned to Tim. "Please stay here, Tim," she pleaded with him.

"And leave you? Nay, Rhiannon, I will not!" he said stubbornly.

"Make him stay, please," she begged Flath.

"He can make his own decisions, Rhiannon," Flath said weakly, but she could see he also wanted Tim to stay. More haunted screams rose on the moist breeze. "Please stay close," she whispered and then followed Ian around the castle and into the kitchens.

Quietly they passed through the kitchens and into the servant's quarters, sending screaming servants scurrying around the halls. They met no opposition and proceeded quickly. "Up this way—less soldiers," Ian pointed to the servant's stairwell. They followed Ian up the stairs and out into a spacious hallway. A few small oil lamps burned offering dim, uneven light. Many doors lined both sides of the hall, and a long, purple rug ran the distance of the hallway. There was no commotion, in fact, it looked deserted.

Ian silently motioned for them to follow him. Slowly they crept down the long hallway, carefully listening for any noise that would announce the arrival of soldiers. The screams from below floated up through unshuttered windows. Rhiannon gripped her sword hilt so tightly her fingers went numb. Desperation boiled in her blood. She knew she had to stop Baobh before she killed all within Sona Tuath. Determined, they picked up the pace and quickly rounded a corner and ran straight into a group of guardsmen! Swords clashed, Luna snarled, and hollers resounded down the hall. Three guardsmen fell instantly, leaving five more.

Rhiannon turned and saw Shih 'Ni run around the corner and quickly slice through one of the men. "Go

Rhiannon, Kyia and I will take care of the rest!" Shih 'Ni called out in Venn. Rhiannon nodded and quickly followed Ian down another hall and up a grand staircase that even in the near darkness was immense and opulent. Thick marble banisters twisted and disappeared into the darkness above. A dark purple rug with scrolling designs in gold gently lay on the stairs beckoning guests to ascend. They were neither guests or in a mind to appreciate such lavishness as they bounded up the stairs and headed towards the queen's chambers.

At the top of the stairs, Ian slowly peeked around the corner, and his body stiffened. He turned back to Rhiannon. "The hall is crowded with soldiers guarding the queen's door," he whispered anxiously.

Flath moved closer and stuck his head around the corner. "Perhaps thirty or so," he breathed. Silently Shih 'Ni and Kyia came up behind them. "More?" Kyia asked.

"Many more," Flath answered. "We will have to fight our way in."

Rhiannon took a deep breath. "Flath, Ian, Shih 'Ni and Kyia will keep the guards occupied while Tim and I slip into the room."

"I think I should go in with you," Flath protested.

"No, your sword is needed with them." Rhiannon shook her head. Another loud smack of thunder shook the castle. A turbulent wind carried screams from below. From somewhere in the din of turmoil she could hear Shankee's voice commanding her war-party. "We must move now!" Rhiannon ordered.

They rushed around the corner and charged the guards,

who were thoroughly taken by surprise but quickly readied themselves. Steel chimed, armor clanked, and bodies thumped to the floor. Angry shouts and fearful cries rang in Rhiannon's ears. She cut through a few enraged guardsmen and carved a path for the door. She could spare no time to look around to see if Tim was following but prayed to Verna that he was. As she reached the door, Tim ducked in front of her, quickly opened the door and slipped inside. She tried to grab him, but he was too quick. She looked back at Flath as another guardsman fell to his sword. She took a deep breath and then ducked inside the door after Tim.

The room was cool and dark. A tiny bit of silvery light shown through a large bank of windows but left many long, dark shadows scattered across the room. "Stay close," Rhiannon whispered. She held her sword high and moved towards the adjoining bedchamber that opened up to the balcony. Her eyes slowly adjusted to the darkness and she started to make out the shapes of furniture. Muscle and sinew were taut as she crept closer, straining to see any movements. She could feel Tim's heat, moving closely behind her and she listened to his sharp, even breaths.

Then she could hear something else. A scraping sound like someone was running something sharp across the stone floor. Her heart leaped in her chest and started pounding out a familiar frenzied rhythm. She moved to the bank of windows, into the dim light so that whoever was following her would also be forced into the light. Suddenly a low growling started to rumble across the room from the shadows. Rhiannon was suddenly very frightened. She said a quick prayer to Verna and peered harder into the darkness.

From out of the void of darkness the shape of a huge tiger formed and sauntered towards them. Rhiannon swallowed hard as she looked into the creature's golden eyes. It moved closer as its long, sharp claws dragged along the hard floor. The sound grated upon her nerves, getting louder and louder until it was the only thing she could hear. The sounds of the dying, of swords clashing, of the battle that was yet raging, were all drowned by the incessant scraping of claws. Angry, jagged claws that were the length of a man's hand from wrist to fingertip! "Stay behind me," she said to Tim.

Without warning the animal hunched its massive hindquarters and leaped at them. Rhiannon jumped one way, Tim the other. Rhiannon was knocked into a chair and almost lost her balance. Swiftly she turned and pointed her sword to the approaching beast while slowly backing up into the darkness. As fast as a bolt of lightning the tiger sprung again, swatting at Rhiannon's sword. The empty, hopeless sound of her sword crashing to the floor and skidding away into the shadows filled the room.

Rhiannon reached for a small axe tied onto her leather tunic on her chest, but before she could get the axe lose the beast leaped again. Rhiannon gasped as she watched him descend upon her—his golden eyes turning blood red with anticipation. Suddenly Tim bolted towards her, his sword bared, pointing at the soft underbelly of the beast. At the last second, Tim shoved Rhiannon out of the way as the animal landed on Tim's sword. A terrible howl rose from the beast as Tim scampered out from under its heaving body, his bloodied sword in his hand.

Bleeding profusely, the tiger sought out Tim's form. Quickly he lashed out catching Tim's leg and throwing him against the wall. "Tim!" Rhiannon screamed and frantically looked for her sword's resting place. Finally, she saw the tiny spark of light from her sword blade as it winked at her from halfway under a large iron chest stand. In two paces she was at her sword and bent to pick it up. She twirled around to see the tiger sinking his teeth into Tim's neck.

As fast as she could, she charged the beast, raising her sword and then quickly bringing it down onto the animal's head hacking off its ear. The tiger screamed and turned towards her. Dizzy with pain the animal shook its head sending blood spraying across the room and splattering the wall. Rhiannon viciously slashed the beast's neck open sending a torrent of blood spilling across the stones. The beast cried and dropped to the floor. Before her stunned eyes its shape started to blur and then shrank and then the body of a dead man lay on the floor in a pool of dark blood.

In a gust of wind and sweet-smelling mist, the double doors to the bedchamber crashed open. The silhouette of a woman stood in the doorway, the curves of her outline painted by a shimmer of moonlight.

"Finally, you have come—I have been waiting long to see you, Rhiannon Kossi, daughter of Sernia!"

CHAPTER SIXTEEN

"The Forest Folk have a very peculiar gift; the ability to shapeshift into any animal in the One God, Ak's, creation. The Forest Folk we have here in Beaynid are the Goyor, and they are a peaceful race who use their powers to tend the Earth. Our Goyor Queen is the exception of course."
—The Forest Folk: Goyor; Sarah Unell

"I have been looking forward to this meeting for a long time, Empress." Baobh's words slipped from icy lips as she stood in the arched doorway. The sound of a battle still waging below was carried on the ocean fueled breeze. The sounds of an angry sky and the morbid screams of her warriors were gone now.

Her chest still heaved with spent exertion as she stared at the tiny beauty that stood before her. She saw Baobh look to the man's body lying on the cool hard stones and saw sadness in her eyes and then a bright spark of maddening anger so hot Rhiannon felt consumed by its intensity. "We have come to claim the throne, Baobh, and my father!" Rhiannon called out.

Baobh laughed wickedly. "Your father is probably already dead. Oh, did you get that gift I sent you? Your father did not want to part with it at first," she shrugged, "but we convinced him you would just love to have it."

A rage started to boil at Rhiannon's spine. She had grown accustomed to it now, even welcomed it, for it made it easier to exact punishment. A hunger rose and spread across her body, invading her blood, penetrating muscle and bone. It was her gift as an Archigos—her right as a warrioress.

"As for Sona Tuath," Baobh paused for a moment. "You have no right to it."

"No, not I. But the people of Beaynid have a right to expect a kind ruler. Someone who will rule with justice instead of vanity!" Rhiannon readied her sword, expecting an attack at any moment.

"I am the only living relative of King Basilias!" she howled. "I am the only one with the right to rule."

"You are Goyor, not Seun," Rhiannon challenged.

"I am but half Goyor," she spat. "I am High Prince Eric's only child. I am Beaynid's rightful ruler!"

"You're wrong, Baobh! Eric and Lorena had a baby who escaped your invasion of Sona Tuath."

Baobh looked startled. "When Eric and Lorena were killed, no child was found." She said with less confidence, then hardened her expression once again. "You put too much trust in rumors, silly girl."

"I have seen the child in a dream, and I know it exists. However, it makes no difference, Baobh. You are still a ruthless murderer, and the people of Beaynid do not want you as their queen."

Baobh laughed again. "And you are here to liberate them?"

"Who better? The prophecy says I will be victorious." She inched closer to Baobh.

"The prophecy is nothing but an ancient tale," she said, unconcerned.

"Then why did you bring me here—to this world? Why have you been looking for me? Why did you try and kill me in Ventra?"

"I should have killed you with your mother when you were yet a child." Baobh balled up her fists in anger. "No matter, I will kill you now and add Ventra to my kingdom!" she said, regaining her deadly composure.

"There is something that stands in your way, Baobh," Rhiannon replied. "There is the matter of a prophecy that will determine your fate." She stopped moving and gripped her sword tightly readying herself for battle.

"I determine my own fate!" she stated, forcefully.

"And I have come to deliver it to you!" Rhiannon charged at Baobh, hoping to take her off guard enough to end the fight quickly. Baobh's lithe form and Goyor reflexes enabled her to jump out of Rhiannon's path with speed and grace.

Baobh whirled around in a cocoon of black hair, and her hand quickly went to the red stones taken from the mysterious Del Nort mines of Ventra that hung around her elegant neck. Her eyes shut, and she silently begged the stones to obey her command as she coaxed them awake. A deep rose glow radiated from Baobh, bathing the room in a tinted light. A thick, sweet-smelling mist hung in the cool air. Rhiannon was shocked that the stones did not need the call of Baobh's voice but answer the call of her mind!

Rhiannon could feel her blade start to jump and quiver as if it had a life of its own. She gripped the pommel tighter, but the sword continued to shake. Suddenly the constant dull aching in her right arm began to throb and cut away at her nerves. She could no longer ignore the pain as she had learned to do. Her arm became weak as it flared up in excruciating pain. Baobh finally thrust out her hand, and like the repelling end of a large magnet, the powerful stones ripped Rhiannon's sword from her hands and sent it flying across the room. Rhiannon watched helplessly as it shuffled along the stones, clattering loudly and finally finding a resting place far from her empty hands.

Her heart pounded in her chest as she looked back over to Baobh. Her brow was wrinkled in heavy concentration; eyes tightly clamped shut. She remembered the vial of Temmer Tree blood that Journey-Of-The-Moon had given her. Slowly she moved towards Baobh while reaching for the pouch she wore at her waist.

Suddenly, Rhiannon felt a heavy pressure that weighed down upon her as if she were being crushed by a large boulder. A violent vibration tore through the air and rose goose flesh along her body. Her knees buckled, and she went down hard, grinding kneecaps into the cool stones of the floor. She felt as if she might be trodden by an overwhelming weight that continued to bear down on top of her.

Rhiannon knew it was the necklace. Her mother's necklace! She felt her only hope was to fight the force of those stones. She clenched her teeth and grunted under the effort to stand. The harder that she pushed, however, the heavier the weight became. Her mouth opened trying to take in air but the weight was too much, and she was only allowed the tiniest bit of oxygen. She grew lightheaded, and her world began to darken. The pressure was too much to bear, her head pounded, and her muscles burned in protest. Her lungs constricted sealing out what she needed the most.

As her body was slowly being crushed, Rhiannon looked up at Baobh. She stared at the woman in disbelief that the prophecy had proven false and that she would soon meet her death just as her mother had—at the hands of Baobh.

Quite unexpectedly Rhiannon could see the form of the black equine; its high, proud horn glistened in the moonlight. She blinked her eyes and tried to focus, sure she was hallucinating. The majestic horse shook its large head, a shimmering black mane cascading down a sleek neck. It looked directly at Rhiannon, and she could easily read the disappointment in the creature's deep, black eyes. Ashamed, she looked away.

"Rhiannon, my daughter, do you give up so easily?"

She was not sure if the voice was in her head or was actually spoken. She raised her eyes to look back up and saw her mother's smiling face. "It isn't like a Kossi to give up so quickly," Sernia chastised, gently.

"It's your necklace, mother, that will be the demise of our people," Rhiannon replied, sharply.

"The necklace has great power, my daughter. However, it cannot take life by itself. Baobh uses it in her hatred to kill." Sernia's voice was low and soothing as she reasoned with her daughter. "The necklace works upon the fears and weaknesses it detects in perceived enemies. The stones hold no power over those who do not fear them."

"Ha! Then tell that to Baobh who is ready to finish me off!" Rhiannon was not sure if she now spoke the words or if they only echoed in her mind.

"You have the power to resist the stones, Rhiannon!" Sernia asserted forcefully. "Will you sacrifice all of Ventra because you're afraid to fight?" Her voice was mocking, biting into the tender flesh of Rhiannon's heart.

"Will you leave me to my own devices again, to live or to die?" Rhiannon accused her mother.

Sernia walked passed Baobh and up to her daughter. Her black eyes shone with tears that spilled down high cheekbones. She reached out a calloused hand and gently touched her daughter's cheek. "My beautiful little girl, I never left you. Not once," she replied softly and then was gone.

Tears dropped from Rhiannon's own eyes, splattering on the stone floor. "Mother!" she cried.

"Sing, Rhiannon! Sing!" she admonished, and then her voice was carried away on the sea-swept wind rushing in from the opened windows.

Rhiannon closed her eyes as the song formed in her mind. The words tumbled out of her mouth as her lungs found the air. Barely more than a whisper, the song danced around the room. Rhiannon found purchase and pushed violently against the weight of the necklace. The further away from the floor, she rose, the louder the words of the song came from her mouth.

Finally, Rhiannon was able to stand, the weight nothing

more than a slight discomfort. She threw it off with vehemence, a renewed anger burned inside. Baobh opened her eyes in shock, her dainty hand desperately stroking the unanswering stones.

Rhiannon quickly removed one of the small axes from the strap on her chest. She flung the sharpened weapon at Baobh. Baobh jumped out of the way as the axe cut through the wake of her hair. Baobh screamed in anger, her shrill voice stabbing at Rhiannon's ears. Before Rhiannon's eyes, the woman's shape melted into the bulky muscle of an enormous lioness.

Rhiannon anxiously looked around for her sword, but it was well hidden. She hurriedly unhooked the last of her small axes and quickly took aim at the beast. She threw it with all her might and watched it bury itself into the lioness's right shoulder. The beast roared sending a shocking vibration through Rhiannon's bones. The lioness swiped at the axe with its left paw and knocked the small blade out of its flesh. Blood trickled down tawny fur splattering on the floor.

Rhiannon slowly started to back away hoping she would come across her discarded sword. The beast followed her with its golden eyes glowing in the moonlight. Suddenly the lioness bunched its haunches and leaped across the distance crushing Rhiannon under its massive paws. The stone floor was hard and unforgiving as the lioness's hornlike claws bit into her flesh.

Rhiannon recalled the vial Journey-Of-The-Moon had given her and quickly fumbled with the pouch at her waist. The beast brought one huge paw up and slapped Rhiannon, sending her rolling across the floor. Dizzy, she tried to focus, but the lioness was on top of her again.

Blood ran from a split in her lip and a deep gash in her thigh. Before the lioness could swing again, Rhiannon wrestled the vial out of the pouch. She fumbled clumsily with the stopper, but it was tightly shut. Baobh raised a huge paw, moonlight glinting off razor-sharp claws and swiped Rhiannon hard across her shoulder. Rhiannon was tossed across the floor again, the vial, freed from her grip, rolled innocently out of her reach.

Instantly Rhiannon was on her hands and knees scrambling towards the vial, but the beast was quickly on her biting into her thick leather war tunic. The lioness's giant teeth penetrated the leather and buried itself into the flesh of her shoulder. She screamed in pain and tried to wrestle herself out of the lioness's mouth. With all her strength she jabbed her elbow deep into the lioness's throat. Surprised, Baobh let go.

Without looking back, Rhiannon fixed her sight on the vial and scampered towards it. Her fingers barely closed on the cool glass container before the lioness was resting on her chest. The weight of the huge cat was crushing the breath from Rhiannon's lungs. All four of the beast's huge paws were grounded into Rhiannon's body, preventing her from moving.

Rhiannon looked up into the golden eyes of the beast and knew Baobh was ready to tear out her throat. She struggled but could not get away. A drop of sparkling clear saliva dripped from the beast's mouth and splattered across Rhiannon's face.

Quickly, Rhiannon pushed the vial down into the palm of her hand and frantically worked the stopper free with her thumb and index finger. Rhiannon closed her eyes with relief when the stopper finally fell from the vial. But Rhiannon could only move her wrist slightly and was not sure that she would be able to pour the liquid onto Baobh at such an angle.

Determined, Rhiannon opened her eyes and stared into the lioness' golden eyes. She felt her hot breath on her cheek as Baobh slowly lowered her massive head towards Rhiannon's throat. Finally pulling an arm free from under Baobh's massive paw, Rhiannon splashed the Temmer Tree blood towards the beast. She felt the hot wetness drip onto her skin and could not tell if she had actually gotten any onto Baobh.

Abruptly the lioness stopped and sat up. An expression of pain formed on the beast's face. It lifted its solid head towards the ceiling and let out a mighty roar that trembled through Rhiannon's body. Suddenly the great form of the lioness blurred and faded until it was nothing more than the body of a small woman, shaking with exhaustion.

In a flash, Rhiannon reached out and snatched the necklace from Baobh's throat. She gave no resistance just looked out at Rhiannon through hollow eyes. With her free hand, Rhiannon pulled a dagger from her boot and deftly planted its blade deep into Baobh's chest.

She howled in pain and anger as Rhiannon removed the blade and Baobh flopped back onto the floor. Rhiannon looked down at Baobh's crumpled, bloody body. She stared down at what was once Beaynid's powerful queen, now nothing more than a dying half Goyor outcast.

"Rhiannon," Flath called out. She looked around towards the open door where Flath and the others had come in. Flath held a small form in his arms, but Rhiannon could not tell who or what it was.

Like the sudden memory of a long-ago nightmare, Rhiannon remembered that Tim had been injured by Baobh's mate. "Tim!" she screamed and scampered across the stone floor on her hands and knees towards Flath.

"No!" she screamed again as it dawned on her that she now held the necklace. She slapped the stones down on top of Tim's lifeless body and started to sing as huge tears streaked her bloodied face.

"It is too late, Greannmhor," Flath whispered. Rhiannon would try anyway. She sang louder and louder, but the stones lay stubborn and cold.

Finally, her song broke off in great sobs as she threw herself onto Tim's body. Tim, the young man who would not leave her on her own in Màrrach. The young man that helped nurse her back to health after she was almost killed. The young man that became her brother and who she shared her thoughts and dreams with. She could not picture a life without him!

Rhiannon's heart was broken. Her chest was tight, and she could not breathe. The bright, hot pain of losing her brother shot through her quivering body. "Tim!" she cried through the hard lump in her throat as Luna gently nudged his body trying to wake the young man.

CHAPTER SEVENTEEN

A young boy lays a'sleeping
Tears splatter as the lass is a'weeping
A young warrior's memory she is a'keeping
Alone, for her brother, she will go a'seeking
But he will go unfound since he is a'sleeping
— Sleeping; Author Unknown

Flath gently lay Tim's body down on the cool stones. His breath came heavy as tears streaked his face soiled by battle. A boy, just burgeoning into manhood, now cut off, never to realize boyhood dreams nor experience life as a man.

Flath could hear the others come into the room. However, he did not acknowledge them. Lost in pain so deep that it dulled his senses, he was not aware of the noise right away. Like the tickling whispers of a feather, he slowly became aware of a fluttering sound. It steadily grew louder as he tried to make sense of it.

The silence of pain was shattered by the slow, long singing of a steel blade being freed from its sheath. Flath looked up in time to see the bloodied form of a great raven take flight from a pool of blood. He drew his own blade only to watch the bird clumsily fly through the bedchamber door and disappear into the darkness. Luna jumped up snarling and charged after the bird.

"She lives!" Flath ran into the bedchamber with Shih 'Ni at his side. Lamps were quickly lit to reveal a very large room. He could see tall glass doors standing open leading out onto the balcony and wondered if she had already escaped. A cool, salty breeze rushed through the doors toying slightly with thick drapes that looked oily black in the darkness. He looked around for the shapeshifter, but large furnishings and shallow lamplight created long shadows distorting his view.

Suddenly he heard the fluttering of huge wings and turned towards an immense, canopied bed. He rushed towards the bird as it hovered above a small cradle. Her haunting, golden eyes turned towards him, and she screeched a harsh warning. With much effort, she lifted a bundle of blankets out of the cradle and tried to carry it towards the freedom of the balcony. He swung his sword toward her but his aim was slightly off, and with surprising agility, she rolled away from his sharpened blade. She squawked again, and the bundle slipped from her yellow clawed talons, thumping as it hit the floor. Quickly she turned and flew out the doors into the darkness.

From the back of his mind, he heard the insistent squalling of an infant but dismissed it and chased after the raven. As he entered the huge balcony, he saw the bird fly off over the sea. The silver light of a full moon illuminated her black form as she floated on the wind. From the corner of his eye, he saw Rhiannon run up next to him as they watched Baobh hover over an angry, churning ocean.

Storm clouds gathered quickly and smothered out the moonlight. A cold, almost acid rain began to fall soaking all of Sona Tuath. Lightning flashed in the distance over the turbulent water sending deafening thunder rolling across the land. A blistering wind rushed up from the Carnaid Sea whipping past the castle and howling in anger as it rushed through the trees of the forest.

In a brilliant flash of hot lightning, Flath saw the form of a huge bird fall like a stone into the hungry waters below. He gasped as he ran his eyes in vain over the darkness looking for Baobh. Suddenly, in another instant of white-bright lighting flash, he saw a woman's body being tossed in the violent waves and let out a long breath. "'Tis over, Greannmhor," he said as he turned towards Rhiannon. "You have won."

The frigid rain descended upon them like a waterfall, but neither moved to take shelter. The once roaring torches that lit up the courtyard below were now extinguished. Lurid flashes of lightning illuminated the gory scene of dead bodies that littered the ground below. Rivers of rain and blood flowed out from the inner castle gates disappearing into the cobbled streets of the city.

"Milady, um, there is a situation that needs your immediate attention." Ian appeared at her side.

The room was now ablaze with light from many oil lamps burning around the room. He noted a slick trail of blood leading out onto the balcony but dismissed it when he saw Kyia holding a crying baby.

"It comes from evil," Shih 'Ni yelled out and pointed at the infant. He held his sword tightly in one hand as if expecting the baby to turn into a wild beast at any moment.

"It's just a babe!" Kyia retorted, trying to quiet the infant. Rhiannon stood numbly watching the situation as if she could not comprehend what was going on. Flath stayed quiet—it was for her to settle, she was their empress after all. It was then that he noticed that she had fastened the Necklace of Verna around her neck. The shiny red stones glinted in the hot lamplight.

Suddenly Shih 'Ni tore the infant from Kyia's arms and held it upside down by one leg. "This child must be destroyed!" he roared angrily as the baby dangled dangerously above the hard, stone floor. He held his sword up high as if to split the baby down the center. Its plaintive wails filled the room.

"Shih 'Ni, no!" Rhiannon screamed and ran over to him, droplets of water dripping from clothes and hair. Shih 'Ni seemed almost stunned that she was in the room, but then his expression quickly faded back into angry determination.

"If you harm that child you will suffer!" she screamed and gently took the baby from his angry gasp.

"Rhiannon, you must destroy it. This child is the product of Baobh and cannot help but share the same tainted blood," Shih 'Ni tried to reason.

"He is a perfectly beautiful baby," Rhiannon said breathlessly as she stared down into its tear-streaked, black eyes. She walked over to the cradle and retrieved a blanket in which she quickly wrapped the tiny babe.

"The son of Baobh!" Shih 'Ni countered.

"An innocent child, just the same," Rhiannon replied angrily. "How could you even think about taking the life of an infant?"

"You are letting your feminine weaknesses influence your decision!"

"Hold your tongue, Master Shih 'Ni, I am still your empress," Rhiannon warned. Shih 'Ni sheathed his sword, folded his arms across his chest and watched the scene in disgust.

"Please find me a wet nurse amongst the servants, if there are any still left in the castle, and bring her up to me immediately," she instructed Ian. The infant had quieted down in the security of Rhiannon's arms. She gently rocked from side to side trying to get the infant to fall asleep while Kyia hunted around for something dry to dress the baby in.

"'Tis done, Flath. The castle has been taken," Teo stated out of breath as he entered the room. His face was heavily smeared with blood and dirt, but Flath could clearly see the deep sadness in his eyes and knew that he had seen Tim's body.

"Then 'tis finally over, my friend," Flath said, giving Teo a strong hug. Flath took him into the next room where Adam, Jon, and Bleen stood over Tim's body. Renewed grief bubbled up into Flath's soul; new tears fell from weary mismatched eyes. "Please prepare our brave comrade's body for transport back to his father," Flath ordered.

"Aye, captain," Teo answered, his own tears spilling on the blood-soaked floor.

"We must find my father." Flath spun around to see Rhiannon standing in the doorway. She walked up to him with a cold look in her eyes. She had given Baobh's son to Kyia.

"Alright, let us go find your father," he replied softly.

After what seemed like an interminable time, they finally found their way to the dungeons. The stench was almost unbearable. The air was heavy with the smell of rotting flesh, urine and feces and mixed with the sharp smell of fish and salt. His stomach heaved with nausea. He could hear the violence of the churning ocean from the caverns below that led up to the back entrance of the dungeons.

The dungeons were quiet except for the sounds of the storm raging outside. They had come across one frightened young guardsman who had surrendered right away. They had stripped him of his weapons and told him to lead them to the old man. Flath looked at Rhiannon as they followed the young man down the narrow halls. Nervous anticipation was etched in the lines of her face. Her brow was furrowed and under her eyes were the dark smudges of exhaustion. She did not expect to find him alive, that he knew. He did not think he could have survived a year and a half in this dungeon.

Three of Rhiannon's warrioress' silently crept behind them. He could not hear them but was aware of their presence just the same. To not be aware of the presence of an Archigos warrior was often the last mistake one made. They stopped in front of a large wooden door. Two torches burned wildly flooding the area with golden, flickering light. The young guardsman lifted a large iron bar that lay across the rotting door. "He is in there," he said and pointed into the cold blackness.

The door swung open, and out of the darkness, such a stench as to knock a person off his feet blasted them in the face. The guardsman gagged and stepped aside; his blond hair looked white in the bright torchlight. Tears welled and streamed freely down Rhiannon's cheeks.

Flath grabbed one of the torches off the wall and entered, Rhiannon followed. One of the warrioress' stayed with the guardsman, and the other two followed them into the damp cell.

"Daddy!" Rhiannon called. Her wavering voice echoed off the wet walls of the large, rock prison. "Daddy!" she called out again, fear and pain ringing thick in her voice.

Flath held the torch above his head, and it guttered in the cold breeze that rushed in through one tiny window hacked way up in the rock wall. The torchlight was weak and uneven in the cavern-like cell. Small eyes glowed back at them in the light and then scampered off with an annoyed squeal.

Rhiannon gasped, and Flath followed her line of sight. He could see the crumpled form of what was once a man. Rhiannon ran to him as Flath quickly followed. She threw herself down onto the damp ground as Flath knelt at her side. "Daddy," she whispered as she turned him over.

Flath tried hard not to vomit or jump away at the sight of the man. He was nothing more than filthy skin pulled tightly over frail bones. Flath swallowed down the bile and held the torch close wondering if the man yet lived, though judging from his condition he was sure he was dead.

"Sernia?" the man whispered, his eyes opening slightly.

Flath jumped at the rough, dry sound of Peter's weak voice.

"Daddy!" Rhiannon cried.

"Sernia, you've finally come!" He reached a shaky hand out and touched Rhiannon's tear-stained face. His fingers were nothing more than dirt and tiny bones.

"Daddy, it's me, Rhiannon." Peter coughed and tried to catch his breath and then looked closer at Rhiannon. His thin, pale lips curved into a smile, cracking at the strain. Blood welled and ran slowly down his chin.

"Rhiannon, it is you," he whispered.

"Everything is going to be okay now daddy. I'm here to take you home."

He tried to take a deep breath but shook with a violent coughing fit. When the spasms quit, he looked as if he had died. "Daddy?" Rhiannon called softly.

Suddenly Peter opened his eyes and looked up at his daughter again. A smile returned to his cracked, bloody lips. "My beautiful Rhiannon. I see the Archigos have found their empress," he said proudly. "You look so much like your mother."

"Daddy, why didn't you tell me?"

"Because I knew you would have wanted to come home," he coughed and took another deep, wheezing breath. "I knew it would be too dangerous for you here and I couldn't bear to lose you too…" His words trailed off and his eyes slowly closed as if he were falling asleep. Suddenly his body twitched, and he was fully awake again. "I am so sorry, my dear," he started. "I knew I should have given you back to your people. But I was too fearful. At first I thought I could hide you from this place, but when that little black colt was born and when you started asking questions about those nightmares, I knew I couldn't keep you from your destiny—but still, I was afraid." Clear, salty tears ran down a filthy, sunken face. "I should have told you," he cried. "I'm so sorry."

"It's alright, Daddy. Everything is okay now." She smiled down at Peter.

"I see you have your mother's necklace," Peter whispered and tried to smile.

"Yes, I do, and everything is going to be alright." She began to unfasten the necklace. "I will make the stones heal you, daddy."

"No!" His voice was surprisingly clear and commanding.

"What?" Rhiannon asked in confusion.

"No, I don't want to be healed."

"Daddy, I can help you," she pleaded.

"No." He shook his head. "I will leave here soon and meet your mother. I do not want to stay any longer, dear Rhiannon." Again, his frail body shook with a coughing fit. When it was over, he looked back at his only child. "I know you don't understand Rhiannon, but my life was over the night your mother was killed. I endured life for your sake." He stopped and took a breath.

"Daddy—"

He cut her off. "I know I haven't been a very good father to you. I was too ruined in my grief to give you what you needed." Rhiannon started to speak, but he interrupted her again. "Now you're grown and have found your destiny." He reached up and took her face between both of his filthy, palsied hands. Flath could see his missing finger. "Now that I know you're safe, and have found your people, I can finally go. I can go to your mother," he whispered. "May the sun smile down upon you. I love you, my beautiful daughter Rhiannon..." He lowered his arms, slowly closed his eyes and died with a thin smile on his face.

The violent storm of the night before had passed, washing away the blood and leaving only leaf litter in the cobbled streets. Columns of gray smoke were smudges across the landscape. The strong marine breeze was keeping the smell of burning bodies from overpowering the town. The bodies had been carried down the steep rocky passageway from Sona Tuath to the beach. A call had gone out for all to come and claim their dead, but out of fear—or prejudice more likely—none of the citizens left their homes. So, Rhiannon gave the order to start burning the dead guardsmen.

All but a few of the rebellion fighters quietly left for home during the night. The few that were left refused to work with the Archigos at their grizzly task of collecting up and burning the bodies. Tired of the bickering, Flath sent his men into Sona Tuath and the surrounding crofts and farms to find men willing to be hired on as his new soldiers.

He did not hold out much hope for new recruits, however until the Archigos had left Sona Tuath.

The dead Archigos were cleaned and wrapped tightly in herbs and cloth for the long travel back to Ventra. Peter Kossi's body was prepared as an Archigos Warrior, ready to be taken to Ventra and buried next to his beloved Sernia. Tim, son of William of Bell, was washed, dressed in new Archigos clothing and placed in a coffin ready to be taken back to his father—the shiny Venturien sword he was so proud of lay innocently on his chest.

Flath's heart ached badly over the death of Tim. He was never supposed to see fighting, that is what Flath had promised William. But Tim had been trained as an Archigos Warrior for over a year, and he had believed the boy safe in the midst of so many warriors.

From where he sat on a rocky ledge overlooking the beach and vast Carnaid Sea, he scanned the horizon again for any sign of Baobh or the famed Beast Rider, Lord Rull, who had mercifully been absent the night before. At dawn, he and a few of his men had gone out to search the beaches for the former queen's body, but the sea had refused to give her up, opting instead to keep her body concealed in the depths of the red oceanic waters. He sighed heavily and scraped his hand through wind ruffled hair.

"Good morning." Rhiannon walked up behind him, squatted down and put her arms around his neck tenderly kissing his cheek. "You sent for me?" Nervously, he cleared his throat and stood up.

He turned around ready to speak, but when he saw her,

he started to lose his courage. She looked so utterly beautiful in the early morning light of Sona Tuath. Her midnight black hair carelessly floated on the salty breeze as two tawny feathers tied in the short strands of her hair looked as if they were going to once again take flight. A circlet of gold and rubies lay gently on her brow sparkling importantly in the sun. The small diamond resting in her nose winked at him as it caught passing light. The red stones and bright silver of the Necklace of Verna glinted in the sunlight. Her black eyes were sharp, looking at him with question and concern.

Not knowing where to start, he looked down and ran his hand through his hair again. He felt the weight of the rings as they lay, almost forgotten, in a pouch at his side. He wondered if it was too late to just toss them into the hungry sea.

"What is it?"

He looked back at her—the time had come.

He took a deep breath. "Something has come to my knowledge that has changed things for us, Greannmhor."

She arched a dark brow in question. "Change things how?" she asked with much trepidation.

"On the way back from meeting with you in Bell, Teo and I came across my family."

"The same family that banished you when you were younger?" she asked sardonically.

Flath nodded. "Aye, but this time I was well met and asked to share their camp and food."

"What changed over all those years? Are they suddenly proud of you now for what you've accomplished with the rebellion?" Rhiannon folded her arms across her chest.

"Oh, aye, they are proud," he answered. "But there was something that my father needed to tell me." Rhiannon raised her brows waiting for him to finish the story. "My father told me something quite remarkable. It seems that I…" His words broke off. He took another deep breath and looked off towards the shimmering white walls of the castle so bright in the summer sun.

He started again. "I am not who I thought I was all these years, Greannmhor." He could see a spark of comprehension in her dark eyes. She gasped, and her hands went up to her mouth.

When she did not say anything, he went on. "I was found by the people I thought were my parents when I was just a babe in the hollowed stump of an old tree…," he reached into the pouch and retrieved the rings and handed them to Rhiannon, "With these."

She upturned the pouch, and the rings tumbled out into her hand. She turned them over marking every detail. "You're Baobh's half-brother then," she breathed in astonishment, still examining the rings.

Finally, she looked back up at him, tears brimming in her eyes. "Then you are to be king," she said softly. He nodded and watched her tears begin to fall. "This changes nothing," she said forcefully, handing him back the rings.

"This changes everything."

"Suddenly you don't love me any longer?" Rhiannon accused.

"I will always love you, Greannmhor. But love does not play a part in this."

"How does love not play a part in marriage?"

"The marriages of rulers? Nay, love does not enter into the equation." He shook his head. "Our people hate each other with a vehemence that will destroy both Beaynid and Ventra."

"Our people will come together eventually, Flath. They will learn to accept us!"

"They will not. You know they will not."

She made no attempt to brush away the tears, just let them run in heavy streaks down her cheeks and drip from her jaw. "They will have to," she tried.

He shook his head again, trying to be strong. "Our people would kill each one down to the last babe before they accepted one another." He spread out his hands. "Look! They even refused to fight together for a common cause!"

"They will change!"

"Nay, Rhiannon, you know they will not. Our people will not accept the marriage of an Archigos Empress to a Seun King," he tried to reason with her, though his heart felt as though it was being squeezed so tightly he could barely breathe. "What of the children that result from this ill-fated union? Do you think they will be accepted as their next rulers? Nay, they would not, and pandemonium would rise!"

"Will you not fight for me then, Flath?" she asked angrily.

"I would fight any force in the heavens or on earth for you, Rhiannon, never doubt that."

"Then why would you discard me so easily now?" she sobbed.

"This is a different situation," he said weakly, the pain of losing her pulsed through his body making him ill. He could feel the cool track of a tear roll down his cheek.

"Any force on heaven or earth, except prejudice?"

"We can do nothing, Greannmhor."

"You're giving up then?" she asked quietly, finally wiping at her tear-stained face.

He swallowed hard, willing himself to go on. "This is a war we cannot win."

"How can you say that? Do you feel nothing for me?"

At that, emotion broke in his voice. He felt as if he was being crushed under the weight of it. "I love you as I will never love another," he breathed.

She walked up close to him and laid her hand on his chest. "And I love you more than anything else on earth. May the gods take pity on us for bowing to the ignorance of our people," she whispered and looked up at him through wet lashes. She let her hand fall and backed away. "It is as you wish, Your Highness, we will leave for Ventra immediately."

She bowed and turned to leave but then came close again, looking hard into his mismatched eyes, as if searching for something. "Remember the dreams I told you were haunting me before I came here?" she asked but did not wait for a reply. "I told you of the images of my mother and a mysterious tree bathed in mist. But what I didn't tell you was that there was a man in my dreams also. That man was you, Flath." She reached over and gently touched his face closing her eyes as if trying to burn the feel of his skin into her memory. Then she reached up and kissed him tenderly. "Goodbye, Flath." With that, she turned and walked away.

"Rhiannon—" he called out to her, but she just kept walking away. He turned and yelled out at the sea, gripping the rings tightly in his hand, wanting nothing more than to pitch them into the red depths of the Carnaid. All his life he was denied the things he wanted because of being nothing but a gypsy, and now, he realized with blistering irony, he will be denied the only woman he had ever loved because he was a king.

CHAPTER EIGHTEEN

"The Goyor, or Forest Folk, are a peaceful race that tend to
avoid outsiders. In fact, it is very rare to actually see one.
Their existence is worshiping their god, Pom Ni, by
protecting and tending to the forest. They live in secret
communes all throughout the Alba Forest."
—Customs of Exotics; Lorn VacLell

He placed a snow-white rose on a plain wooden
coffin made of knotty pine. It was completely
unadorned of any mark or trinket that spoke of the man that
lay inside. A young man that was so vibrant in life now lay
in the quiet anonymity of death's solace. Her hand began to
shake as she slowly stroked the smooth wooden cover
hoping to rub away time—back to a time so very near when
he yet lived.

She kneeled and wept silently, bowing her head in
supplication to Verna on Tim's behalf. Her world would
forever be changed in so many ways. So many sorrows
weighed her down like a huge stone tied around her neck,
pulling her deeper into a bottomless sea. Tears splattered on
a dirty floor and glistened in beams of warm sunshine. She
felt tired and weak under the crushing pain of Tim death.
Sorrow crowded her mind and clung to her heart so tightly
that it was the only thing she could feel or see. She felt as

though someone had carved out everything inside her, yet purposely left her damaged heart so that she would suffer and die from the pain.

Finally, she stood and wiped the tears from her face. It was then she saw his shadow splayed across the stone floor. She looked up to see Flath watching her. She looked at him coolly, not letting her composure fall to him. "I will be leaving in the morning to take Tim back to his father," he said quietly. She nodded her head. He looked down at the floor, then back up at her. "Greannmhor—" he started.

She put up her hand and shook her head. "Please, don't call me that anymore," she said sadly. "I'm still not sure what it means, but to me, it was a word of endearment, meant for lovers, which we are not."

He took a deep breath, suddenly annoyed. "Alright, Empress Kossi, will you be taking the infant back to Ghroc, then?"

"Yes, Your Majesty."

He blanched at the title but then let the expression fade. "Thank you."

"The child is your nephew, you know," she said after a moment.

"Aye, I guess he is," he nodded.

"Do you know what he is called?" she asked, hopefully.

"The nurse called him Kaat, I believe."

"Good. I will tell Journey-Of-The-Moon. Maybe someday when he's older, he'll have an interest in seeing all of this," she spread out her arms to indicate the whole of Sona Tuath. "And meet his uncle, the king."

"Hopefully when he does come, it will not be for the throne or worse—revenge."

When they fell into an uncomfortable silence, she turned to leave, then stopped and turned back around. "It seems Baobh was bleeding Sona Tuath dry. I've sent a bird back to Màrrach with a message ordering as much food as we can spare, along with money to be sent immediately. I've asked that it all be taken to our military outpost on the eastern shore. I understand that Sona Tuath has a few ships and the trip is much faster by sea."

She clearly read the shame on his face. "If we were not in such a sorry state, I would refuse, but I will thank you for your generosity, Empress Kossi."

"People are starving, Your Highness, I would help no matter how they felt about the Archigos. And besides, not all of Beaynid hate us."

"Aye, I guess there are two or three that do not wish for your slow, painful deaths."

At that, she genuinely laughed. "May the sun smile down upon you, Flath," she said softly and then turned to go. A pain so immense and hopeless filled her mind and body that it made it hard for her move.

As she reached the door, she met Teo. "Are ye leav'n now, lass?"

"Yes Teo, we must be heading home," she said slowly.

"I'll miss yer smil'n face," he said sorrowfully, then wrapped her in his broad arms.

"I'll miss you too," she said, blinking away a tear. "I bet your family will be happy to have you home now."

He laughed. "Weel, I've sent fer them ta come here, as Flath will be need'n me still for a while, I'm sure."

She smiled again. "I'm sure he'll need you now more than ever before." She looked over at Flath who was now kneeling by Tim's coffin as she had just been doing. "Take care of him for me, Teo."

"I will, Rhiannon," he said quietly. "The man is a fool fer not listen'n ta his heart. No good will come of it."

"Oh, Teo, maybe he's right. Maybe our people will never come together," she sighed. "I see so much hate in these people. They would kill the very ones that liberated them! If delivering them from Baobh won't soften their hearts, nothing will."

"Time, lass. Time will change people like noth'n else."

She put her arm on Teo's shoulder. "Then maybe there's hope for me and Flath yet."

He laid his wide, warm hand on hers. "There's always hope, Rhiannon. Give the lad some time. He'll come around."

"We are ready to depart, Empress," Kyia said as she walked up to them.

"Please watch over him, Teo." She looked over at Flath once again. He still kneeled over Tim's coffin. Teo nodded sadly, and Rhiannon turned and walked away.

The violent, turbulent waters of the great Carnaid Sea had long since tamed into cool pink tides with lazy foamy waves, and in a short time the castle, its walls, and in fact the entire city was washed clean. No trace of blood or battle was found in all of Sona Tuath. Her white walls and blue roofs gleamed in the sunshine as children played summertime games. What was left of the Sona Tuathan Royal Guard stood at their posts as if nothing had ever happened. The lavish temple that Baobh had constructed for the worship of Pom-Ni was pulled down, and construction was started on a proper Sona Tuathan Kirk for the One God, Ak. Even as Beaynid sighed in relief and tried to put the memories of Baobh's rule out of their minds, deeper and darker feelings started boiling up into their hearts.

As promised aid had arrived from Ventra by way of hired ships that followed the jagged coastline south to Sona Tuath. People were hungry and in need of many things, but as they stuffed their mouths with Ventra's sweet bread and meat, they cursed the Archigos—even while guzzling their fine imported liquor.

Ancient childhood fairytales of blood-thirsty Archigos Warriors were revived as the vivid retelling of exaggerated stories filled Sona Tuath and the surrounding countryside. Children were afraid to sleep in their own beds and women did not venture out at night. Men armed themselves with swords, spears, bows or anything else they could find.

This weighed heavily on Flath. They did not trust him yet as ruler, though none dared challenge his right. Most accepted him as the rightful heir, though his partnership with Ventra was not understood. Rumors that their king and Ventra's empress were to wed flooded the streets and caused much talk in taverns and shops.

As the weeks passed the rumor would not die, and the

people's voices grew wrathful. Flath stood in a small room he had made into his private study. It was small, unadorned and had no windows, thus offering no distractions to his dark thoughts. This was the place he retreated to when his heart was heavy. This was the place that he increasingly spent so much time.

He looked down at the signet ring he wore: a tiny but intricate image of a grand castle on the cliffs of a dark sea, and on each side of the ring, jewels glimmered in the soft lamplight. The smaller ring—his mother's—was up in his bedchamber. He wished that it could have been Rhiannon's someday, but knew that was not to be. He sighed heavily and wondered how different his life would be had he not been the offspring of royals, or had his gypsy parents not found him that bloody day almost twenty-six years ago, or even if he had not met up with his family that late afternoon in the forest.

He gritted his teeth and balled up his fists. Why has this come to me? He did not want the rule of this kingdom any longer, if he ever did, but did not know how to change things.

"Sorry ta bother ye lad, but there's a ship on the horizon," Teo spoke softly as he entered the study.

Flath looked up sharply. "What kind of Ship?"

"Actually, several of them. From Yellow Island."

"Yellow Island? What could they want?" Flash snarled.

"Ta wish the new ruler well?" Teo shrugged thick shoulders.

"After they slaughtered thousands of my men, now they come to me in peace?"

"Laddie there's many things in politics that ye'll never understand." Teo put an arm around the younger man's shoulder. "But I don't think it would be a good idea ta make an enemy outta Yellow Island."

"They chose a side when they came up against us!"

"Aye, 'tis true but things are much different now, ye ken?"

Flath dragged his hand through his hair. "Aye, I suppose they are."

"Would it have been smart fer Yellow Island ta make an enemy of Baobh by join'n wi' a bunch of rebels?"

Flath took a deep breath and let it out slowly. "What shall I say to this King of Yellow Island?"

"I dunno." Teo shrugged. "I guess that depends on what he wants."

Less than an hour later, Flath sat and looked around the sun-filled room as he sat on the throne of Beaynid. The ornate jewel studded seat stood next to a smaller one, made for the queen, and both sat atop a large dais that ran the length of the room. The three steps to the dais were huge and were built with the same gray stones that made up most of the castle.

"Don't look so worried, lad," Teo whispered with a smile as he stood next Flath.

"I hate this!" he hissed. "When is the old man going to get his bum off the ship and get this over with?"

"Get used ta it, yer a king now," he chuckled.

"I was a better gypsy," Flath answered.

Teo looked over and laughed out loud. "Weel, ye

wouldn't get ta wear that fancy hat and sit yer arse on that fancy chair either!"

After what seemed an interminable time, the castle guards ushered in many brightly arrayed servants, all wearing the yellow and black signal on their tunics and carrying bottles and chests and bolts of exotic fabric. Flath sat silently as gifts began to pile at his feet. He could feel the sweat start to bead on his lip as he concentrated on not balling up his fists and keeping a placid smile on his face. Rare spices, herbs, teas, enough soft, rich fabric to dress every woman in Sona Tuath, sparkling gems and crystal vases were all placed on the foot of the dais cleverly leaving a small path for their king to approach—if he ever arrived, that is.

Finally, a tall skinny servant with dark hair approached Flath and bowed deeply. He informed Flath that King Umar had also brought spirited, strong horses, intelligent hounds and quick hawks, all for King Basilias of Beaynid. Umar had also gifted the throne with cows, goats and sheep and much food and wool. Flath was shocked as he looked around at the growing pile of pricey offerings.

Just then a small inconsequential man stepped into the room. "May I present to you King Umar of Yellow Island!" he announced so dramatically Flath suppressed an urge to laugh. He sat up straight as King Umar's entourage—which included approximately twenty-five highly armed guardsmen—marched into the room.

The short, squat man was dressed in a violet colored, elegantly embroidered coat with pearls sewn in at the cuffs and neck. A profusion of feathery white lace erupted at his throat and spilled out the front of the coat and at his wrists. His trousers were also violet and heavily embroidered. A rectangular piece of silk ran down from his right shoulder to the left side of his waist. It was red with a yellow center and a rather life-like picture of a hog's head in the middle. He wore thick golden ropes around his neck, and a large gold crown sat atop his gray, thinning hair.

Umar wasted no time. He quickly approached the dais and climbed the stairs. "It is so wonderful to see you were successful in your acquisition of the throne, King Basilias." Umar kneeled and took Flath's hand and kissed his signet ring.

Flath squelched the urge to pull his hand away from the small man's wet lips. "You are well come, King Umar, I assure you."

Umar stood up and looked at Flath with a humble expression on his face. "Had I known you were a Basilias, my lord, I would have never sent my army after you and your men. My most humble apologies." The small man broke out in a sweat.

Flath wanted to laugh. He knew the only reason Yellow Island did not come to Baobh's aid again was that of Rhiannon's threat. "Your apologies are accepted."

"I bring you many gifts!" His chubby violet arms swept the throne room that was now full. "These goods are the very best in the known world, Your Highness. Yellow Island has strong trade alliances with many faraway places," Umar stated dramatically. "And now Beaynid will benefit also." He bowed again and came closer to Flath. "I have come to suggest an alliance between our two great lands." Flath raised brows in question. Umar nervously turned and motioned for someone to approach. "Please allow my daughter, Princess Jocelyn, to approach."

"Of course," Flath said uneasily. A tiny mouse-like young woman climbed the stairs up to Flath. Shyly she looked at him and then quickly looked away.

Her dress was violet, like her father's and the bodice of her dress shared the same embroidery and pearl work. A thick golden torque encircled her long neck encrusted with large diamonds and tiny rubies, ear bobs to match hung from her lobes. The same scarlet banner with the yellow circle in the center hung from her waist down to the lacy hem of her dress. Instead of the hog's head, though, there was a white flower. Her brown hair was swept up in a network of braids and coils that were held in place with pearl-encrusted pins. The tiny crown she wore was very delicate and boasted rubies and yellow and white diamonds as well. Her face was powdered too heavily, and her lips were painted a bright red. The delicate bones of her cheeks were shaded with pink, and her eyelids were powdered with a sheer green color.

"I am offering the Crown's debts canceled." Umar smiled broadly. "Queen Baobh ran up a considerable amount of debt. It seems she had a taste for the finer things." Umar went on, "I am also suggesting a union between you and my daughter sealing an alliance between Beaynid and Yellow Island."

Shocked, Flath looked over at Teo who stood without expression. He looked back at King Umar. "You waste no time, do you?"

"Forgive me King Basilias, I am but an old man and the sea travel has made me weary. I wish to get the business over with before the pleasantries of a feast."

Flath wrinkled his brow, not recalling any mention of a feast. "I have just started my rule. I think 'tis too early to think of taking a wife."

King Umar lowered his voice. "Even from Yellow Island, I have heard the rumors of you and Ventra's new empress. Your people are not happy, Your Highness." He shook his head. "Now would be the perfect time to give Beaynid their queen...it will stop the rumors. They grow irate and might start entertaining thoughts of stripping you of your kingly rights." He looked around as if whispering a secret. "Your army is still not strong enough to prevent a successful coup d'état."

Flath sighed and looked out the window at the huge ships docked in the bay that had brought King Umar to stand before him with this outrageous offer. Flath knew he was right. The people of Sona Tuath were not happy. The angry talk and accusations grew louder by the day. Taking a wife would stop tongues from wagging. He took a deep breath and thought about Rhiannon and a brand-new stab of pain pierced his heart and tightened his stomach.

"She comes from good stock, Sire," Umar went on. "Her mother birthed me six sons. She is not yet ten and six and will be a good breeder for you," he announced proudly as he placed his small, dainty hands on his narrow hips and smiled.

Flath looked down at the girl who stood watching him with small green eyes. Her skin was as white as ivory, and her face was rather drab. She had no remarkable features at all. She was like dull standing water that was neither hot nor cold. He thought of the bland taste of porridge when he looked at her. Within her eyes, he saw a spark of something he thought was revulsion. He smiled sweetly at her in a mocking manner. She stared back at him venomously.

He took a deep breath and knew this would close Rhiannon out of his life forever. I have already lost her. His chest was heavy, and it was suddenly hard for him to breath. His throat painfully constricted and his mind raced. He had to stop the pain. He had to get her out of his blood. "Fine! 'Tis done. An alliance shall be made between Beaynid and Yellow Island."

Teo choked so loudly everyone in the room looked over at him, expecting him to expire at any moment. "A word with ye, Your Highness?"

Flath looked back over to Umar who had a supremely offended expression on his sallow face. "Excuse me," he said apologetically and got up and followed Teo into a corner of the room. "What was that all about?" he demanded.

"Ye can't marry that girl," he said indignantly.

"Why not? Does Sona Tuath not need a queen?"

"Not that queen," he argued.

"What does it matter?"

"Princess Jocelyn has a…reputation."

"What kind of reputation?" Flath asked suspiciously.

Teo's face grew bright red. "Weel, if she's already wi' child, I won't be surprised."

Flath scrubbed a hand through his hair in agitation. He

looked over at the young woman and then back over to Teo. "I do not have a choice, you have heard how the people talk! I must get this over with," he said and tried to walk away.

Teo reached out and grabbed his arm. "Lad, ye are mak'n a big mistake."

"Then it will be my mistake, Teo."

"What about Rhiannon?"

Flath looked down at the floor, then looked back up at his old friend. "What about her?"

"Will ye let her go so easily?"

"'Tis time to rid her of my life," he said quietly and then walked back to Umar.

"An alliance will be made between Sona Tuath and Yellow Island!" Flath announced again. Umar smiled happily. Jocelyn scowled.

"Ian, go down to the kirk and fetch us a vicar. We will have a wedding."

"No need, sire, for I have brought my own priest."

"Very well then, let us get on with it!"

Flath heard the dainty sound of disapproval coming from Jocelyn's direction and looked over at her. She stood scowling at him, her skinny arms tightly folded across almost nonexistent breasts. He smiled to himself. This will be easier than I thought, she already hates me.

Rhiannon walked down the familiar trail that was nothing more than a rabbit track, really. She held tiny Kaat closely to her bosom trying not to jostle the babe from his peaceful slumber. Tanya, the young wet-nurse, had fed the child just before Rhiannon started down the "path" to Ghroc. This time she went alone. The threat of Baobh now gone, she felt she wanted a little solitude. Shih 'Ni did not agree at first, but that did not surprise her.

Without warning the dense forest started to give way to the gentle, colorful village, she knew as Ghroc. "Empress! Empress!" the children cried and surrounded her.

"You have come to visit us again!" Singing Brook giggled happily.

"I have, and I've brought someone to come and stay with you."

Fox's eyes grew wide, "Who is it?"

"Is it an Archigos warrior?" asked Bear Paw.

"No," Rhiannon chuckled. "He's not quite as scary as that."

"Who did you bring us?" Singing Brook asked.

Rhiannon sat on the ground, still holding the infant quite tightly. Finally, she peeled back the blankets to show all the little children what she carried in her arms.

They all gasped when they saw the tiny little face nestled contentedly in his blankets. Round, wonder-filled blue eyes peered back at the children, and then petite little lips and plump cheeks swelled into a smile.

"He's so cute! What's his name?" Singing Brook asked.

"His name is Kaat," Rhiannon answered.

"Why are his eyes the color of the sky?" Fox innocently asked. "None of us have eyes that color."

"Well, his grandfather was not from Ghroc," Rhiannon whispered, taken aback by the sheer beauty and perfection of the tiny babe. Suddenly she wished with all her might that she was holding, instead, her own child. Something deep within her stirred and a desire grew—a desire that she had never noticed until that moment. Quite unexpectedly she wondered if she were doing the right thing. Perhaps she should take the child and raise it as her own.

"So deep in thought, Rhiannon Kossi?" Journey-Of-The-Moon's soft voice brought her out of her frantic thoughts. She looked up at the older woman suddenly confused. For a second she did not remember where she was. She looked around and saw that all the children were now gone.

"I'm sorry…,"

Journey-Of-The-Moon laughed. "You will have your own children soon enough, my dear." Rhiannon hugged the babe to her bosom and stood up. She felt strange—oddly detached—as if she were watching the scene from high up in the treetops. "I see you have brought us someone." The older woman's smile was very warm.

"Yes," she said slowly. "I hope you don't mind me bringing him here. He's without parents now and will need to be instructed in your ways." Slowly she handed the infant to Journey-Of-The-Moon and experienced an immediate emptiness.

"Baobh and Eagle's son," Journey-Of-The-Moon stated rather than asked.

"Yes. His name is Kaat."

Journey-Of-The-Moon looked up at Rhiannon. "We are indebted to you, Empress, for bringing one of our children home."

Rhiannon smiled. "If my child were missing I would hope someone would do the same for me." Startled, the Goyor looked up at Rhiannon. "What is it, Journey-Of-The-Moon?" The woman's composure faltered for a moment, and Rhiannon read something in the woman's eyes that she could not understand. "Is everything alright?" Rhiannon asked cautiously.

Journey-Of-The-Moon smiled, her face once again a mask of kindness. "I am fine, do not worry."

Rhiannon crinkled her brows. "Do you know something that you'd like to share with me?"

Journey-Of-The-Moon laughed, her black eyes shining in the sun. "I need to tell you nothing that you will not know soon enough, my dear. True knowledge is only gained through experiencing life. Experience life, Rhiannon, and you will never have any regrets."

Rhiannon looked at her suspiciously. "So, you can still see my future?" she asked.

"Some of it I do see. Some of it I do not."

"And you won't share with me what you can see?" It was more of a statement, for she already knew the answer.

Journey-Of-The-Moon shook her head. "I cannot." She smiled again as a bright beam of light poked its way through the tree boughs. The light shone in Rhiannon' eyes and warmed her soul.

"Then I guess I'll just have to wait until things happen." Rhiannon smiled and shrugged.

"For the kindness that you have shown this newest Goyor, you may keep the Emissary beads I had given you in your dream, Rhiannon Kossi, so that you may always find your way back to our home."

"Thank you, Journey-Of-The-Moon!" Rhiannon's hand went up to the beads she still wore around her neck next to her mother's necklace.

Journey-Of-The-Moon closed her eyes and balled up her small fist. Slowly she turned her fist over and opened her hand. In her palm lay a small amber colored stone intractably carved into a rose and fastened onto a strand of gold. "Please give this to the young nurse. Tell her it is our gift to her for caring for one of our children. It will ensure the healthy birth of her future children."

"Thank you, Journey-Of-The-Moon. For all you've done."

"I thank you, Empress Kossi for what you have done for Beaynid." She looked deeply into Rhiannon's eyes. "Did you accomplish all that you set out to do, Empress?"

"I guess the most important things, yes," Rhiannon sighed.

"But you return without the one you had hoped to be your mate?"

"Yes."

"I am sorry, Rhiannon." The Emissary's expression turned to one of compassion.

"Did you know Flath was the baby you showed me in the dream?" Rhiannon held her sad gaze.

"Yes," she replied.

Rhiannon nodded, "Farewell, Journey-Of-The-Moon. May the sun smile down upon you," she smiled again and turned to walk away.

"Empress! Empress!" a small voice called out from behind her. She turned to see Bear Paw running towards her, his little legs and arms swinging as fast as they could. "Take me with you!" he cried.

Rhiannon looked up at Journey-Of-The-Moon who was watching with an amused look on her face. She bent down next to the little boy, so eager to leave. "I would love to take you with me, Bear Paw, but you're needed here."

"But I want to be an Archigos Warrior! I want to go to Ventra with you and Shih 'Ni!" he pleaded.

Rhiannon ran her hand over the tight coils of his black hair. "You're such a brave young man, willing to leave your family and all your friends behind for a place so far away and full of peril". His round, black eyes widened. He suddenly looked like he was not so sure he wanted to leave. "There're no other Goyor in Ventra so you'd be by yourself most of the time." Bear Paw was quiet. "All we do in Ventra is fight and eat huge amounts of food and beat each other up for fun." The little boy was still silent. "You're needed here much more, Bear Paw. There are not nearly enough Goyor to protect the whole forest. If you leave, who will shepherd the little animals and protect the fragile plants?"

"I guess my turtle and bunnies would feel sad that I left them," he reasoned.

"Yes, they would. And think about how sad your

parents and friends would feel about you leaving them?" He looked as if he would cry, so Rhiannon took him in her arms. "You're such a handsome young man, and the forest wouldn't be the same without you. You're going to grow up to be a very important man who does some very important things." She let go of him and looked into his little black eyes. She wondered what her own son would look like. She sighed and wondered if she would ever have children of her own.

"Will you come back?" he asked in a small voice.

"I will come back, Bear Paw, I promise." She kissed his forehead, stood and walked back into the forest.

CHAPTER NINETEEN

"Prior to the War of the Gypsy, Sona Tuath was heavy with debt. Queen Baobh threw elaborate parties and lived in utter luxury. It has also been rumored that Queen Baobh siphoned from Sona Tuath's coffers to bestow gifts of monies upon Lord Rull and his Forest Folk from a faraway land."
—*Sona Tuath; Thomas Ulln*

They had just enough food to last the winter—food for Sona Tuath that is—nothing for the towns and villages of Beaynid whose crops had been raped by Baobh's greed and incompetent rule. Beaynid would suffer for sure. He had since found out that Baobh's alliance with Lord Rull involved large monetary gains for him. He still did not understand their relationship beyond the money Baobh had been giving him, and he did not know what Rull had provided Baobh in return. Could it have simply been payment for aiding her in The Great War twenty-six years ago? Or could it have been extortion? Could it be that this Lord Rull knew something that she did not want anyone else to know? He thought not, for look what she did to the Prophecy Keepers to keep the prophecy from being widely known. No, she would have just eliminated whoever got in her way.

Flath rubbed his eyes and let his mind drift. He looked over to the oil lamp and watched the plump flame flicker and then grow into a long thin finger as wisps of black smoke curled around unseen wisps of air.

He raked his hand through his hair and stared at ancient cracks as they poetically crept across plastered walls. Long shadows swayed and flashed as torches burned higher up on the walls of his study. The room was quiet and remote from the busy chaos that permeated the castle. Far below him lay damp passageways and dungeons carved from the rock. Above him towered the massive castle of Sona Tuath. He sat in the middle. Symbolic of what his life had become.

He took a deep breath and started looking over the ledgers again. Baobh had not only ravished the nation's resources but burdened Beaynid with debt that was owed to a half dozen lords, kings and merchants of other lands. It was not only the money she had given Rull but the overly lavish lifestyle she kept for herself: jewels, clothes, parties, and drink. It would take many good years to finally pay off what was owed. He leaned back in his chair and stared up at the shadowed ceiling. Large cobwebs hung in the still air.

Word spread quickly of the Archigos Warriors and their tiny servants showing up at villages and small towns all over Beaynid. They provided food and protection to unthankful inhabitants. Flath prayed to the gods that Ventra would continue to help his citizens through the winter. He had granted lands and titles to men throughout Beaynid to help keep some sort of order. In return governing the people of their region, they not only received large parcels of land and had manors built for them, but they were allowed to charge a small duty to cover their expenses incurred by their new positions. In contrast to the harsh taxes Baobh had demanded, the Beaynidans were more inclined to pay the new lords. Some of the tax money, of course, would have to come back to Sona Tuath, but it would hardly be enough to get the castle town through winter let alone to start paying off the debt.

An oil burning lamp flickered in the breeze when the door to his study was opened and then quietly closed. He hoped that it was not Jocelyn.

"Ye've been pour'n over them papers fer days lad, 'tis time to take a break." Teo's jovial voice boomed across the silent study.

Flath scrubbed dry hands down his stubbled, exhausted face. "Has there been any more reports of outlawry?" he asked.

"Ha! Wi' all those Archigos warriors roving about?" Flath shook his head. "The lass has done much ta restore peace ta the land," Teo cautiously observed.

"Aye, she has," Flath replied tightly.

"She and her warriors have worked hard ta bridge the chasm between Ventra an' Beaynid," Teo stated, with a little more courage.

"I was riding into Jeil a few days past and saw a handful of children playing in a meadow. When I rode closer, I saw a few children of the village happily playing with Archigos children and those of their little pale servants." Flath sat back in his chair, stretched his arms and then intertwined his fingers behind his head.

"Ye look like an auld man, lad. Have ye giv'n up on sleep, then?" Teo asked.

"The dreams keep me up at night."

"Ah, yer still hav'n those wee nightmares, are ye?"

"Aye, and they grow in color and intensity every night." Flath leaned forward in his chair and spoke softly as if even mentioning the dreams would conjure one immediately.

"Ye need to go and visit my poor auld mother, lad. Shee'l set ye straight."

Flath shook his head. "No need. We both know why I suffer." Teo looked down at his boots and remained silent. "The day she left she told me that I was in her dreams. The dreams that brought her to me." Teo looked back up at his friend but offered no condolences. Flath took a deep breath. "Ah well, the wheel of time ever moves us forward, not behind," Flath concluded with a forced smile. He sighed and sat back trying to relax a bit. He looked at Teo thoroughly in the glowing light. "You look happy, old friend." He gave his friend an easy smile.

"I am," he said, triumphantly. "Shawna is wi' child again." His face split into a broad smile, barely visible underneath the explosion of unkempt beard.

Flath got up and walked over to Teo. "Congratulations!" he said and slapped him on the back. "Babe number five."

"Aye! One more barin to add to the pack," he said proudly.

Flath looked down at the stone floor. "I would like to have children someday," he said ruefully.

"Ye will soon enough, lad. Yer queen is quite wi' child," Teo stated pensively as if reminding Flath.

"Oh, yes. I guess she is. With whose child, we will never know," Flath answered bitterly.

Just then the door to the study flung open with a crash. Flath sighed, knowing immediately that Jocelyn had entered the room. She marched up to him and thrust tiny fists onto plumping hips and looked up at him. "Are you going to eat with us tonight, Your Highness, or take your dinner elsewhere, as always." Her tone was demanding. "I had informed you last week that we will be having guests on this night."

"I do not have much of an appetite, Jocelyn."

"I am your wife!" she screeched. "Yet, I see so little of you as to not even know who you are. And now you will shame me in front of our guests?"

"I am a busy man," Flath said and sat back down at his desk pretending to look over his ledgers.

"You are not living up to your husbandly duties!" she screamed in a rage, arms flailing in the air. "You even refuse to share the marriage bed with me, but on the night we were wed!"

Flath looked up at Jocelyn. Her green eyes were livid with anger. "Leave me," he stated very clearly. Jocelyn stared at him but said nothing. After a while she grew bored and left, slamming the heavy door behind her. "If I were a heartless man I would have that woman killed," he whispered.

"She is the mother of yer child, like it or no," Teo counseled and sat down beside Flath. "She will give ye yer babe soon enough, lad, then you may send her away."

"You do not believe the child is mine and neither do I,"

Flath answered in a huff. Teo sat back and looked at Flath. "I voice what we both feel. Do I not?"

"Aye, but there is a chance she does carry the heir."

"I suppose so," he acquiesced. "However, I will keep a close watch on the date of the child's arrival. If it does not coincide with the natural period of time, then I will know for sure." Teo nodded slowly. "Then I will send her away shamed and will never have to look at the vile creature again."

Teo was silent, offering no advice or rebuttal and that annoyed Flath, though he did not know why. "I do not want to waste any more time thinking of things that I cannot change."

"That would be wise, for you'll drive yerself mad!"

"Mayhap I will travel a bit. Visit settlements farther away." He leaned back in his chair and reached behind cradling his head in his hands once again. Mayhap I will stay away until the child is born."

"You will travel in the dead of winter?" Teo asked skeptically.

"Have you already forgotten how many winters we have spent in the wild?" Flath laughed. "Do you think I have grown soft?"

Teo smiled. "Ye will never grow soft, lad."

Flath sat atop his horse on a small hill that skirted the many broad roads leading into Tel' Rhia. It was almost February, and the land lay dormant and vast. The deep green pine trees of the forests had thinned and finally given way to oak, hemlock, and maple, all now ghostly bare with their bent arms reaching toward the heavens. The snow was a good four feet deep almost all the way down to the docks. None had seen a winter so ferocious as this.

An eagle flew high above hungrily searching the depths of white hoping for a meal. Suddenly it folded its giant wings and quickly dove out of sight. A chilly wind blew up off the ocean, and Flath pulled his coat tighter. He kneed his horse, and they started down the road to Tel' Rhia. He had been staying in the busy shipping city for over a month now but was getting anxious and increasingly had to spend time in the quiet of the frozen countryside to clear his mind. He was thankful for his anonymity in Tel' Rhia, for none knew the King of Beaynid by sight or really cared much, at that. He blended in with the general populace, drinking in the pubs, wandering the endless streets of merchants and even taking part in a game of chance or two. He was bored and restless, but the alternative was sleeping on the cold ground while traveling between towns, or even worse, returning to Sona Tuath.

Ian frequently traveled between Sona Tuath and Tel' Rhia delivering messages and news from home. The queen became more spiteful and angry as her belly grew and Ian always had a note from her to deliver. Flath never read them. Teo took over while he was away and assured him all was well, though Flath kept thinking he had been gone too long and should return, worrying that his people will have thought their king had abandoned them.

The day was drawing to a close as the achromatic sun slowly sunk towards a gray horizon. Flath led his horse down into Tel 'Rhia. Merchants began to close up their shops as taverns and whorehouses started to fill. As Flath rode closer to the inn, he had been staying at he saw Ian patiently waiting for him.

"Greetings, Your Majesty!" he yelled when he caught sight of Flath.

Flath slipped off his horse, and a stable boy took the reins. "Ian, 'tis good to see you!" He hugged the young man, and they walked inside. They sat at a table, and a chubby innkeeper with a friendly smile quickly placed food and wine on the table. "What news do you have of Sona Tuath?"

Ian scooped up huge piles of food and stuffed it into his mouth as if he hadn't eaten in weeks. "Everything goes well my King," he answered, then hastily shoved more food into his mouth. "There has been some sort of sickness with the townspeople, but the surgeons are not too alarmed," he said between bites.

"A sickness?" Flath quit eating and looked at the young man waiting for more information.

"Aye, however, I am sure 'tis nothing but an outbreak of flu or some similar illness." Ian looked up at Flath. "Do not worry. The surgeons will see to it that the people recover." He smiled and took a long drink of wine. "Oh, and I almost forgot." He put down his fork and dug around in a small purse. "This came for you. 'Tis from Ventra." He handed over the parchment to Flath and then started eating again.

It was not a letter in an envelope, but a rolled-up

announcement on thick parchment paper. He carefully unrolled the gold colored paper, its thickness, and quality he had never seen before. The royal symbol of Ventra embossed at the top in a deep, rich purple tone. The words of the announcement were formed with such great care and intricacy that they were a piece of art in themselves. They were not of mere ink that could smudge or fade during a long journey, but as if burned into the paper.

Flath read it quickly and then re-read it again slowly. "It seems Rhiannon is inviting me to a Fiann."

Ian looked up again. "Aye," he said with a smile.

"What is a Fiann?"

"Teo said you would ask that." Ian laughed. "It is the celebration that is held when an Archigos empress officially takes the throne. Or at least that is what Teo said."

He shrugged and sat back in his chair, his food all eaten. "So, I expect you will be accompanying me back to Sona Tuath, then."

"Aye, I reckon I will be, young Ian." Flath smiled widely and carefully rolled up the parchment. "I must ready myself for the long journey north," he said excitedly. "We will leave at dawn!" he announced.

"Good, the queen is greatly anticipating seeing Ventra again."

Flath's smile quickly deflated. "Jocelyn has asked to come?"

"The queen asks nothing, Your Majesty, she demands."

"She will not accompany me!" Flath stated angrily.

Ian looked out the window, the sun was completely gone, and Tel' Rhia was now glowing in the light of hundreds of lamps and torches placed all around the town and docks. "I have ridden with much haste to reach you expediently," Ian said. Flath leaned in as if to say something, but remained quiet. "The queen has already left."

Flath slammed his fist down on the table making the utensils jump and the bottle of wine fall and shatter on the floor. "As I live and breathe, I will kill that woman!" Patrons of the inn quickly looked over at the disturbance but seeing there was to be no violence they resignedly returned to their interrupted conversations. "We will leave immediately!"

"I thought you might want to, my King," Ian said as he jumped up and followed Flath from the smoke-filled inn.

CHAPTER TWENTY

"The Fiann is the Archigos coronation ceremony where a new empress takes the throne of Ventra. It is a wonder to behold! One never forgets the deep thunder of hundreds of giant drums or the rhythmic chanting of thousands of warriors as sweet-smelling smoke from sacrificial fires fills the valley. It is steeped in mysterious pagan rituals that honor the many gods and goddesses of that warrior nation. Among the most popular goddess is Verna along with other gods and goddesses that bless war, fertility and good luck."
—*Customs of Exotics; Lorn VacLell*

The Great Hall was silent as she slowly walked towards the Archigos Ceremony Keeper. The old woman stood tall and proud, her long gray hair was braided and snaked around the floor at her feet. Her four young apprentices stood on either side of her, watching their empress approach. Rhiannon followed a path of bright orange flower petals past thousands of guests and Archigos alike.

The hall was immense and ran the whole length of the palace. Sunlight from windows that stretched from floor to the soaring ceiling lit the room. Thick brightly colored carpets were brought in and laid on the floor where the audience sat. The room was filled with loud chanting and warrioress' pounded on drums and shook tambourines. Kyia walked in front of Rhiannon, sprinkling water taken directly from the roots of the Tree of Eternal Spring, while Shankee walked behind dropping feathers from sparrows. Both actions symbolized fertility and good fortune.

Rhiannon's onyx hair had grown enough to be braided into tiny strands and pinned up into loops. Gems were woven into her hair and winked in the sunlight. A circlet of gold and amethyst wrapped around her head in signification of power and war. She wore a tight strapless short blouse called a choli. It was low cut to show the bright red diamond and blue scrolling tattoos that pronounced her an Archigos Warrioress and Empress. The choli was the color of rubies and was heavily beaded and studded with diamonds. It came up just below her breasts and was hemmed with golden tassels. An oval-shaped amethyst was placed in her navel, and a long skirt, called a lehanga, hung around her hips. Tiny bells hung from the hem of the lehanga and quietly chimed as she walked. A thick chain of gold wrapped around her waist and a heart-shaped, deep purple amethyst hung down from the chain to rest at the junction of the legs. Amethyst was said to be given to the Archigos by Sin'trah the goddess of luck and fertility and was used in many ceremonies to assure the quick birth of an heir and luck in a peaceful rule. The beaded ruby colored lehanga split open at the thigh to expose her legs and trailed upon the floor behind her. Chains of gold were wrapped around both ankles, and diamond rings were fitted to her toes.

Finally, the chanting and music stopped as she reached

the old woman and was handed a jeweled goblet of sacred tea which she quickly drank. The Ceremony Keeper took a long, thin pipe and drew in until her lungs were full then slowly blew the smoke into Rhiannon's face. The old woman then handed the pipe to one of her apprentices and began to chant, softly at first, but growing in intensity and volume. Still chanting, she dipped her old, withered hands into a jar of water taken from the Tree of Eternal Spring and placed her hands at Rhiannon's temples, then slowly went down her body to her breasts, her belly and finally over her pubic bone.

The Ceremony Keeper stopped chanting and stood erect, looking deeply into Rhiannon's eyes. She bellowed a few sentences in ancient Venn, and then Rhiannon recited them back. The old woman instructed Rhiannon to kneel, then she turned and took the Necklace of Verna as it rested upon a pillow. She carefully placed the necklace around Rhiannon's neck and said a few words. Then she turned to another of her apprentices and took the crown of Ventra and finally placed it upon the head of the new Empress of Ventra.

The crowd erupted in great cheering and applause for it had been a long time since there had a Fiann, most of the people—guests and warriors alike—had never witnessed one. Rhiannon turned to her warriors and guests and could not help but smile. She thought of all that they had accomplished and how far she had come. She thought of a distant life on a Montana ranch, the day she stepped through the Tree of Jur, the day she met Flath, and the first time she saw Màrrach. She thought of those she lost: Tim and her father and even her Gypsy King, Flath Basilias of Sona Tuath.

The ceremony now over, the old woman and her many times over granddaughters left the hall. Oread began serving drinks and food, and the hall became loud with talking and laughter. Rhiannon walked over and sat on the throne, grateful the Fiann Ceremony was now over, and the celebration had begun.

"Do you see him?" Rhiannon scanned the crowd.

"I'll tell you if I see him," Kyia answered as she walked up to Rhiannon. "If he has come at all."

Rhiannon turned to her cousin. "You don't think he's here?"

She shrugged. "Perhaps."

Rhiannon sat back and sighed. "Maybe he didn't come," she admitted.

Kyia placed her hand on Rhiannon's shoulder but did not speak. Rhiannon looked over at the windows and saw the gray smoke from the sacrifices that were being offered throughout the day. To keep them all appeased, every god and goddess was being offered something today. "My mother sat on this very throne after she became empress," she finally said.

Kyia smiled at her. "Your lineage is very long, Rhiannon, and very royal."

"So is yours!" she challenged.

"Yes, but I was born of the wrong mother."

"Wrong? Right? None of it matters it's just who comes out with the birthmark. It could have been you just as easily as it was me."

Kyia laughed. "I don't believe that."

"Why not? You're certainly smarter than me, and infinitely more patient," Rhiannon argued.

"Anyone who takes one look at you, Rhiannon, can discern the difference between a mere woman, and an empress," Shih 'Ni climbed the stairs and sat down next to her in the gaddi, a smaller throne that was usually reserved for the tjaty (the empress' mate). He took her hand and tenderly kissed it.

"I'm not sure that I agree with you, but thank you for the compliment anyway." She smiled at him. "It was a compliment, wasn't it?" She looked at him sideways.

"Most assuredly, my Empress." He held on to her hand. "You are more beautiful now, at this moment, than any woman could ever hope to be," he said softly, looking into her eyes.

"Oh brother, here it comes," Kyia said and rolled her eyes.

"Ha! You're such a smooth talker!" she laughed and brushed him off as she took her hand from his grip.

He leaned in closer to her, "Any man who can resist a woman like you is naught but a soulless fool," he whispered and kissed her cheek.

She leaned back and looked at him in shock. "You have had too much to drink, Master Shih 'Ni," she said angrily and wondered what prompted him to act in such an uncharacteristic way. Shih 'Ni was nothing if not serious and proud. This shameless display of affection was not the Shih 'Ni she knew.

Suddenly, out of the noisy din, she heard a familiar voice

call her name. Her heart slammed in her chest, and she held her breath as Flath walked up to her. He looked haggard and much too thin. His skin was pale and lacked the healthy, sun-kissed glow it had when she saw him last, a half a year ago.

She stood, slowly descended the stairs and walked over to him.

"I was afraid you wouldn't come," she whispered, not taking her eyes off his face which had a hollow, sad expression.

"There is a wasting disease in Sona Tuath, and many have taken ill and died. I did not think it was the most opportune time to leave, but Teo insisted." His words were clipped and seemed forced.

"I'm so sorry, Flath. I didn't know there was illness in Sona Tuath. I'll get Tess to ready medicines to take back with you."

"Nay, Yellow Island has sent a shipment of medicines and physicians."

She nodded. "Yellow Island has lent a lot of help to Sona Tuath this past winter. I've heard they sent in some of their soldiers until you can build up your own army."

"Aye, King Umar has been generous," he swallowed hard.

"He must be feeling guilty. But it's much better to have them as an ally, huh?" A wide smile crossed Rhiannon's face. Flath's morbid expression did not change.

She studied his face and thought that he might be ill as well. "Are you feeling alright, Flath?" Her brow furrowed in concern.

"Aye," he replied shortly.

She changed the subject. "We have been working hard in Beaynid too. I'm sure you've noticed the change. Things seem to be working out just like I said they would," she said, happily.

"Aye, I have noticed, and I thank you graciously for your generosity towards Beaynid. We would have suffered, and many would have probably died off this winter had it not been for your help," he said, nervously looking around. "Rhiannon, there is something I must tell you." He reached out and touched her face tenderly.

"Alright, tell me," she coaxed, smiling brightly. Her smile faded when he looked like he was incapable of speaking further. "Are you sure you're not ill, Flath?" she asked. "You look tired." She put her arms around him suddenly very concerned for his health.

Rhiannon, I—."

"My lord, will you not introduce me to the empress, now? I have waited long enough." A shrill, almost childish voice called from Rhiannon's elbow.

Rhiannon let go of Flath and looked down at the petite, young woman. She looked up at Rhiannon with a shockingly venomous smile on her thin, pale lips. Small, delicate hands where exaggeratingly placed on top of a belly that had begun to swell. Rhiannon narrowed her eyes; she looked vaguely familiar. Suddenly a wave of nausea washed over Rhiannon as she looked back at Flath who had gone white.

"Rhiannon, uh," he choked. "Rhiannon, this is Queen

Jocelyn...of Beaynid," he swallowed audibly as sweat trickled down his brow.

Rhiannon looked back down at the young woman who resembled a plump mouse and then back up at Flath. "Q—queen?" she stuttered and started to tremble. "You took a wife?" she whispered, accusingly.

"Will you not wish us well on the birth of our child, the heir to the throne of Beaynid, Empress Kossi?" The woman's poisonous voice echoed in Rhiannon's ears. Rhiannon slowly backed away, but her heels hit the step of the dais. She was trapped and could not move. The hall started to spin; she found it difficult to breathe. All she could think of was getting out of the hall and away from Màrrach.

She bolted for the door then tripped and fell hard onto the cold floor. Her crown clanked on the marble and then quickly rolled out of sight. She jumped to her feet and ran out of the hall, a silver she-wolf silently followed.

Shih 'Ni was standing on the dais and watched the young woman walk up. He had seen the Seun enter earlier. His attempts to distract Rhiannon had failed. He slowly descended the stairs and stood near enough to Rhiannon to offer help if she wanted it—or to pull her off the girl—whatever the situation demanded. When he saw her backing up he knew she was going to run and then Rhiannon was gone in a flurry of scarlet colored skirts leaving a trail of surprised gasps behind her.

Shih 'Ni quickly walked up to Flath. "Why didn't you just stay in Sona Tuath?" he demanded angrily. "Why did you have to ridicule her so publicly with your unfaithfulness on this special day?" he demanded, in Ska.

A swarm of guests started to gather around; kings and queens and lords and ladies of different lands along with rich merchants and politicians, all of whom traded with Ventra. The hall that was once busy with cheerful conversation and merry music was now silent. King Umar pushed past whispering onlookers and stood next to his daughter.

"I—," Flath started. "I never meant to hurt her," he offered weakly.

"You put this viper, heavy with your spawn, on display as if to mock her! How did you think she would react?" Shih 'Ni shouted angrily. Jocelyn gasped and hid behind her husband, timidly peeking out around his elbow.

Flath clenched his fists. "I love her!" he howled. The crowd gasped, and low murmurs filled the hall.

"Is this how Seun men demonstrate their love for a woman, by mating with another?" Shih 'Ni shouted for all to hear as he threw his arms dramatically in the air.

"I will go to her and explain the situation!" Flath ripped his arm out of Jocelyn's jealous grip and started after Rhiannon.

Shih 'Ni quickly jumped in front of him. "You've done enough," he said and turned to leave. The crowd parted as he quickly left the room and ran from the palace.

CHAPTER TWENTY-ONE

"It is a naïve misconception that the male Archigos Warrior is a weak man, either mentally or physically. Because theirs is a matriarchal society, it is a popular belief that the men of Ventra are emasculate, submissive or obedient. Nothing can be farther from the truth.
The male Archigos Warrior is one of the most formidable, dangerous forces that one may encounter. Your only hope of survival is that he is on your side in a fight. He is quick of wit and body, and though always in subjection to his empress, is head-strong and independent. One cannot look at an Archigos Warrior and not realize his might, virility, and mystique."
—*Ventra, Land of Ice and Warriors; G. P. Love*

A huge, glowing disk floated high in the bitterly cold night sky. He knew where she had gone—he was not concerned that he would not find her. He felt that he knew her better than he knew himself.

Shih 'Ni silently slipped through the trees like the most dangerous of predators, quickly moving deeper into the densest part of the forest. The snow impeded his progress, but he pushed on with a frantic urgency he could not fully understand. The moon did its best to inject cool beams of light through thin conifer needles, and the snow-covered forest floor seemed to glow in the cold light. He needed no light, however. He knew the forest like he knew his own body. Snow quietly crunched under his feet as he moved further into the pines.

She was there, lying on the lush, soft grass beneath the Tree of Eternal Spring where snow dare not enter. Ancient pine trees ringed the serene willow as if to offer shelter and protection from the harshness of the forest. An opening in the tree cover allowed bright, luminous moonlight to spill down upon Rhiannon and the tree. Luna sat quietly near Rhiannon, her fluffy tail wagging in acknowledgment of his presence. Rhiannon's body shook with quiet sobs, her tears bathing the soft grass under the willow.

After watching her for a moment, he moved into the clearing and quietly sat next to her. Her dark hair had fallen, and a sprinkling of rubies around her head winked in the moonlight. Ropes of gold encircling her waist shimmered like a sunset. Torn skirts were bunched up around naked thighs. Shih 'Ni reached over and took her into his arms.

"I'm such a fool," she cried as she buried her face in his neck and his long, black hair. He said nothing, just gently stroked her hair. Her tears were wet and warm against his neck. He took a deep breath and suddenly felt guilty. He had long wished for this, but now seeing her so devastated he knew he had been wrong. He cursed Flath and then himself. "How could I have been so blind?" she finally asked. "I'm so stupid."

"He is a selfish, disloyal man," Shih 'Ni breathed into her hair.

"I thought he loved me," she whispered.

Shih 'Ni was silent. He did not understand why Flath had taken that runt of a girl to wife, but he did know Flath still loved Rhiannon—he saw it in the Seun's eyes and heard it in his desperate pleas to go after her. She slowly sat up and looked at Shih 'Ni. Her face was wet and shiny. Thin slivers of hair were stuck to her face, and tiny bits of grass littered her hair. He tenderly took her face in his hands. "My beautiful, perfect Rhiannon," he sighed. "The man is a fool and does not deserve you."

"But I love him!" she cried, the tears started to stream down her cheeks again.

"It will pass in time," he said softly.

"No," she shook her head in his hands.

"It will. I promise."

"But we were meant to be together," she cried, "It was him that I dreamed of, Shih 'Ni!"

He took her hands in his and took a deep breath. "You can't control the actions of another. He's chosen someone else, and there's nothing you can do to change it now."

"This is not how it's supposed to be." A single tear hanging from her chin shivered then fell splattering on Shih' Ni's fingers. "We were supposed to be together," she murmured.

"Sometimes things don't work out the way they're supposed to, Rhiannon." Shih 'Ni brushed the hair from her face. "You must make your own destiny."

Her eyes turned downward. "Tim has died, my father is gone, and now I have lost Flath. I have no one," she whispered so softly.

A sharp pain stabbed at his heart. "You have me!" he blurted.

She looked back up at him. "I'm sorry Shih 'Ni, I misspoke—I know you'll always be here for me." She smiled warmly at him. "I'm so grateful for your friendship. You mean more to me than you could possibly know."

"I want more than your friendship," he stated in a low, even tone. She was silent. "You've known for a long while that my feelings for you run very deep. I want much more than mere friendship, Rhiannon." When she did not speak, he went on. "Do you remember last year, right here under this tree, I first made my feelings known to you?"

"Shih 'Ni—" she started.

"No," he stopped her. "Please listen to me," he implored. "I know you love the Seun. I know you were hoping for a match, but things have changed. He has taken another mate, and she now carries his child." Tears welled in Rhiannon's eyes and fell in obscenely large drops from her jaw. She said nothing but kept looking at Shih 'Ni.

"Maybe you were supposed to be with the Seun. But now, unless you are content to be his mistress, that can't be. You have been planning and working so hard for the survival of Beaynid, and now it's time to work on Ventra's future. Your future." A slight breeze started to flow through the trees, rustling sleeping leaves.

"Are you going to tell me it's time to give Ventra an heir?" Her voice was soft; hopeless.

"I will not—you are Ventra's empress—you know what she needs."

Rhiannon looked over at Luna who had crawled up into

a fluffy ball, her winter coat thick and shiny, and had fallen asleep. She sighed and looked back up at Shih 'Ni. "She needs an heir," she whispered. "She needs a tjaty to help her empress rule," she conceded.

"I love you, Rhiannon. I have loved you since we were children. If you let me, I will make you forget Flath. I will help you rule Ventra and give her an heir."

As if the forest herself were answering for Rhiannon, the breeze grew into an unusually warm, sweet wind as it softly whistled through the rigid branches of the pine trees and ruffled the long, green ribbons of the willow. He studied her face, so pale in the moonlight. The desperate grief had passed, but a mellow pain still existed in the depths of her dark eyes. "It wouldn't be fair to you," she finally said. "I will always love Flath." Her words were dripping with sorrow.

"Not forever, Rhiannon. I will make his memory fade."

Her lips formed a sad smile. "You are a good man, Shih 'Ni. Would you enter into a marriage with a woman who loved another?"

He held his strong chin up high and looked into her eyes. "I would," he stated without hesitation. Rhiannon sighed and stared into the darkness of the forest as if she were watching something. She nodded her head slightly and then looked back up at Shih 'Ni. She inched forward and tenderly kissed his lips—Shih 'Ni could see that she had made her decision.

"You were born to be a tjaty, Shih 'Ni. If you accept me —knowing I love another, then you'll be Ventra's new tjaty." Her expression was as sharp as the tip of her sword, her eyes weary and darkened by defeat.

Shih 'Ni smiled and gently kissed the back of her hand. "You will not be sorry for your decision, Rhiannon." He gently touched her chest at the resting place of her heart. "All wounds will heal in time, my Empress."

Rhiannon looked out the large window of her bedchamber. Long, heavily embroidered drapes ruffled in the unseasonably warm breeze. Most of the snow had melted leaving only patches of whiteness under the still bitter shadows of trees.

In the morning light Shih 'Ni and Rhiannon had returned to Màrrach. Most of the guests had stayed, and so they had made the announcement that Empress Kossi had selected a mate and the Nikah would follow within the next few days. Not wanting to miss any more scandal, almost everyone stayed. Gossip spread through Màrrach like poison. Rhiannon cared not.

Kyia had told her that Jocelyn and King Umar had left Màrrach amid a torrent of angry howls that night. She did not care, for she never considered Yellow Island an ally. His army did not pose a threat to Ventra, and they certainly did not depend on Yellow Island for their traded goods.

Rhiannon assumed Flath had accompanied his pregnant wife back to Sona Tuath and she sighed heavily as she watched guests meander around the grounds outside her window taking advantage of a warm day in the middle of winter. Her head pounded as she gently rubbed at tender temples. Shankee told her Shih 'Ni had insulted Jocelyn quite nicely. And Rhiannon could not help but laugh at that. She looked down at Poeso who lay on Rhiannon's grand bed contentedly nursing her cubs. A knock rumbled at her chamber door. "Come in!" Rhiannon called, knowing it would be Kyia.

"It's almost time," Kyia said softly as she walked up to Rhiannon.

"I'll be glad when this is all over."

Two girls rolled in a tub of water, not only from the Tree of Eternal Spring but also waters from an ancient pool of water from deep inside the mines of Del Nort. The powder of finely crushed herbs and gems were added to the water. Rhiannon disrobed and climbed into the tub of steaming water. The Ceremony Keepers' apprentices washed Rhiannon in a slow, deliberate manner, keeping silent, their dark heads bowed at their work. Shih 'Ni was going through the same treatment in his chambers with the other two apprentices.

Finally, after the ceremonial bath was completed and the negative and evil spirits were washed away, Rhiannon climbed from the tub and dried off.

She still was not entirely sure about all the beliefs of the Archigos, even after what happened the night of her Fiann. She had not been raised as a religious person, so she found it hard to have faith in all the Archigos gods and goddesses but, as their empress, she had to try. She would be glad when all these ceremonies were past her, and she could go back to living her life.

The girls dressed Rhiannon and carefully brushed the strands of her sleek, black hair. They weaved in flowers said to be sacred and blessed by many gods and goddesses, and attached soft sparrow feathers and tiny claws from female rabbits. The Royal Crown of Ventra was placed on Rhiannon's head, and many ropes of green gems and pearls were wrapped around her arms. Bands of red and pink stones were strung across her forehead. The Necklace of Verna and the Emissary Beads still hung around her neck. The girls attached more ropes of gold and gems to Rhiannon's wrists and ankles honoring the never-ending list of gods and goddesses—Shih 'Ni would wear the same bracelets and anklets.

Finally, they rubbed a paste made of herbs and the water from the Tree of Eternal Spring, across her cheeks and forehead. The herbs were for the healthy birth of children. The herbs Shih 'Ni would have pasted across his face were for sexual desire and potency.

"Do you think you're doing the right thing?" Kyia asked after the girls had finally left.

Rhiannon looked at Kyia sharply, but then softened her face and just shrugged. "It's for the good of Ventra." Rhiannon strolled to a window and looked towards the jagged teeth of the Vel 'Kur Mountains. "I'll be thirty-three years old this year, and while I'm hardly old, I'm not getting any younger. I could get sick and die, or get injured, or a hundred other things could happen to me. Ventra needs her heir." Kyia walked over to her and took Rhiannon's hands. "There's something you want to say, isn't there?"

"I'm not sure if you are making the right decision Rhiannon."

"You don't think Shih 'Ni will be a good husband?"

"Shih 'Ni is a good man, he'll make a fine tjaty, but you don't love him."

Rhiannon sighed and was quiet for a long while, but finally spoke. "I do love Shih 'Ni and I always will." She took a long, sad breath. "But not the way a wife should love a husband." She shook her head.

Kyia looked down at her feet. "You need to consider the dreams."

"The dreams were wrong."

Kyia looked up again. "The dreams are never wrong. They called to your parents and our grandparents. They're how the gods and goddess let us know which path to take."

Rhiannon could not help but snort, but it would have been sacrilege to question the will of the gods, especially as an empress. "They didn't see which path Flath would take, I guess."

"Maybe it's not over between you."

"I'd say it's pretty much over...he's married to someone else."

Flath loves you, you know." Rhiannon was surprised that Kyia used his name when she always used the term Seun or gypsy.

"I thought he did," she said quietly.

"Will you not wait for him then?"

"I will not!" Rhiannon replied sharply and let go of Kyia's hands.

"Is it your pride that prevents you from going to him, or do you wish to get even with him?"

Rhiannon put her head back and laughed. "What should I do, wait for him to get rid of his queen? What kind of man would put aside a woman he vowed to love and his child?"

"Psh! From what I saw it was merely a business arrangement between Beaynid and Yellow Island, and I doubt he vowed to love her."

"That's even worse! He bought a woman like he would cattle or a measure of grain, then?" Rhiannon was growing angry at Flath; her eyes flared with indignation.

"This might be good for Ventra, but it will be bad for you," she hesitated. "And, in the end, for Shih 'Ni."

"Shih 'Ni knows I love Flath and he still agreed to marry me."

Kyia shook her head angrily. "You're being stubborn, and I have a strong feeling that this will end badly—especially for Shih 'Ni!" Kyia turned and quickly left the room.

Rhiannon sighed and walked out onto her large marble balcony. The air was cool but not as bitter as it should have been. Spitefully she looked towards the purple mountain range that divided Beaynid and Ventra. She hoped that on their long journey home Jocelyn would fall off the highest peak and die amid the spikes of sharp rocks that would end her fall—then she felt immensely guilty. She most likely came by ship anyway since the mountain trail was still impassable this time of the year. She wondered why Flath had made the swift decision to marry. By the look of

Jocelyn's belly, he must have married the minute Rhiannon had left him in Sona Tuath.

Tears welled in her eyes and poetically fell from damp lashes. "How could you betray me like this?" she bitterly asked, as a soft breeze started blowing from the south. She closed her eyes and pictured his face in her mind. She tried to picture him as he was when he had found her in Beaynid, but all her mind would conjure was the pale, sunken image of a broken man that stood before her at the Fiann Celebration.

Suddenly she was aware of voices. At first so faint that she thought it might be the wind, but when she listened harder, she could tell they were coming from inside. When she walked into her bedchamber, the voices became insistent, though not raised. She approached the large doors that separated her bedchamber from a larger room that was used as her living quarters. It was slightly ajar allowing the voices to be heard.

She heard Flath's voice, and her heart began to pound wildly in her chest. She resisted the overwhelming urge to open the door and put her ear closer to hear what was being said. She recognized the second voice right away.

"Please, I must see her," Flath implored.

"You may not!" Shih 'Ni was unyielding.

"I must explain myself."

"She has seen enough to know that you have thrown her aside—your pregnant queen is proof of that!"

"I need to tell her that I made a tremendous mistake." Rhiannon took in a sharp breath and held it. Blood was pounding in her ears so loudly as to almost drown out the voices, so she moved closer.

"It's too late, Seun," Shih 'Ni countered. "She has chosen who will be her mate."

"I am going to send Jocelyn away after the birth of her child and have the marriage annulled." Flath's voice was full of emotion. Rhiannon's tears fell freely, splattering on the marble floor.

"So, you expect the empress to patiently wait for you to dispose of your wife and child and shame herself and Ventra?" Shih 'Ni's voice rose slightly. "You have cut her to the bone, Seun. Go home to your queen and forget about Rhiannon. It's time that Ventra leaves off from the uncertainty of a chance union between our lands. You have chosen, and now, so has she."

Rhiannon moved away from the door as if it were on fire. She backed up so quickly she ran into a stool and fell hard upon her back. Tears drenched her face as she scrambled to get up to her feet and then ran back out onto the balcony.

When Kyia appeared half of an hour later, Rhiannon was fully composed as she stared blankly out into the cool afternoon sky.

"I'm sorry, Rhiannon," she said softly.

Rhiannon turned and took Kyia's hand. "You told me how you feel. Don't ever be sorry for that. Who knows, you may be right." Rhiannon shrugged.

"Bes will bless you and Ventra with luck and Ceres will bless your union with an heir." Kyia smiled. "I worry too much." She made a sound that could have been a small laugh. "We must go now. They're ready for the Nikah to begin."

Rhiannon adjusted the skirt of her bright, cerulean blue lehanga and tried to smile. "Well, I guess I have a ceremony to attend." As she left her bedchamber and moved across the huge room of her living quarters Shih 'Ni suddenly appeared at her side.

"What are you doing here?" Kyia asked annoyed. "You should be downstairs!"

"I must talk to you, Rhiannon." He took her by the arm preventing her from continuing. "Alone," he said to Kyia.

"Well, hurry Shih 'Ni, everyone's waiting." Kyia shook her head and walked out the door to the hall.

"Changed your mind?" Rhiannon joked. Shih 'Ni gave her a severe look. "What is it Shih 'Ni," she prodded when he did not speak.

"I must tell you something before we're joined."

"Okay…" Rhiannon lifted her eyebrows and opened her palms in a prodding gesture.

Shih 'Ni took a deep breath then finally started to speak. "The Seun tried to see you earlier. I prevented him."

Rhiannon looked at him blankly. She was sure that he would not tell her of the incident. Finally, a humorless laugh slipped past her lips. "If he had truly wanted to see me I doubt that even you, Shih 'Ni, could have prevented him." Shih 'Ni raised an eyebrow and crossed thick arms across his chest but did not argue. "So, he didn't leave with this wife then?" she asked nonchalantly. Shih 'Ni shook his head. "Well, what did he want?" she asked.

"He says he will send the woman away as soon as the

child is born and have the marriage annulled," Shih 'Ni recited quickly, as if not to lose his courage.

Rhiannon raised her chin in defiance. "And I suppose he wishes I wait for him?" she asked angrily.

"Yes."

She snapped her head back and laughed aloud resounding sound that echoed across the opulent marble room. "Then I guess he's a fool!" she stated with bitterness. Shih 'Ni's shoulders visibly lowered, and she heard him expel a breath in relief. She moved closer to him, wrapped her arms around his waist and laid her head on his chest. She listened to his heartbeat—so strong and insistent.

"Did you think I would cast you aside so easily?" she asked in a quiet voice.

"He still loves you." Rhiannon felt Shih 'Ni's warm breath on her cheek.

"That he may, however, he will have to live with his choice," she said quietly.

Finally, there was a knock at the door, and Kyia entered. "We have people waiting if you two don't mind." Shih 'Ni kissed her cheek and then quickly left the room. Rhiannon looked back to the door of her bedchamber where, not even an hour earlier, Flath stood. She sighed and looked back at Kyia. "Ventra awaits, my Empress."

CHAPTER TWENTY-TWO

The time is finally right for her to choose a mate
An heir, the empress, must produce before it is too late
Baobh is after our empress; her hatred is too much to sate

Ventra's most powerful are lined up in a row
All vying for a chance for his seed to sow
The heir must come, and it cannot be slow

The Nikah is performed, and now it is done
The tjaty is on the throne under the setting sun
Now we must all be patient for the heir to come
— An Heir for Ventra; Kyia Kossi

R hiannon walked out onto the smooth sandstone steps leading from the palace. A haunting, deep cadence of drums and harsh chanting filled the valley but now came to a sudden stop. Struck with awe at the crowd assembled before her she slowly began to descend the steps. The girls that had attended her earlier dutifully walked behind her. Her warriors and guests stood silently before her as she followed a path clearly marked with white flower petals. Ahead of her were a handful of her most powerful warriors, standing in a row. It was customary for the empress to pick a mate from these warriors. They stood tall and straight under the bright afternoon sun—their chests were bare to show the tattoos of their rank and importance. They wore nothing but deep green loincloths.

Mates, however, were almost always already chosen by that point but the Archigos—determined to hold on to the Old Ways—kept the ancient custom. The guests stood in amazement at the ceremony, so thick with ritual. Young girls and old women alike giggled as they watched the powerful warriors awaiting their empress.

Finally, Rhiannon reached the warriors and stopped before Shih 'Ni. She smiled up at him, but his face remained serious. Slowly she took out a length of gold rope with an idol of Dionysus attached (an Archigos Goddess) and carefully tied the golden chain around his waist. Then Shih 'Ni bent and tied around her waist the birthed umbilical cord that once connected she and her mother in the womb. Hanging from one of the ends of the cord was the golden image of Baubo—yet another goddess of fertility. This idol had the body of a woman, but the head and tail of a rabbit.

She took Shih 'Ni's hand, and the Ceremony Keeper's apprentices sprinkled sparrow feathers and water from the Tree of Eternal Spring on the path before them as they walked together. They approached great stone bowls that were used in sacrifices, and Rhiannon grabbed a burning torch from a warrioress standing near the huge altar. Together Shih 'Ni and Rhiannon went down the line of altars lighting each offering ablaze honoring the many gods and goddesses of Ventra, many of which Rhiannon still did not know.

As the last of the offerings went up in large golden tongues of fire, a man stepped out of the crowd in front of Rhiannon. Gasps and murmuring spread through the people. Rhiannon stopped short, and she felt Shih 'Ni's hand tightened around hers. Flath walked up to them and stood, painfully looking into Rhiannon's eyes.

"You cannot do this without hearing me out," he finally said

"I don't wish to hear what you have to say." Rhiannon's heart began to race, and the air seemed too heavy. She panicked and wanted to run away.

"I have made a mistake, Rhiannon. A mistake that I will make right." Rhiannon saw the agony in his mismatched eyes. His face was so pale and etched with sorrow.

"How can you make right a betrayal so vast and a wound so deep that it has threatened to swallow me whole?" She shook her head as tears ran down her cheeks and answered for him. "You can't", she whispered.

"I love you, Rhiannon," he beseeched.

She began to quake and Shih 'Ni moved closer to her. Her throat tightened when she looked up at Shih 'Ni and saw him looking at her with such pure, poignant emotion that it was something of such grotesque beauty. She knew now that he would offer no objection but waited, as did Flath, for her answer.

She took a deep breath and turned to Flath. "You have made your choice and now, so have I." She echoed the words Shih 'Ni had said a short time earlier.

"Rhiannon, I never meant to hurt you, you must believe me."

"I don't care what you meant to do." She wiped a tear from her cheek, smudging the herbal paste across her hand. His clothes were simple, not the garb of a king. The golden panther head around his neck and the slithering serpent in his ear both gleamed in the sunlight. She ached so badly to hold him and wash away his pain. She craved his closeness, and at that moment, she wanted nothing more than to feel his touch. His stare was intense and intimate, and she felt as though she were melting. He was close to breaking; she could see that, but she was just as close.

"Go back to your queen and leave me be," she said bitterly and walked past Flath to the marble altar where the ceremony would continue. Her steps were purposeful but filled with such pain she could not see where she was going. Shih 'Ni guided her closer to the old woman who waited to make them man and wife. Shih 'Ni said nothing, for what verbal comfort could he offer? In her mind's eye, she could see Flath staring after them, tears running down hollow cheeks, then turning to leave her...forever.

The rest of the Nikah went by in almost a blur. The Ceremony Keeper took deep draws from her ever-present pipe and blew the blue smoke into their faces. She chanted and sprinkled water on them and burnt incense. Finally, she took an ornate dagger and carefully slit a line in their left palms. Rhiannon could see the small white scar that she had made when she and Tim became sister and brother.

The old woman grabbed a chalice and took some blood from both she and Shih 'Ni. She swirled it around and sprinkled some powdered herbs into the red-black liquid. She handed the cup to Rhiannon who brought the blood up and wet her lips. The tangy, copper taste almost made her gag, but she repressed it. She handed the cup to Shih 'Ni who did the same. The Ceremony Keeper took the chalice back and stuck her withered, bent thumb into the blood. She sang a soft song which Rhiannon did not know and then carefully smudged the blood mixture onto Rhiannon's and Shih 'Ni's foreheads and kissed their hands. Slowly she got to her knees, with the help of her apprentices, and bowed deeply to them. Rhiannon heard her warriors start to chant and the drums began to beat out into the valley again—it was then she knew it was finally over.

She turned to face her warriors and guests, half expecting to see Flath, but she did not. Shih 'Ni squeezed her hand, and she looked up at him. He smiled at her with a kind and vulnerable expression that she had never seen on his face before and she could not help but smile back. "You are tjaty now," she whispered, and he kissed her lips.

The festivities afterward seemed to drag on, in fact, they were still going on downstairs and would continue for days. Rhiannon sat on her balcony again as she watched a man quickly walking towards the stables. He would not be slowed, though his steps were slightly uneven from an old injury. She watched as his horse was brought to him and he mounted the beast with swiftness and anger. Then she watched him ride away without even a backward glance.

From behind her, she could hear her husband's steps then felt Shih 'Ni's warm hand on her shoulder. The sun had set, and the land was rapidly being swallowed by a cold night. Rhiannon was exhausted. He sat down beside her, and she could feel him studying her.

She finally turned to him and smiled. The torches had been lit, and now their erratic light danced in Shih 'Ni's black eyes. Shadows flickered across his long, narrow nose and high cheekbones causing his dark skin to take on the red hue of fire.

Rhiannon took a deep breath. "Shih 'Ni, I knew Flath had tried to see me even before you told me." Shih 'Ni's brows rose in question, but he did not speak. "The door was slightly open, and I heard you two talking..." her voice trailed off.

"Why didn't you go to him?" he asked quietly.

"I don't know," she replied.

"Are you sorry now?"

She smiled and kissed his cheek. "No, my tjaty, I am not."

"Do you feel you've made the right choice then, instead of waiting for the Seun?"

"I have made the right choice, Shih 'Ni." He silently nodded and looked out over the land that was now in almost complete darkness.

"I do not expect you to love me the way you love him," he said quietly. Rhiannon felt the sting of pain in her heart for both Flath and Shih 'Ni. How had things got so complicated? She wanted to say something to him, but no words came to mind, so she took his hand in hers and said nothing, for she knew he was right.

Flath might have left Màrrach and Ventra behind, but

she knew that not even time or space could erase the love that still smoldered within her. His touch still burned her skin as if she were on fire. His memory had branded her for an eternity—for that, she was sure. The night was growing deeper, and she felt as though she were drowning in it. She felt so alone as if she were the only one in the world. With every beat of her heart, a nagging ache moved through her body and mind—a sickness for which there was no cure.

Ventra would have her heir, the warriors of Màrrach would have their tjaty—but Rhiannon would find no relief.

EPILOGUE

The desert was awash in white heat as the sun sailed above in a deep blue sky. It was not yet summer across Katlom Desert, but the oppressive heat drove all within its reach to seek cover. Transparent waves danced off great white dunes that rose out of the desert sand like the humps of a sea serpent and then disappeared off into the distance.

The young woman turned from the harshness of the desert and walked out onto the lush, soft grass that lined the banks of an underground river that bubbled up from the depths of the earth and fed the large Sangron Oasis. She sat under the deep shade of a palm tree swaying in the afternoon breeze. Dipping a slender hand under the blue waters, she felt the cool, rejuvenating powers of the river. A black snake slithered out from under a thick green bush and made its way to the river where it drank to its full. Gulls that had gotten lost in the violent winds of a long-forgotten ocean storm now hovered over a small lake in the center of the oasis ready to capture a neglectful fish.

Her long curly hair, not black as it once was, but white as mid-winter snow, ran down her back and pooled onto the grass. She took her hand from the water and ran her wet fingers over the jagged scar across her chest—a wound that had almost taken her life. Her skin, once dark and flawless, was much too pale now.

She had lost everything but her life, and during her long months of recovery, she did not even cherish that. She remembered the cruel storm as it mocked her and threw her into the frigid waters of the red ocean. She recalled how the salty water burned her eyes, flooded her nose and rushed down her throat. She took a deep breath lost in the memory of how it felt to have water filling her lungs. She was so afraid and completely helpless as she slipped beneath the sea. Her lungs burned as if they were on fire and almost burst from her chest. Finally, the sweet darkness had taken her, and she felt neither pain nor cold anymore.

She watched him now as he strolled from the large sand colored, smooth-walled dwelling. He walked up to her with careful, long strides and she thought back to when she finally awoke, weeks after she had drowned in the Carnaid Sea. Her eyes were burned by poisoned salt and blood water, and she could only make out the shape of his face but knew his voice immediately.

He had brought her here, to the Sangron Oasis in the middle of the Katlom Desert in the southernmost region of Beaynid. Now, eight languishing months later, she was fully recovered, her eyesight as keen as ever. She had been but a breath away from the silence of death when Karha Rull pulled her from the violent red waters of the Carnaid Sea. But just why Lord Rull had saved her, she did not know. She was useless to him once she had lost Sona Tuath.

He sat down next to her and looked out over the green oasis. She turned to him and watched his brown hair flutter in the wind. His beard was neatly trimmed, and his clothes were fastidiously clean and neat, ne'er a wrinkle could be seen. His black boots shined in the hot sun as he stretched out on the cool grass. He looked over and watched her though he said nothing.

She imagined she could see herself from his green eyes —so different from the woman she had been. Defeat and sorrow lay heavily upon her so that even death seemed favorable. Not only on the inside had she changed, but her appearance had morphed as well. Her hair and dark eyes were bleached white, her skin even paler than a Seun's! Maybe it was the harsh, cold waters that almost took her life, or perhaps it was the devastation of losing all: her kingdom was gone, her mate laid waste, and even her tiny son was taken from her. The Empress of Ventra had robbed her of everything!

The agony of living with such flesh-piercing loss had finally consumed her spirit and fire and left her with a putrid rotting numbness that was always with her. Something neither here nor there, almost like a whisper on the wind that your thoughts only vaguely heard. Her life was over, and she was just waiting for death. Just how that death would come she did not know nor care; she just waited.

"My Sgàth has brought word of your son," Karha said.

"What news has he brought?"

"He is well in Ghroc; growing quickly." She looked past him to a growing thunderstorm on the horizon. "I can have him brought here," he offered.

She looked at him sharply. "You would bring him here

to die in this desert?" She shook her head. "No, he is better off where he is."

"We are hardly dying here, Baobh."

"I am already dead," she whispered.

"You will live again. The prophecy has gone unfulfilled."

She looked at him again. "I am as good as dead; the prophecy has been fulfilled."

"You are living and breathing right before me!" Karha dramatically spread out his long arms. "The empress has not caused your death."

"Of what good is my body when I have nothing inside?"

He reached out and grasped her arm. "We have made an alliance once before, you and I. We will make one again."

She ripped her arm from his grip. "We will make no agreements, for I have nothing you want." She looked at him sharply. Karha was of the Forest Folk, as she was, but from a wholly different creation. He was from far away, from the kingdom of Kyell. There was none like him in Beaynid or Ventra. He had certain powers, as she did, though they were very different. While she wielded the powers of the earth, his kind used gems stones and metals to do their bidding. Karha Rull was a great Beast Lord from a land far to the west. His skin was neither light nor dark, and his face was rather unremarkable. He had the slim nose, high cheekbones and pointed ears of the Forest Folk, but was taller and leaner, much like that of a human. He was not the dark, impressive god that so many in the land painted him as. Yes, he was an evil man, but you could not tell it by looking at him.

He was silent for a moment and then spoke again. "The queen is near to giving birth. I believe the king will send the child away and, who knows, maybe kill its mother."

"How does this concern me?" Baobh looked away from the man out over the empty desert.

"I will give you a child for the one that was taken away from you,"

She quickly looked back over to him, and her brows shot up. "What madness is this, that I should take a Seun child as my own?"

"The child will be the heir to the throne, even if its father denies it." Baobh stayed silent. "You and I, we do not age as humans. Therefore, we can be patient. The child will quickly grow into a man and will be outraged when he is told of what is rightfully his. Then we will simply aid him in his bid for Sona Tuath. The man will be but a puppet king. A king only in name, for you, shall rule Sona Tuath once again."

Something began smoldering in her eyes. "But what of the prophecy? Have you forgotten? What is to prevent Ventra from coming to Beaynid's aid once again?"

Lord Rull shook his head. "The new king has alienated the Empress of Ventra; they will not interfere."

"They need only to turn their eyes upon me, and the prophecy will be fulfilled," she said sorrowfully.

"You still do not understand, do you?"

"Understand what?" she demanded.

"The prophecy is not about the current Empress Kossi —it is about the daughter she will bear," he said succulently.

Baobh sucked in her breath, and her pale eyes grew wide. "This cannot be true!" She leaned away from him. "Do you tell me lies only to get me to cooperate with you again?" she howled.

In an instant Lord Rull was on top of Baobh, she felt his hot breath on her cheek. His eyes were wild, and she knew she had pushed him too far. "I do not lie, for I do not have to!" He sat up and lifted Baobh up with him, her arms painfully clasped in his iron-like hands. "You will take the Kossi babe when the empress gives birth, for she has already taken a mate, and this time dispose of the child before it can be your undoing. Then we will carefully mold the Seun child into our puppet king." The red in his face began to recede, and his green eyes grew cool.

Baobh's mind began to race as she thought of the possibility of taking Sona Tuath once again. Her mind drifted to her son growing into a child within the confines of Ghroc. A pain she had not known since she went down into the waters of the Carnaid stabbed at her heart. Anger and deadly scorn grew within her for the woman who had taken her child away.

"She will know the pain I have known, and weep for her child as I have for mine," Baobh whispered, and Lord Rull smiled.

Continue with Rhiannon and Flath on their journey with the third book in the Sword of Rhiannon series:
Sword of Stone: The Sword of Rhiannon: Book Three
https://amzn.to/2IQ3lfY

Get your copy of *Sword of Stone: The Sword of Rhiannon: Book Three* today!

Please feel free to look me up on any of these social media sites.

http://www.melissaebeckwith.com/

https://twitter.com/M_E_Beckwith

https://www.facebook.com/AuthorMelissaEBeckwith

https://www.goodreads.com/user/show/15959449-melissa-e-beckwith

https://www.pinterest.com/M_E_Beckwith/

www.linkedin.com/in/melissa-e-beckwith-Author

https://plus.google.com/u/0/109438403164764731559

ACKNOWLEDGMENTS

I have so many people to thank for giving me my creative life and making my books a reality. Since I wrote War of the Gypsy at the same time I wrote The Empress of Ventra, I would like to thank a lot of the same people—people who gave me the much-needed support and encouragement that we writers crave because our egos can sometimes be delicate. *grin*

First, I'd like to thank my husband of thirty-one years for putting up with all my quirks and standing by my dream to become an author. His support has been invaluable and ever so much appreciated.

Again, I'd like to thank my very first beta-readers from all those years ago: my beloved sister, Amy Marshall-Waddell (who is also my official Proof Reader), and my friend, Shawna Fernley.

My dynamic editor, Courtney Cannon (who is also responsible for my stunning cover design and creating my beautiful website) has been a huge source of information and support and has worked tirelessly on all my projects, including my book launches. This self-confessed technophobe thanks you for your patience! Please find her here: www.fictionatlas.com/

Again, thank you to the extraordinarily talented Cornelia Yoder for my magnificent map of Ventra and Beaynid and her seas. It is thrilling to see a world that I created in my head actually appear in such a beautiful, professional map! You can find her at: www.corneliayoder.com

A big thank you to the always effervescent and accomplished Charles Renne from Under Production Multimedia for making me look so good in my professional headshot. Connect with him here: at: https://www.facebook.com/UnderproductionMultiMedia/

Thank you again to my daughter, Annie Beatty, from Mirrors and Chairs Salon for doing a terrific job taming my tresses and making me look so spectacular for my photo! You can find her here: www.facebook.com/annieatmandc

I'd like to give a huge thank you to all the ladies from the group, Women Fiction Writers on Facebook, for all your help and advice and patiently answering all my questions along this publishing journey of mine.

Once again, I'm sending out a huge thank you, to YOU, my loyal reader, for remaining with me on this journey into the lives of Rhiannon and Flath and their friends (and even Baobh).

As always, reviews are so important to authors,

especially us Independent Authors, so I'd be very grateful if you'd take a moment to leave me a review. I'd also love to hear your thoughts and feedback.

ABOUT THE AUTHOR

Melissa has been writing books since before she had learned to read, in the form of picture books, and planned to be an author at age four. She spent her youth penning short stories, poems and writing in her diary. At nineteen she married her high school sweetheart and started her family. Born and raised in beautiful Southern California she and her husband now live along the Ohio River in Indiana to be near their beloved grandson, Bryar.

Melissa enjoys the outdoors and nature, especially camping. She has an interest in the natural world, particularly the wonder of birds and bugs. She can't grow plants to save her life, though she likes to try. She loves art and paints a little herself. She has a great interest in history and plans on trying her hand at historical fiction in the future. Someday she hopes to travel the world starting with Scotland, Ireland, Africa and Australia.

Melissa loves to listen to heavy metal, Irish rock, and Celtic music...well, anything Celtic really. She loves renaissance fairs, crystals, dangly earrings, bright clothes, the color red, yellow roses, orange cats, and little dogs, like her fuzzy Shih Tzu, Abby.

Most days you will find her tapping away at her

keyboard, doing research for her next great novel, or catch her with her nose stuck in an epic fantasy or historical fiction story.

Melissa E. Beckwith
Fantasy Author

www.melissaebeckwith.com

Printed in Great Britain
by Amazon